After a paranormal encounter in his youth with someone from his future, Collin Frey sets his sights on getting to Marke Staple University. Now eighteen and with a full scholarship to the prestigious university, Collin hopes to find an explanation to that life-changing event. Unfortunately, it only leads to more questions.

Finding out he's there to study magic is the first surprise. The second is his roommate, Terrence, looks identical to the person who started him on the path to Marke Staple.

Collin's more than willing to sell his soul to get closer to Terrence and uncover all the secrets hidden there. Can knowing a man will change after making a horrible mistake ease the pain of betrayal? Collin is going to find out.

SCARLET GAZE

Foster Bridget Cassidy

A NineStar Press Publication

Published by NineStar Press
P.O. Box 91792,
Albuquerque, New Mexico, 87199 USA.
www.ninestarpress.com

Scarlet Gaze

Printed in the USA
First Edition
April, 2020

Print ISBN: 978-1-951880-89-7

Also available in eBook, ISBN: 978-1-951880-90-3

Warning: This book contains sexually explicit content, which may only be suitable for mature readers.

For Jeremy

Prologue

Six years ago

Scarlet eyes: the color of molten lava and just as violent. A jagged scar cut across pale skin from Adam's apple to left ear: healed, but still ghastly in its proportions. A horrible sight to behold, especially when I was so young.

I saw him on the ski slope, our last night in Copper Mountain. That year, I was twelve, so Mom and Dad let me venture out by myself. No one looked after me to make sure I stuck to the West Village, which was filled with beginner courses. I wanted a challenge, so I headed for the Center Village, which had more advanced declines.

At the top of the slope, the sun began its descent behind the mountains, throwing bright orange rays across the snow. I prepared for the drop, anticipating the squirm in my belly, the air whipping past my face, bits of hair flapping from beneath my beanie. As I started to push off, a glint of light caught my eye. Metal, half buried by snow. Curious, I left the edge of the slope and shuffled toward the object.

Holding both my poles in one hand, I bent and used the other to wipe away the snow. Beneath was an old coin, judging from the semilegible words and faded, half-visible image. I lifted it up to the dying light. A building with a spire stood in the center, and I read the name beneath:

Marke Staple. I flipped the coin, hoping the other side offered more clues to its value or origin.

One look and I yelped, dropping it as if it burned through my glove. It fell back into the snow, landing head's up.

My face stared up at me from the silver coin. An older face, more mature. How I'd look as a young adult, but unmistakably mine. Same snub nose. Same hereditarily thick eyebrows. Same birthmark on my chin.

A sudden noise pulled my attention from the coin. At the edge of the slope was a thicket of trees, eerily silent of animal chittering. Only the crunch of snow came from among the pines.

"Where is it?" asked an accented voice. British. A moment later, a young man emerged. On hands and knees, his fingers splayed into the snow, searching for something. He must have spied my skis, because he looked up sharply.

He wasn't dressed for the weather, wearing jeans and a gray short-sleeved shirt; his brown ear-length hair had no hat to keep away the chill. His face was free of blemishes or wrinkles, but a horrible scar peeked out from the neckline of his shirt. It zigzagged across his pale flesh like shark's teeth. The gash turned my stomach, and my appraisal lifted to his eyes. Red irises stared back at me. Red like blood. Red like fire. Red like anger, and sin, and the devil himself.

I screamed and tried to back away. My skis tripped me, and I fell backward, landing on my side in the snow. I frantically turned toward the man—the monster—ready to fend him off with my poles. But he hadn't moved. In fact, he stared at me with just as much horror. His eyes were wide, and he'd pulled back, huddling against himself.

His crimson eyes blinked rapidly a few times; then he swallowed, making the scar along his throat bob. "Collin?"

I flinched from him again. My heartbeat drummed loudly in my ears. I must have heard him wrong. How could this monster know my name?

"Collin," he repeated. "It's you, isn't it?"

My tongue froze to the roof of my mouth, leaving me unable to utter a word.

The man's stiff posture deflated. He sagged as if no longer capable of keeping his body upright. His shoulders lowered, and he put his face into his hands. He shook, and I realized he was sobbing.

"I'm so sorry," he babbled, voice breaking with sorrow. "You were right, and I'm so sorry I betrayed you."

I opened my mouth to speak, several times, but no words formed. At least the feeling of immediate danger passed, so I got to my feet.

As I moved, he raised his head and looked at me. Tears streamed down his face, making his cheeks ruddy too. Then, he spied the coin between us. He started forward on hands and knees, and I hastily retreated a few steps. He wasn't coming for me though. He stopped at the coin, cradling it in his hands as if it were a treasure.

"I'll find my way back," he said, his eyes glued to the coin. "I hope... I hope you can forgive me."

Then, he pinched the coin between his pointer finger and thumb and was gone. Only the indentations in the snow offered proof he'd been there.

I couldn't recall going down the slope. When I got back to the ski lodge, I was shaking so hard Mom made me drink a hot cocoa. It wasn't the chill. It was those unearthly eyes. The familiar way he'd uttered my name. The broken sobs he'd cried.

They haunted my dreams for years after the encounter.

Chapter One

Mom and Dad chatted softly as I gazed out the taxi window. Occasionally, the driver would point out a well-known sight, or something of interest. My parents oohed and aahed, but I barely registered the words. My thoughts focused inward, to the red-eyed man, his desperate pleas for forgiveness, and the total absurdity of the situation. When my mind dwelled on the event from my youth, the rational side wanted to dismiss it as a daydream, or some sort of hallucinated episode. The man had disappeared. That sort of thing didn't happen in real life.

Yet here I was. Following the clues that could easily turn out to be nothing more than a figment of my imagination.

"And 'ere we are," the cabbie said, pulling the car to a stop. "Marke Staple University. Very prestigious." He turned around and smiled at me. "You're a lucky one to get in."

Mom leaned forward eagerly. "Not lucky at all! Collin got a full scholarship! He's very bright."

I wrinkled my nose and unbuckled my seat belt. "Thanks for the ride."

I climbed out and gazed upon the school's gothic spires. They sent ominous shadows stretching across the school grounds. One at the center of the campus stood higher than the rest. I recognized it from the school's website. And the coin. The familiarity of it made my heart ache. So close.

The driver got out of the car and opened the trunk. He lifted our bags out and set them on the sidewalk. Dad slipped him a few American dollars, which he took with a wink. "Thanks a lot. And good luck in your studies." He waved before climbing back inside and disappearing the way we came.

"So, here it is," Dad said, following my gaze to the spires. "Kinda creepy."

Mom lightly smacked Dad's shoulder. "Travis! Don't say things like that. It's an old school, with old architecture."

"And old ghosts," Dad muttered, then shot me a mischievous grin. "I hope you don't venture out at night."

I laughed, and the tension filling me lessened. A bit.

Dad threw his arm over my shoulder and pulled me in for a side hug. "Come on, kiddo. Let's check this place out."

A man in a butler-type uniform headed our way, a trolley in front of him. He stopped in front of us and gave a formal bow. "Mr. and Mrs. Frey? I'm Stephen, Mr. Helmer's coordinator. We sent a car to pick you up, but apparently they were stuck in traffic and didn't make it on time. You'll be compensated for the fee, of course."

"Don't worry about it," Dad said.

Stephen dipped his head, graying hair falling over his eyes, but when he rose, he didn't look happy with Dad's dismissal of the taxi fare. "Mr. Helmer will be here shortly, but he sent me ahead to collect your luggage."

"Thank you," Mom said as he loaded our bags onto the trolley.

"I'll get them delivered to your rooms." Another bow, then he scampered off.

"That's awful nice," Mom added. "A car to pick us up—even if we missed it—and a butler to carry our things. What else will they do for us?"

"Well, they're giving me a full scholarship," I said, walking forward. "That should be plenty." The tuition here was enormous. I *had* been lucky they'd offered me a scholarship, or else I never could have afforded this place. Millionaires sent their children here. Mom and Dad barely made enough to send Mindy—my older sister—to Florida State. This was on the other side of the Atlantic.

Mom and Dad followed my lead. We stepped past the stone gate and onto campus. As soon as my foot touched the ground on the other side, a tingle ran up my spine. I glanced around, wondering if they had a laser or infrared camera pointed at us. Nothing looked out of place. No obvious surveillance. With the next step, the chill vanished, so I dismissed it as a fluke and pushed it from my mind.

The campus was constructed of stone buildings, most sporting tall spires. Nothing in Florida even came close to this. In age or in design. An odd sensation permeated the air, almost like the change in air pressure on an airplane. A hum sounded just a decibel below hearing.

"Which way should we go?" Dad asked.

Mom pointed to a small sign in the grassy area in front of us. "Freshman orientation. That way." She gestured to the right.

We started in that direction, but an older gentleman jogging toward us slowed our steps. I recognized his face—Patrick Helmer, the dean.

"Mr. and Mrs. Frey," he called out, waving his hands over his head.

We stopped and allowed him to catch up. When he did, he smiled broadly, adding more wrinkles to his kindly face. "And Collin, of course," he said to me. "I'm glad you made it in safely. I'm Patrick Helmer, the dean." He shook all our hands enthusiastically. "I must apologize for the mix-up with the car. We must have copied your flight time incorrectly."

"It was no problem," Mom said. "The cab driver got us here quickly."

"We wanted to do more, Mrs. Frey, to show how excited we are to have Collin here."

Mom smiled, happy for someone to be singing my praises.

"We were just heading to orientation," I said, gesturing in the direction we'd been going.

Helmer waved his hand dismissively. "No, that's for the ordinary students. You don't need to listen in. If you don't mind, I'll give you a tour of the campus."

"That would be lovely," Mom said. "Are you sure you're not too busy?"

"Never too busy to assist our new literature students. We take pride in both our programs, but literature is the jewel in our crown. Collin won't want for anything while he's in our care, Mrs. Frey."

Some of the tension left Mom's shoulders at his words.

"Now, this way." He led us deeper onto campus. "Marke Staple is a very old, very selective school."

"I know," I said. When we'd returned home from Colorado, I had looked into this place. I had the whole history of it memorized. And when I'd found out they only had two degrees—literature and business—I had applied myself to my studies and set my sights on getting here. "You only select five students a year to be in your literature program."

The dean grinned. "Correct. And we are very happy you selected our school, Collin. I know you had plenty to choose from."

I nodded, but it wasn't true. Oh sure, my grades were so fantastic I could have gone to almost any I chose, but Marke Staple was the only place for me. My encounter with the red-eyed man cemented it.

"This"—Helmer said, lifting his hand toward the closest building—"is Lapris Hall. It's the administrative building. My office is in there, as well as all the other teachers'. If you have any problems, you can find your solutions there."

The building was two stories, with a dozen windows on this side. At each corner, elegant spires rose twice the height of the building. Atop each spire was an animal statue. A dog. A cat. A bird. A turtle. Curious. Most ancient buildings like this put statues of people or crosses, or at the very least gargoyles.

Helmer noticed my study of the spires and leaned close to me. "Wards," he said softly. "They protect us."

I shivered again, wondering what a university would need protection from.

He continued walking. Mom and Dad followed, but I lingered. Something about the building...wasn't right. There was a haze that drew the eyes to the top, to the spires.

"Come on, Collin," Dad called.

I pulled my gaze away and hurried after.

"This," the dean said at the next building, "is Regalia Hall. All your classes will be in here. Besides the Staple

Spire, it has the most original stonework. Only the west wall was affected by an earthquake in 1734."

This building had one spire over the entrance, although several cats sat atop the buttresses. If four protecting Lapris Hall were enough, why did this building need a dozen?

"English departments are all the same," Dad said, lifting his chin to study the detailed stonework. "And I bet the teachers all look like Dracula. That's how it was at my college."

Helmer laughed. "We don't have any vampires on staff. A few hybrids, perhaps, but nothing dangerous." Then he met my eyes and winked.

We continued around the rectangular campus, passing the café, and then the math building, the economics building, and other places the dean said I would have no use for. With only five students in each year, the literature program hosted twenty students total. The business program had four hundred. Naturally, most of the space would be devoted to their courses.

Finally, we reached the dormitories. There were three: lined in a row on the south side of campus. The school's rock-wall perimeter stood just a few feet from the rear of the buildings.

"The men's dormitory is on the left," Dean Helmer said, gesturing. It was two stories, lacked any spires, and was identical to the one on the right. "The women's dorm is on the right. The staff's in the center." The staff's building was taller, and had two enormous statues peering down at the students' dorms.

"Let me guess," I said, nodding up toward the statues. One was a lion, the other a tiger. "They're meant to keep us in after curfew."

The dean chuckled and clapped a hand on my shoulder affectionately. "Ah, Collin. I do wish we could set them to that task. Unfortunately, we rely on resident assistants to enforce the curfew. Our statues are simply meant to ward off any danger."

"Ah," I said as if that made perfect sense.

"Now, why don't we leave you to get settled into your room. You've got your room assignment?"

I wiggled my phone. "Yeah, it's in my email."

Helmer nodded, then turned to my parents. "Mr. and Mrs. Frey? If you'll join me in my office, I'll go over the finer points of Collin's scholarship. Give you our emergency contact information. Get yours in return. That sort of thing."

Mom looked at me, hesitating. "Will you be okay on your own?"

"I'm fine, Mom. I don't want you and Dad being overbearing when I meet my roommate."

Helmer glanced at his watch. "We can meet in an hour at the cafe for dinner? Will that suit you, Mrs. Frey?"

She nibbled her lip, but dipped her head. "All right. We'll see you in a bit."

The dean smiled. "Wonderful! Michael is your RA, Collin. Ask him if you have any questions."

Chapter Two

Mom, Dad, and Helmer walked back the way we'd come, toward Lapris Hall and the campus's entrance. I watched them for a moment, then returned my gaze to the dorm on the left. The lion loomed above it, almost leaning out and over the roof of the men's dorm. A ward? What sort of danger were they expecting?

Shrugging my shoulders, I headed inside. The dorm lobby looked exactly like I had expected: a television showing a soccer match, with a couch positioned to see the screen. Two winged armchairs beside an empty fireplace. A pool table. A vending machine with soda against one wall, one with snacks along the other. Everything your typical college student needed.

A tall man with dark hair nodded to me as I walked in. I assumed it was Michael, so I returned the gesture. Straight ahead were the stairs leading to the second floor. My room was two hundred eleven. As I climbed the steps, I wondered if that butler guy had managed to get my things here already.

On the second floor, I followed the numbered doors until I found my room. It was on the outside wall, on the east side of the building. That would put us almost directly under the lion statue. An odd tingle ran up my spine thinking about it. This school was weird; of course, I'd known that, just from the red-eyed man and his mysterious coin.

I knocked on the door two times before pushing it open. It was empty, but a shirt on the left bed suggested my roommate had claimed that side already. Sure enough, my two suitcases were by the foot of the bed on the right.

I surveyed the room. Weird to think this would be my home for the next year. Maybe longer. Most students only lived in the dorm their first few years, but they were likely to be locals. I'd have no other options, besides renting an apartment. The unnecessary worry seemed silly now, so I banished it from my mind. I focused on the present, and on my task of unpacking.

The room was like a mirror image, the left flipped and perfectly replicated on the right. Smallish beds were pressed into the corners with a dresser right beside their heads. At the foot were desks, with chairs and a lamp. Against the far wall was another door that led to a tiny bathroom.

I entered the space. It held a toilet, a rectangular shower stall, and a sink. My whole body barely fit in front of the sink. My roommate and I would have to go in shifts once classes started. Two people would never fit. I mentally prepped to set my alarm at least a half hour earlier.

When I went back into the room, I started to unpack my bags. Mostly clothes, a few books, my laptop, and my sketch pad were all I brought. I wasn't a great artist, but the medium was the only way I could replicate the red-eyed man's features. Keep them fresh in my mind.

I pulled the pad from beneath my shirts and flipped it open. The first drawing was Horseshoe Beach, back home. A decoy. The next, an old storefront with awnings over the windows. The next five or six were the same, boring landscape scenes. Whenever anyone looked at my sketches, they only viewed the first few. After that, I let my real intent out.

I'd drawn his eyes. Red and haunted. The horrible scar along his throat. The brown hair falling to his ears, blowing in the chilly wind. The coin with *Marke Staple* scrawled, almost illegibly, beneath the spire.

All the clues, assembled here in my sketch pad.

So close. I knew he was here, somewhere.

There was a knock on the door, followed by the arrival of my roommate. He entered back first, pushing the door in with the sole of his shoe. I rushed forward to grab the knob and propped my foot along the base to hold it for him.

"Thanks," he said, his voice thick with a British accent.

"No problem. Can I help?"

He spun into the room, his hands laden with a large box. "Nah, I can manage." He placed the box on his bed, then turned to me. "Good to meet you."

I started to extend my hand, but I froze midmotion. It was *him*. The red-eyed man. I'd spent so many years dwelling on his features; I'd recognize him anywhere. Except...

His short brown hair fell in front of clear blue eyes. While on the slope, they'd been molten lava; now they'd were as cold and piercing as glaciers. He smiled, but the sharpness in his gaze didn't lessen.

I stared at him, shaken and confused. This was *him*. The same ugly scar marked the skin above the collar of his shirt. His high cheekbones. His narrow nose. Arched eyebrows. Thin lips.

But...his eyes? What happened to his eyes?

Since I hadn't completed my move toward him, he came to me. He scooped my hand up into his and gave a firm pump. His skin radiated warmth. It thawed me from my sudden paralysis.

"G-good to meet you too," I said, my voice trembling. "I'm—"

His grin deepened, but it still didn't alter the harsh glint in his eyes. "Collin. I know. I'm Terrence Smith."

He released my hand, and my skin broke out in goose bumps. "Have we met before?"

He'd turned back to his box, but at my words, he regarded me again. His eyes roamed over my face, and I had to put my hands behind my back to keep them from shaking under his scrutiny.

"No, I'm sure we haven't."

He went back to his box.

I sat on the edge of my bed, uncertain whether my legs could continue to hold my weight.

"At a ski lodge? In Colorado?"

This time, he didn't even glance at me. "Nope. Never been to the States. I've lived in Lewes all my life. It's only twenty minutes from here."

I was silent for a long moment, staring at his back. He'd begged me to forgive him, promised he'd come back to me. And now...he didn't even know who I was.

Finally, Terrence glanced over his shoulder. I averted my gaze.

"You've got it bad for this guy, huh?"

I made a noncommittal noise.

A grin played at the corners of his lips, and he faced me, arms folded across his chest. For the first time, some emotion danced in his eyes. It was the exact opposite he'd shown me on the slopes. There, he'd been repentant, broken. Now, he was mischievous. Or something more sinister.

"So, you're gay?"

I shrugged my shoulders. "Demisexual." The identity took a long time to make sense. Once my sexual hormones kicked in, I began to think of the red-eyed man in a new way. I remembered his desperation, the vulnerability on his face, the raw and broken spirit he showed me. The experience formed an emotional connection, and once I became old enough to process it, the feelings morphed into sexual desire—but only for him.

Terrence nodded. "I'm bi."

I swallowed past a lump in my throat.

"So, tell me about this guy," Terrence said. "He's not your boyfriend?"

I shook my head.

Terrence's smile showed just the hint of teeth. "Good. Means I have a chance."

Instant heat flooded into my cheeks. My heart beat fast, and I tried to control my breathing. The feeling of elation evaporated when I met his gaze. Six years ago, I'd seen him honest, raw, and bare. Right now, that openness wasn't present in his features. He was lying.

I wanted to growl with frustration. My head hurt from the logistics of this absurd situation. My heart hurt from his overwhelming beauty. My soul hurt from the words he'd uttered—even if he hadn't meant them.

I turned away, lifting my sketch pad into my lap.

"Is that where you're from, then?" Terrence asked.

"What?"

"Colorado?"

"Oh, no. I'm from Florida. Cross City."

I flipped to the first sketch of the red-eyed man. I'd filled the drawing with colored pencils, showing off the suppressed fury lurking in his irises. I quickly glanced from the paper to Terrence and back again. Identical, besides the eyes.

"So you fell in love with this guy there?"

"Not really." It'd taken me ages to put a name to the emotions the red-eyed man stirred within me. And it had been more a reflection of his own love that kindled my interest in him.

Terrence smiled again. "This sounds complicated. I want to hear the details."

Sighing, I closed the pad and tossed it beside me on the bed. "It is complicated, but there's not much to say."

Terrence shrugged, but I could see the glint in his eyes as he filed away the information. So different from what I expected. But...

I'm so sorry. The red-eyed man's words played through my mind. *I'm so sorry I betrayed you.*

How was I going to figure all this out? Who could I tell this to without sounding nuts?

"You wanna go get a drink?" Terrence asked suddenly. "There's a great pub down the street."

I shook my head, genuinely disappointed. "My mom and dad are with Dean Helmer, signing papers. They should be back soon."

Terrence's face contorted. The feigned sincerity vanished completely. Only for a moment the look of loathing lasted on his face, and then he covered his feelings with his default mask. "Oh. Well, maybe next time. I'm gonna head off before they get back."

"Sure. See ya."

He booked it to the door. He paused before leaving, and the mischievous grin was back, playful and dangerous. "Once you're drunk, I bet you'll tell me all about this mysterious guy you're so fixed on."

Then he was gone.

Chapter Three

My alarm pulled me from restless sleep. My dreams were feverish, dark, and hazy. Luckily, upon waking, only the lingering dread stayed, not the images that had haunted my mind.

I sat up and hit the button on my phone that killed the invasive chimes. Groaning, I put my feet over the edge of the bed. I rubbed at my eyes, then glanced at Terrence.

His posture was similar to mine, though his arms were stretched over his head. The hem of his shirt crept up, revealing the pale skin of his stomach.

I inspected the flesh, roaming slowly over what I could see. Terrence caught me staring, and I looked away. Out of the corner of my eye, I saw his smirk.

"Good morning," he said, standing from his bed.

"Morning," I mumbled.

"Mind if I take the first shower?"

"Go ahead."

He grabbed a change of clothes out of his drawer before heading to the adjoining doorway. Pausing, he eyed me with his head slightly tilted. "Unless you feel like joining me?" His slow grin added a gleam to his eyes.

My stomach squirmed at his invitation, but I shook my head. I wanted nothing more than to see more of his bare skin, yet my mind knew better than my body. Jumping into something with him wasn't my best choice at the moment.

It'll happen eventually, my eager hormones tried to reason. *You know he betrays you, and to do that something needs to develop.*

"Next time, then?" Terrence said, laughing. He slipped through the door and shut it behind him.

I groaned and flopped back on my bed. This was going to be a nightmare.

After Terrence showered, shaved, and brushed his teeth, he emerged in a fresh set of clothes. I did a double take at seeing him in the faded jeans and light-gray shirt. This was the exact outfit he'd been in when I saw him on the slopes.

Noticing my gaze, Terrence shifted to peer at his clothing. "What? Have I got a stain?"

I swallowed. "No. It's... I'm getting in the shower."

I grabbed my own clean outfit and dashed into the bathroom. I prayed he'd be gone when I was finished, but no such luck. When I emerged, he was sitting on his bed, looking at his cell phone. He met my eyes and grinned.

"I figured we'd have breakfast together this morning," he said, standing. "As long as the dean isn't going to join us."

I picked up my cell phone and deposited it into my pocket. "He shouldn't, as far as I know. My parents would love to meet you."

He winked and got up from his bed. "Parents always love me." He went to the door and pulled it open.

We walked down the hallway side by side.

I texted my parents to let them know I was heading to the cafe now. We'd discussed it last night, but I wanted to make sure they were awake. It wasn't unheard of for them to miss their alarm. Mom always called me the responsible one of the family.

Outside, I squinted up at the sun, barely over the school's eastern wall. My body fought the jet lag from our long day yesterday, between layovers and flights to get here. Three days until school started; I had better adjust by then.

We arrived at the cafe and headed inside. Mom and Dad weren't there yet, so Terrence and I selected a table and sat.

"Sleep well?" he asked, glancing around the nearly deserted room. The last few days of freedom, so the students were likely sleeping in.

"Not really," I confessed. "New place. New bed."

He met my gaze and nodded. "Understandable. You'll adjust soon. Must be overwhelming, coming from the States and all."

"Yeah."

"If you need to cuddle, just let me know. You're welcome to share my bed."

I shrugged nervously. It would be easy to give in. Resisting was much harder.

With another grin, Terrence continued. "Why'd you pick Marke Staple? There are plenty of similar programs in your area."

To find you, but it would have been too weird to say aloud. He wouldn't believe me. Or maybe he would. I didn't know which would be worse. "Ready for a change."

"I'll help you make the most of that. Let's head to the pub later today."

"You mentioned that last night, but I'm underage."

Terrence snorted. "You do realize you're in a different country? Legal age is eighteen."

My cheeks heated for not concluding that on my own. "Sure. I'd like that."

Mom and Dad arrived then. We stood to greet them. Terrence laid on the charm and had Mom blushing within the first two words. Dad shook his hand and smiled widely.

"Don't you worry, Mr. and Mrs. Frey," he said, leading them to our table. "I'll keep a close eye on Collin. Show him everything he'll need to know on campus."

"Thank you, Terrence," Mom gushed. "But, please, call me Diane."

"And I'm Travis," Dad added.

Terrence showed off his white teeth. "Maybe I'll just call you Mom and Dad too?"

They all laughed. My eye twitched.

After that, they were all trading phone numbers. Terrence even clicked a photo of my parents to add to the contact picture. Mom insisted on getting one of him and me together for hers.

Terrence threw his arm around my shoulder and leaned in. His head rested against the side of mine. His heat radiated into me, and my heart thudded against my rib cage. So close. I could smell the scent of cinnamon on him.

"You boys look so darling," Mom said, sitting back down. "Now, why don't we eat?"

"You sit," Terrence said, getting to his feet. "I'll bring you back something. Anything off-limits? Food allergies?"

"Just coffee for me," Dad said.

Mom smiled, basking in the attention. "Anything is fine."

Terrence turned toward me. "Collin?"

"I'm not picky."

He nodded, then raced off.

My stomach lurched. The whole time, his eyes had been calculating. There hadn't been a speck of humor or good will in them. Why was he doing this? What did he want to use me for? I was so insignificant. There was nothing special about me. Why go through this trouble? Charming my parents? Seeming like a nice guy when I knew he was going to betray me.

"You okay, Collin?" Mom asked. She leaned toward me and put her hand on my forehead. "You look pale."

"I'm fine. Just nerves."

And just like that, Mom was sobbing. "I'm so sorry we'll have to leave today." She wailed loudly, and Dad had to pull her into his arms. "You'll be all alone."

It was endearing, despite how it drew the eyes of the few people in the cafe. I knew this would be hard on them. With Mindy at Florida State, at least she was close. I was across the ocean.

"It'll be okay, Mom," I said, reaching over to pat her back. "Just think of all the privacy you and Dad can have. It'll be like a second honeymoon."

That made her snort.

"Think of all the money we'll save on groceries," Dad added. "Not having to feed a growing young man will do wonders for our budget."

She giggled and pulled away from Dad's hold. "That's a good point. We'll be able to order pizza every night and not worry about proper nutrition."

Terrence returned with a tray filled with plates of pancakes and mugs of coffee. He set them on the table, then dished them out to us.

"Looks like I missed all the emotions," he said as he sat with his own plate in front of him. "You doing okay, Diane?"

Mom dabbed at her eyes with a napkin. "Oh, you know how mothers worry."

He nodded. "I do. Though mine's only a twenty-minute drive from here; not too much for her to worry over."

Mom shook her head. "She still does. I can guarantee it."

"I'm sure the dean told you how the literature students are cared for. Collin's safety and happiness will be his top concern. Besides, there'll be other first-year students coming in with him. He'll make friends, no problem."

I cast a quick glance at Terrence out of the corner of my eye. He knew exactly what to say to ease her concerns. The tension left her shoulders, and the creases in her brow vanished. That was a good thing, but I wished I knew the reason behind it.

"You're going to be a great friend for Collin," Mom said. "We'll have to plan on getting the two of you home for Christmas."

Terrence laughed and put his arm around my shoulder again. "Sounds good to me. Will I get to bunk in Collin's room?"

Mom completely missed his innuendo, though Dad's lips twitched slightly. "Oh, no, Collin wouldn't have to sleep on the couch. We have a guest room."

"Too bad," Terrence whispered in my ear as he pulled away. Then, to my parents, he said, "I'm assuming the dean has ordered you a ride to the airport. Would it be all right if Collin and I tag along?"

My mom's eyes turned misty again. "Terrence, you are a sweetheart. You sure it won't be an inconvenience for you?"

"There's nothing I'd rather do."

Chapter Four

After seeing Mom and Dad safely to the security checkpoint at the airport, Terrence, the driver, and I headed back to the car. On the ride there, Terrence had sat up front with the driver, leaving me smooshed between my parents. Now, Terrence climbed with me into the back seat and squished *our* bodies together.

"Can you take us to the Swift Unicorn?" Terrence called up to the driver.

Her lips pursed together briefly before she dipped her head.

"It's close to school, so it's not that far out of the way," he told me. "I can't wait for you to see it, Collin. It can be our hangout."

He moved just a bit closer, our hips and thighs aligning.

My heartbeat increased at the lingering scent of him. "What are you doing?" I blurted out.

He flashed me a grin that put a glint into his eyes. Not friendly or flirty, hungrier. "Getting comfy. You mind?"

"No," I said quickly, lest he pull away. "I just, I don't understand why you're doing this."

"Doing what? Being friendly?" He showed me more of his teeth.

"Friendly's not what I'd call it."

He pulled away, with a lightly muttered, "I can stop."

I reached out and gripped his arm, stilling him. "No!" My cheeks blushed at the pathetic whimper of my word. "I said I don't mind. But, we just met. Why are you...?" I trailed off, unsure of how to say it. Looking at me like a piece of meat was an apt comparison.

"I like you, Collin. And I know you like me because I remind you of that bloke you met in Colorado."

"I don't—" I cut off, knowing I couldn't honestly finish that sentence. He grinned in triumph. I pressed on, ruffled by his assurance of success. "How did you get that scar?"

The tangent in topic threw him. His face twisted to a horrible mix of fury and pain. His pupils dilated, making the blue irises seem larger. He immediately put his mask back on, but the smile was obviously forced.

"Boating accident. When I was little."

I nodded, accepting the lie. Even if I hadn't seen him at his most vulnerable, I would have known the statement false.

I knew that scar. And through the fabric of clothing, I could trace it without fail. The temptation to run my fingers over his flesh to strip off Terrence's mask again with such a bold move was strong. Instead, I clenched my hands together. "So, what's so special about this pub?"

Terrence's grin was back in force. "It's great! They give discounts to literature students. A sort of club off campus."

"But you're not in the literature program."

Terrence's lips thinned, becoming almost a sneer. "Just because I'm not in the program doesn't mean I don't know my stuff."

My cheeks warmed with embarrassment. "I didn't mean to imply—"

He waved off my comments, but his face didn't lose its rigidity.

"Honestly, I wasn't trying to dig at you. I'm sure you know just as much Shakespeare as me."

Terrence snorted. "Right. Shakespeare."

I looked at him quizzically. "Then, Dickens?"

All resentment left his features, and he turned to me, eyes wide. "Dickens?"

"Yeah. I assumed you'd prefer the British writers, but maybe you're a fan of Faulkner?"

"Literature greats?"

I blinked at him in surprise. "Of course. If you're so offended you're not in the literature program, we can still discuss the masters. I'm partial to Thoreau, myself."

Terrence laughed. A chuckle at first, but it escalated. His body vibrated, and his cackles brought the eyes of the driver in the rearview mirror.

"Collin," he panted. "Oh god!"

I squirmed, unsure of how I'd made an idiot of myself. I didn't like being the butt of his personal joke.

"What's so funny?" I demanded.

It made him laugh harder.

The taxi pulled to a stop along the side of the road. "Here we are," she said.

Still scowling at Terrence, I climbed from the back of the car. He followed, but slowly, his body sluggish from his mirth. He still tipped the driver a couple of paper bills before wobbling to the building beside us.

"Well?" I asked when he made to push past me into the pub. "You gonna let me in on the joke?"

His grin was mischievous. And dangerously beautiful. "Oh no. I'd rather you discover the punchline yourself. It'll be funnier that way."

Then he sidestepped me and pushed on the large, wooden door that led into the Swift Unicorn. My only option was to follow, or be left behind.

The inside was much the same as British-style pubs in America. I never made a habit of barhopping, being underage over there, but I'd visited a few locations—Mindy's twenty-first birthday party, for instance. This pub had a large stone fireplace against the far wall. The drab, gray stones made up the entire wall. The three others were wood, colored with age. To the right, a bar took up the length of the room, with padded bar stools spaced intermittently. The rest of the room was filled with round tables and simple, wooden chairs.

A piney, smoky scent filled the air, despite the fireless fireplace. Every table was empty, implying they were closed. Terrence didn't care; he walked into the room as if he owned it.

"Hey, Alfie," Terrence called.

A man popped up from behind the bar, a rag and mug in his hands. He wore a shirt and vest, with the sleeves rolled up to show off Celtic-style tattoos on his forearms. A shaggy beard hung from his chin, with bits of red mixed in with the brown.

"Terrence," he greeted jovially. "Didn't expect to see you here today. Not with school starting soon."

Terrence's smile became predatory as he threw his arm around my shoulder. "This is my roommate, Collin. He's in the literature program."

Alfie nodded somberly. "Nice to meet you, Collin. Welcome to the Swift Unicorn."

"Thanks," I said.

"This is the best pub in all of England," Terrence told me.

Alfie's smile returned, and he beamed at us. "A pint for both of you?"

"Ta," Terrence answered before I could say anything. Then, he tightened his hold on me and pulled me toward a table.

We took our seats, and Alfie hurried over with two mugs of pale ale. He set them in front of us with a flourish. "Anything else?"

Terrence considered a moment but shook his head. "Maybe some lunch later, but for now, we'll stick with this."

"Just let me know."

Alfie retreated to the bar, leaving us alone.

Terrence lifted the mug to his lips and took a long pull. He set it down with a sigh.

"What is this?" I asked, eyeing the amber liquid.

"It's called Tipsy Gnome. It's an ale they brew themselves. Potent."

Slowly, I took an experimental sip. I wasn't a complete angel; I'd had beer before, smuggled into school dances or classmates' parties. This, though, tasted unlike anything I'd had before. It was thick with a surprisingly sweet aroma. I caught hints of apples, cinnamon, cloves, and nutmeg. Like Thanksgiving in liquid form.

"Wow," I said.

"Great, isn't it? The food's just as good. This place is amazing."

I nodded and took another, longer, drink. "Why did Alfie think you wouldn't show up? You come here often?"

"Nearly every day this summer. Nothing else to do in this area. Full of tourist traps." He gave an exaggerated shiver. "I told you this place is special for literature students. It draws a specific crowd. Some of the older students wouldn't like me being here. But if I'm with you, they can't throw me out."

Could this be the betrayal? I thought. Him simply using me to get things he couldn't on his own? *Not likely*. That wouldn't drive a man to the torment I'd witnessed in him all those years ago.

The bar's door opened, and two young women walked in, dressed in the uniforms of Marke Staple. The one in the lead was tall with brown hair falling past her shoulders. She wore a pointed frown as she gazed over at us. The one in the back was shorter with red hair and freckles covering almost every inch of her face. Her green eyes opened wide as she almost collided with the one in front.

"Why'd you let him in, Alfie?" the taller woman said. "You know he's not supposed to be in here."

The barkeep wrung his hands in apology. "He does no harm, Lisbeth."

She scoffed. "And who's the sprog?"

I knew she meant me, but before I could say anything, Terrence said excitedly, "This is Collin Frey. *He* invited me here."

The two women's scrutiny of me increased. I tried not to squirm.

Finally, Lisbeth nodded. "I saw Helmer's files. He looks like Collin Frey." She didn't look happy about it. "Two pints, Alfie."

She walked toward us, and the other woman followed. Without asking, they joined our table.

"I'm Lisbeth, and this is Maggie. We're literature students too."

"Nice to meet you," I said.

Alfie approached our table hesitantly. He held the two drinks out in front of him as if they were a shield. "Remember, you can't study outside of school."

Lisbeth snorted. "This sprog's a new student. He wouldn't dare try to study with us."

That hardly seemed to placate Alfie, but he nodded and retreated.

I glanced after the barman, more confused than ever. "What's he mean we can't study here? Is it illegal to read in British pubs?"

The two women stared at me for half a second before they both began to laugh. Terrence's eyes shone, and I could tell he held his mirth inside. My face reddened with embarrassment.

When the women finally stopped laughing, Lisbeth's cheeks were pleasantly pink. "And I heard Americans lacked a sense of humor." She grinned at me, obviously warming up to my presence. Then she glanced at Terrence and sneered. "Why've you attached yourself to him? Plan on getting a free ride?"

Terrence's eyes widened, feigning shock. "Of course not. He's my roommate."

"Convenient," Maggie added, her voice thick with an Irish lilt.

Terrence spread his hands, innocently. "I'm not responsible for that."

"No, but you certainly had access to your father's files," Lisbeth said.

Maggie added, "And you're the type to scheme your way as close to the literature program as you can get, since they won't let you in, no matter who your father is."

I looked between them, trying to follow the conversation. "Who's your father?"

Terrence groaned, and the women pounced on his sudden discomfort.

"Dean Helmer, of course," Lisbeth answered smugly. "The dean's own son can't get into the program. How sad."

I glanced at Terrence in confusion. "But your name is Smith, not Helmer."

"I've got my mother's last name."

"They divorced when he was little—*because* of him," Lisbeth said. "Of course he'd want to start here at his father's school once he turned eighteen this summer. But he had to come in as a business major, not literature. He got special treatment though, like getting to stay in the dorms a month early."

I glared at her. I wasn't grasping all the nuances of what they were saying, but this I could understand. It wasn't right for them to make fun of Terrence because his parents split up, and worse, blame it on him. I turned sympathetic eyes to Terrence. "I'm sorry. That's terrible."

He didn't look at all miffed. "Lots of people have divorced parents. It's no big deal."

"It does when it gives you daddy issues," Maggie said. "Then you chase after all the literature students, hoping some of it will rub off on you so you can join Daddy with his studies."

"The dean teaches literature?" I asked. Wasn't he too important to waste his time teaching students?

Lisbeth nodded. "You won't find a more accomplished person at the university."

"He's not that great," Terrence mumbled.

"Daddy issues," Maggie stage whispered to me.

I sat back, letting everything they said sink into my brain. It was complete gibberish. The only reasonable, logical thing I could gather from the whole conversation was that Terrence's parents were divorced and he had grown up without his father. I pitied him.

"Are you seniors?" I asked, hoping to move onto a topic I could understand.

"Yeah," Lisbeth answered with a self-satisfied grin. "I'm top of the class. I'm guaranteed a position in the government."

"With only four people to compete with, it's not difficult to be on top," Maggie said, but again, she said it softly to me.

Lisbeth shot her a frown, and Maggie grimaced abashedly.

"Why do you want to work in the government?" I asked. She implied it was what literature students strived for. It sounded boring to me. Bureaucracy and paperwork.

"You'll understand in time," Lisbeth said, leaning forward to gently pat my hand. A tremor ran through my body when her fingers touched me, like a spark. She snatched her hand away, shaking it as she did so. She glared at me. "Watch it."

"Sorry," I mumbled, rubbing my hands on my jeans. "I must have had a static electric charge from the carpet or something."

She huffed. "Maybe." She downed the rest of her ale, then looked at Maggie. "Ready?"

Maggie's drink was only halfway gone, but she nodded.

"See you tomorrow at the meet and greet," Lisbeth said with a not-so-pleasant grin. Maggie waved.

Once they left, Alfie rushed to our table to clear their glasses.

"Please be careful," he warned us. Or maybe it was Terrence he was speaking to.

Either way, I was ready to go back to our dorm. Instead, Terrence ordered us another round.

"I don't have a lot of money," I said after Alfie set two more mugs on our table. "And what I've got has to last the whole semester."

"Today's on me," he answered.

"Thank you."

He waved away my words.

"You're not on good terms with your dad?"

He wrinkled his nose. "Not the best topic, Collin."

"I understand. If you want to talk about it, let me know. It could help. Especially if this is all starting to get pulled up now."

"It's not as bad as Maggie made out. I just didn't see him a lot growing up."

"Will it be hard seeing him more now?"

"Not sure. We'll have to see."

I dropped the subject. Plenty of my friends back home had gone through divorces. I was the oddity with parents still married. But each person was different—some wanted to be consoled, and others wanted to be left alone. Terrence seemed more the latter.

"What do you plan to do with your degree?" I asked.

"Not sure. Stockbroker or something." He turned his pale eyes to me. "What do you want to do after you graduate? Stay here in England?"

I chuckled softly, surprised by the question. "I haven't thought about it. I was so intent on getting over here, I never considered what comes next."

"Why is it so important to be here? You don't even understand why this literature program is so special."

I looked away, unable to answer the question. The less I told him about the red-eyed man, the better. He must have guessed, based on my reaction.

"So this guy you met in Colorado? You think he's here? Why?"

"British accent."

Terrence smirked. "You know," he said, the accent completely gone from his voice, "people are able to change the way they speak. Actors do it all the time."

I shook my head. The man had been too wounded, too vulnerable to put on a mask. That was his real tone, his real words, his real soul.

Terrence laughed. "Another round, Alfie! And why don't you bring us some food."

Chapter Five

We wobbled out of the pub. Night had fallen. How long ago? I had no idea. A brisk wind blew, and I was glad I'd brought my jacket. I pulled it on as we walked and nearly ran into a light pole. Terrence grabbed my arm and steadied me. The heat of his touch was unreal. His skin was like a furnace, his body temperature higher than mine.

"Are you sick?" I asked. My words came out slurred, and even I had trouble deciphering their meaning. "You're hot." No, that wasn't any better. "Fever?"

He laughed. He didn't look nearly as unbalanced as I felt. "No, I'm fine. My body runs warm."

"Must be nice in winter."

"Terrible during summer."

I laughed and nearly fell off the edge of the path.

"Easy," he said, pulling me closer. He smelled of cinnamon—a scent I associated with the ski lodge in Colorado. "We better get you back to your bed. Too much fun for one night."

I shook my head and the world lurched. I clung tighter to Terrence. I was feeling too keyed up from his presence. I wasn't ready to call it a night. "What else can we do? You know this area. There's gotta be something."

He glanced at me, and there was a twinkle in his eyes, but the hint of something darker lingered beneath. "There *is* something, but it might be risky."

Any red flags in my head were dulled by the alcohol, so I nodded. "Yeah, let's do it."

"I didn't even say what."

"Let's do it," I repeated.

"Well, Professor Evoy is a notorious drunk. I was going to suggest we sneak into his apartment and steal a few more cans."

I hiccupped. "More to drink? I don't think I can fit any more inside me."

A high-pitched giggle came from Terrence. "It's obvious you're inexperienced, but we can make it work if we try hard enough."

My cheeks reddened, realizing he wasn't just talking about the alcohol. "Is it smart to break into a teacher's room?" I asked, sticking to the original topic.

"No."

"Then why do it?"

"It'll be fun. And if we succeed, I'll let you kiss me."

My eyes immediately went to his lips. They were red and inviting and curved up in a beautiful smile. "Let's do it."

When we got back to campus, it was nearly deserted. A few students milled about, but the lack of people gave the place a haunted feeling. The buildings loomed more so than during the day. And I could swear eyes looked out of the empty windows.

I shivered and nearly fell over.

"You can barely stand," Terrence said. "Maybe this isn't a good idea."

"No! I want to give it a try."

He paused but eventually nodded. "If you insist." His hesitancy was obviously feigned. I wasn't sure why he bothered when I already knew his true goal.

Use me. He's going to use me. The beer made the situation surprisingly clear. But it also left me free from caring.

He led me around the back of the teacher's dorm. My parents had a room in here last night. I suddenly missed them.

"Come on," Terrence said, slipping his hand in mine. His fingers tightened, and I soaked in his warmth. It was perfection, having him so near. I was half afraid my mind, now free of inhibitions, would allow me to reveal more than prudent.

We walked to a back door. The security light didn't flash on as we passed under it. My heartbeat sounded loud over our footsteps. At the door, Terrence dropped my hand. He pulled two pieces of metal out of his pocket and slipped them inside the lock. The soft clink reached my ears as he fiddled the thin picks around. After an audible click, he turned the knob with a satisfied smile.

"After you."

A knot formed in my stomach, and the buzz in my head stilled somewhat. The thought of a kiss as a prize pushed me on. I walked inside.

It opened into a dark laundry room. One of the washers vibrated softly, which meant someone was close by or coming back soon.

"Maybe this isn't such a good idea," I said.

"If you think so," Terrence answered easily. Too easily. "We can go back."

I steeled myself, thinking of what I could get if I went through with this. "No. Let's go."

I could make out his smile, even through the darkness.

"This way," he said.

He knew the layout of the building well and took me to a back stairwell. We climbed to the top floor. Terrence peeked out the landing door before pushing it open and walking out.

I raced past him down the hallway, wanting to hurry this excursion along. I got three doors in before I remembered I had no idea where I was going. I turned back and looked at Terrence.

He grinned. "Eager, aren't we?"

"I'm here on a scholarship. I don't want to get kicked out." That fact should have kept me from doing this in the first place, but it was hard to remember that when I looked at Terrence.

Surprisingly, he snorted as he joined me, then continued down the hallway. "They wouldn't kick you out of here for any reason, Collin. Believe me. You'll find out what I mean at class on Monday."

That didn't sound right, but a lot of what I'd learned over the past twenty-four hours didn't make sense.

We walked to the room at the end of the hall. Again, Terrence pulled the metal picks from his pocket and set to work on the door. It opened more quickly than the first.

"How do you know he's not here?" I asked quietly as we entered the room.

Terrence closed the door behind us, then turned his attention to me. "Because he had a meeting with my father. They'll go on and on for hours yet. Let's go. Kitchen is this way."

The room was a den of sorts, with an armchair and a tiny television. To the right was a short corridor, and that was where Terrence headed. Off the hallway was a single room. As we passed, I saw a small bed. Not the best living quarters for a tenured professor. Even mine and Terrence's bedroom was bigger.

At the end of the corridor was a kitchen. Terrence hadn't been kidding about the man being a drunk. Almost every inch of counter space had a bottle of alcohol. Gin, rum, vodka, whiskey.

"We drink that, we get sick," Terrence said. "We have to stick with beer for the night."

I nodded, worldly enough to know that rule.

He crossed his arms and leaned against the wall. "In the fridge."

So, he set this task to make me prove myself. Fine. I went to the fridge and pulled it open, not at all shocked to see dozens of brands of beer. I had enough cunning to grab two cans from the back, where their absence wouldn't be noticed. I put them into the interior pockets of my jacket, then hurried to Terrence.

"Let's get out of here," I whispered.

He didn't argue, only started back the way we came. As we passed by the bedroom, the front door opened.

"Forgot to lock the door again," said a deep, male voice. "Bugger it."

My eyes flew open wide, and I froze. Terrence looked petrified as well. Luckily, he recovered first and grabbed my hand. He pulled me into the bedroom and pushed me roughly to the floor.

"Under the bed!" he whispered urgently.

I wiggled on my belly and wedged myself between the carpet and low box spring. The tight space pressed on my chest, and I had difficulty drawing in breath.

Terrence crawled in beside me, on his stomach, and angled his head so I could see his face. Despite the initial shock, his eyes now shone with excitement. He was enjoying this? He had to be crazy! My only thought was how fast they'd put me on a plane back home if caught.

Terrence couldn't be correct in stating I'd never be expelled.

My body began to shake.

Likely sensing my inner dread, Terrence reached his hand out and gripped mine. The heat of his skin calmed me instantly. He raised his other hand and put a finger to his lip. As if I didn't already know that.

The professor entered the room, singing a song with resounding vibrato about King Arthur. His footsteps went around the bed to a side door. I followed his movements with my eyes, expecting him to drop to the ground at any moment and discover us.

Instead, he went into the bathroom. The sound of a showerhead turned on and drowned out his lyrics, if not the melody.

Terrence gave my hand a squeeze, and I glanced in his direction.

He motioned with his head to back out. I looked back to the bathroom and heard the change in the pattern of the falling water, a sign the professor had gotten into the shower. I scrambled backward. Once free from the bed, I didn't wait for Terrence; I bolted to the front door.

Fortunately, Terrence was only a few seconds behind me. I opened the door swiftly, and we raced into the hallway. My dread fueled my flight, and I reached the far stairwell before Terrence. I took the stairs two at a time, nearly stumbling on the second-floor landing. Still, I pressed on. I had to get out of there.

I threw the back door open and gasped for air. The cool inhalation stung my lungs. I leaned forward, resting my hands on my knees.

The heat of Terrence's hand touched my back. "You're quick when you want to be. Come on. Let's go finish our drinks."

His hand lingered for just a moment more; then he set off, away from the building. He didn't head back to our dorm room, but toward the edge of campus where trees clumped together atop a low hill.

I followed him to the trees. He selected one and sank to the ground behind it. The thick trunk would block us from anyone who decided to gaze in this direction. I sat in front of him.

"Hand 'em over," he said, gesturing with his hand.

I shook my head. "You said if we did this, I could kiss you. That first."

The area was lit by a single lamppost next to a bench, several trees over. The little light that reached us threw odd shadows on Terrence's face. Still, I had no problem seeing the smirk on his lips.

"Okay. Go ahead."

I swallowed, suddenly nervous. I'd played the kissing games during school, but I'd never had feelings invested before. I'd only ever felt sexual attraction the red-eyed man. It was obvious to me that he and Terrence were the same person, somehow. That meant I could love Terrence.

I moved closer, shifting my body so I was on my hands and knees in front of him. His eyes never left mine. I leaned in. My eyes fluttered shut. I felt the residual heat of him before I made contact. My lips touched his. Softly. I brushed them back and forth before opening my mouth just a bit to feel more of him. He tasted as good as he smelled, of cinnamon and strong spices, plus the lingering scent of beer from the bar.

He kissed me back, just as lightly. His hands lifted and gripped my biceps. To keep me from getting closer or keep me from pulling back, I didn't know. The kiss went on and on.

Eventually, Terrence placed his palm on my shoulder and gently pushed me back. I went willingly.

"The beer," he said.

I tried to hide my heavy breathing, my shaking limbs. I removed the two beers from my pockets and handed one over. He opened it and took a swig. I did the same with my can. The taste of it was bitter compared to the kind we'd had at the Swift Unicorn. Still, I chugged it.

Terrence finished his and tossed the empty can over my shoulder. It clattered against a tree, then rolled down the side of the hill.

"You ready?"

I finished mine and set the can on the ground. "Yeah."

I had trouble getting to my feet. The rush of overwhelming emotions and the extra alcohol wasn't the best combination. Terrence slipped his arm through mine and pulled me up. He stayed like that, pressed close to me, as we walked down the hill.

When we entered the building, Terrence waved to Michael, the RA, and he waved back. That meant we were in before curfew. Though it was likely a close thing. Many students filled the lobby, most gathered around the television watching American football. A few called out to Terrence, and he lifted his hand in greeting.

"I can make it up to the room by myself," I told him, in case he wanted to stay with his friends.

He shook his head. "I'm ready to call it a night."

With his arm still linked in mine, we made our way upstairs.

Once in our room, I didn't even bother changing out of my clothes. I collapsed onto the bed and nuzzled my head into the pillow.

"Night," I mumbled.

Terrence laughed softly. I felt his heat draw near; then his hands removed my shoes. He lifted the blanket and covered it over me. "Good night."

I smiled contentedly and snuggled further into the warmth of my covers. I fell asleep almost instantly.

Chapter Six

I woke with a blinding headache. I thanked every god and demon in existence that classes didn't start until tomorrow. I opened one eye experimentally but closed it again as the morning rays of the sun struck it. The light pierced my brain, frying at least half of my brain cells. Or maybe the beer had done that.

"Good morning," Terrence said cheerfully.

I flinched at his words, covering my ears with my hands. I forced my eyes open again and saw him dressed and ready for the day. He sat at his desk, a book in his hands.

"Uhh," I answered. Anything else was beyond me.

Terrence laughed. "Can't hold your liquor. Pretty pathetic, Collin."

I groaned at his words, not the insult they carried. His voice echoed through the empty caverns of my head.

"Shh."

He snickered but didn't say anything else.

Fighting the pain in my brain and my body, I got into a sitting position. I glared at him through squinted eyes, but he'd returned his attention to his book.

"Why are you in your uniform?"

"Meet and greet starts in an hour. The business program might not be as prestigious as literature, but we still have one."

"Fuck," I said with feeling.

Terrence gave me an approving glance. He stood and came to my bed. "You need some help?"

I started to shake my head but thought better of it. "No. Give me a minute."

"I was going to grab breakfast. Want me to wait for you?"

The idea of food roiled my already fragile stomach. "You go ahead. I'll see you later."

He left me alone in my misery. With him out of the room, I finally let go of my breath in a big rush. The half-hazy scenes from last night, of my lips pressed to his, had hit me hard when our eyes met. I couldn't think with him in the room. I *had* kissed him. I remembered the heat from his lips.

I raised my fingers and touched where our mouths had met. It had been intense, and the memory of it seared in my mind.

The red-eyed man loved me. I knew it. I could feel it in every fiber of my bones. But Terrence wasn't that man. *Yet*. He'd told me he'd come back to me. I had to wait for him. I couldn't rush this, couldn't smother him with memories *I* had, but he did not.

"God, this is too confusing. What the fuck is going on at this crazy school?"

Thinking about this topic hurt my brain while sober. Dwelling on it now was futile.

I rose from bed and stumbled into the shower. The scalding water helped clear my head, as did the motions of washing off yesterday's grime. When I climbed out, I felt better, more like myself. I brushed my teeth, shaved off what little stubble there was on my chin, and dressed in my slacks, shirt, and blazer.

The meet and greet for the literature program was in Regalia Hall, right next to my dorm. The dean had said all my classes would be there as well. About time I poked around.

As I passed the side of the building, I gazed up at the cat statues. Why cats? Each figure posed differently: one stretched lazily, one stood regally, and one had a mouse clutched in their paw. All of them, though, had eyes that peered down and seemed to follow me as I rounded the corner.

At the front of the building, I saw a few other students heading into the main entrance. I hurried to follow them inside.

My first sight of the hall made my jaw drop. Expecting an old, Gothic-style decor, I still wasn't prepared for the vaulted ceilings and the fluted columns around the perimeter of the large entrance room. The floor was a mosaic of millions, if not billions, of half-inch colored tiles. I couldn't make out the pattern from here, but I knew if I gazed down from the second floor it would be clear. The effort involved to construct it was impossible to comprehend.

Along one side was a buffet table, filled with breakfast finger foods and cups of coffee. Most of the students milled around it, snatching up tiny muffins and shoving them into their mouths. I made to go that way when a voice stopped me.

"Collin!"

I glanced around and saw Dean Helmer approaching me. He reached my side and clapped a hand on my shoulder.

"How are you, lad? You're looking pale. Did you sleep okay?"

I swallowed. "I'm fine, Dean Helmer."

He gestured to the room. "So what do you think? Is it up to your standards?"

"It's beautiful. I was admiring the mosaic."

"Most of it is original," he said, nodding. "A few repairs over the centuries." He lifted his gaze and ran it around the room. "Have you met any of your fellow classmates?"

"No, not yet."

"I see Tabitha over there. Shall I introduce you?"

I followed his gaze to a petite, young blonde woman who stood admiring a painting on the wall.

"If you don't mind."

"Not at all. Come along."

I walked beside him feeling nervous. Terrence had filled my mind since I first saw him, so the anxiety accompanying the start of a new school year in a foreign country had faded to the background. Now it raged forward, demanding I pay attention. There were only five new students enrolled in the program this year. What if they didn't like me?

"Tabitha?" the dean said as we approached.

She spun to face us, a large smile on her painted lips. "Yes, Dean Helmer?" Her accent was thick, not British, but French. It was odd to think that I wouldn't be the only foreign student.

"I'd like to introduce you to Collin Frey. He's from America."

"Nice to meet you. I'm Tabitha Fabron."

I stuck my hand out and vaguely wondered if it was a culturally acceptable gesture. I almost sighed in relief when she shook it.

Tabitha smiled at me, putting dimples in her cheeks. "What school did you come from?"

"Uh, Dixie County High School."

She nodded as if that was what she expected. "I'm from Maison de Verre."

"Oh," I said as if that was what I had expected.

"And here's Laura," Dean Helmer said.

Another woman joined our group. She was tall—taller than me—and lanky. Her long brown hair hung loose and covered her left eye.

"Laura Ammar," the dean introduced. "This is Collin Frey and Tabitha Fabron."

We all shook hands. Her grip was strong, and the single brown eye I could see looked focused.

"Where are you from?" Tabitha asked.

"Ontario. Canada," she added when Tabitha continued to stare.

"I'm from Florida," I said.

Laura nodded. "Another student is from America. I met him last night. Omar. Have you seen him yet?"

"No, I haven't met anyone but my roommate."

Dean Helmer shifted at that, and I recalled that he was Terrence's estranged father. Was it weird to mention him around the dean?

"I'll go see if I can find Omar and Sammuel," Helmer said. He wandered off.

That was probably my fault. I'd have to watch what I said from now on.

"That's an amazing painting," Laura said, turning to the portrait Tabitha had been admiring before we joined her. "Is it de la Mar?"

"It is," Tabitha said excitedly. "I'm surprised you recognize his work."

I gazed up at the artwork. Renaissance in style, but it featured a fat grub sitting in a chair instead of a person. "I don't know that artist."

I studied art as a hobby, but only to build my drawing skills and fuel my selfish desire of recreating the red-eyed man. My passion came from drawing the lines of his face, the rubies of his eyes, not the contemplation of other artists' skills or styles.

"He's pretty obscure," Tabitha said. "Even in our circles."

Laura laughed at that, and Tabitha joined in. I attempted a polite chuckle.

Tabitha pointed at the lower half, showing a floor that resembled ground instead of tile or carpet. "I always admired his use of detail. You can see the different veins in each of the leaves."

"I like the color scheme," Laura said. "Earth tones, but with a hint of cool in the blue drapes. His *La Fleur Qui Pleure* is one of my favorites."

Tabitha made a noise of agreement.

Before I could give a vague comment to feel included, Dean Helmer returned with two other men. The first was tall with charcoal skin and nearly black eyes. His dark hair was cut short to his scalp. The second was almost his opposite in coloring but his equal in height. Skin as pale as milk, dirty-blond hair, and light-blue eyes.

"This is Omar Jones and Sammuel Larkspur. Omar is from Georgia."

I reached forward and shook Omar's hand. "I'm Collin Frey, from Florida."

He grinned. "That makes us neighbors."

I smiled, too, relaxing at his easygoing response.

When I let go of his hand and moved onto Sammuel, my anxiety returned. His grip was unnecessarily tight, and his smile never reached his eyes. "I plan on being top student in our year. Plan accordingly."

His voice, when he spoke, had a near identical accent to the dean's. A local. The only one in our year. Was that a good thing, or a bad thing?

I pried my hand out of his. "Sure."

The women shook the men's hands, and Sammuel whispered the same threat to each of them. Tabitha glared right back, but Laura seemed unperturbed.

"Good, good," Helmer said jovially, paying no attention to the hostile undertones. "Now that we're all acquaintances, I'll leave you to it."

He left us and I shifted from foot to food awkwardly.

"Where about in Georgia are you from?" I asked Omar.

He folded his arms across his broad chest. "Remerton—a suburb of Valdosta."

I nodded. It was pretty close to the Florida border. "I'm in Cross City."

"We vacationed down that way a few years ago. Horseshoe Beach."

"Yeah. We drive there almost every weekend. My dad is an amateur surfer."

Omar laughed. "But not you?"

"I'll swim occasionally, but my balance is shit. Can't stay on the board."

"I hear ya. Never even wanted to try surfing."

"Football?"

His smile deepened. "Yup. Linebacker. The only thing that made me consider not attending Marke Staple. This is one of the best schools for people like us, but there's no football team here."

I wasn't sure what the *people like us* statement meant, but I understood not being able to play football. "Tough choice, huh?"

He shrugged. "In the end, I had to think about what would serve me long-term. I'm decent at football, not great, so I couldn't bank my future on the slim possibility of going pro."

"Well, maybe I can help keep your skills fresh. I'd love to toss around the ball. I was second string quarterback for my high school team."

His eyes crinkled in delight. "Serious, man? That would be awesome. Maybe we can find enough to fill out a team."

I barked a laugh. "How many Americans attend here? I bet they'd all be down."

"There are five, so we'll have to recruit more." Before I could ask how he knew that, he pressed on. "We'll have to see once school gets started. I wouldn't want it to interfere with studying. That would kind of defeat the purpose of choosing Marke Staple."

"Attention!" called Dean Helmer.

We both spun. The dean stood on the steps that lead to the upper floor. He had his hands raised. The noise in the room quieted.

"Welcome to the start of a new semester. A special welcome to our incoming freshmen." He glanced in our direction and nodded.

"To start, I feel I should remind you of the rules. A few of you older students need a refresher." His eyes shot to a group of boys beside a pillar. "There is no alcohol allowed on the school grounds, even for those old enough to drink."

A collective groan sounded through the students.

The dean pushed on over the din. "Same with tobacco products. We want our students to devote their minds to studying, not burning their potential with these substances.

"Men are not allowed anywhere inside the women's dormitories. Any man caught on the premises will face immediate expulsion. Women are allowed in the men's dormitories up until nine o'clock at night. Any woman found inside after those hours will face a suspension.

"Curfew is ten thirty on weeknights and midnight on the weekends. No exceptions. Anyone breaking curfew faces suspension. This applies to all students at Marke Staple, but it's especially true for those in the literature program. It is paramount that you follow this rule. You cannot be outside your dormitories after midnight."

I shivered at the seriousness of the warning, but the gathered students looked bored now as if they'd heard these rules a thousand times. A few whispered to each other, not even bothering to pay attention.

"And finally, please remember that you are not to study outside of the school's walls. If I get even a hint of that, students will be banned from the school, without even a trial to defend themselves. This is a very serious matter."

Helmer's eyes met mine briefly, and I stared back, puzzled. He moved on, singling out all the other freshmen. What could possibly be bad about studying off campus? It made no sense.

"Now, I dare say I've taken enough of your time. That concludes my announcements. Please stop by the buffet table if you haven't yet."

The dean descended the steps to a sprinkle of applause. I noticed that Lisbeth and her group of seniors clapped hardest.

Laura and Tabitha went back to discussing art. Sammuel joined them. I turned back to Omar.

"Can you tell what the mosaic is?" I asked, gesturing to our feet.

He glanced down. "No. I haven't been upstairs yet."

"I'm curious. You wanna see it too?"

He shrugged.

I started toward the stairwell that Dean Helmer so recently vacated, and Omar followed after me.

"The architecture is beautiful," I commented.

"Yeah. All the schools are similar, keeping to the same themes."

I thought of Florida State, where Mindy currently attended. It didn't resemble this at all.

The steps were marble, white with veins of gold and silver swirling throughout. The banister was antique wood, polished but still showing its age. They tried so hard to make it intimidating. I was afraid to rest my hand atop it as we climbed.

When we got to the second floor, I eagerly turned to look at the pattern on the floor. My jaw dropped.

"Pretty cool," Omar said. He leaned forward and put his elbows on the banister.

Below, the mosaic took on the shape of a whirlwind, pitch black on the outskirts, but bursting with color as it reached the center. Along the edges there were starbursts that offset the darkness. Like the battle of good versus evil. Was it biblical in nature? The Creation?

Then, at the center, was a cluster of white tiles. There were two lines, and they crossed over each other, forming an X. I had no idea what it could symbolize. Just one more thing I didn't understand.

"I skipped breakfast," I said, still gazing down at the awesome display before me. "Do you want to go get some food?"

"Sure," Omar said. "So far, nothing's compared to my mom's cooking."

I laughed, and it seemed to break the spell the floor had cast on me. I turned to him. "I think England is known for its bland cuisine. I don't think anything will be as good as back home."

He shook his head and grinned. "My mom is a terrible cook. The food here's been an improvement."

We set off for the buffet table.

Chapter Seven

Talking with Omar cured a bit of my homesickness—a feeling I didn't even realize was inside me. We chatted about football, television shows, films, hobbies. His easygoing nature was infectious and our conversation flowed smoothly.

"So your roommate isn't a literature student either?" I asked after I nibbled on a tiny bite of a biscuit. My stomach still felt tender.

Omar shook his head. "I think they discourage that to minimize competitiveness. Can you imagine sharing a room with Sammuel?"

I'd only met Sammuel briefly, but I could tell his type. And Omar was right. It would be awful being stuck with that all day and night.

"Your roommate's nice?" Omar asked.

"I'm in love with him," I answered without thinking. Once my brain realized my words, I fidgeted nervously.

Omar's eyes widened for an instant before he forced them back to normal. "That's fast."

"It's complicated," I said with a sigh.

"How's he feel about you?"

"He loves me too. Just not yet."

Omar raised his eyebrow. "Confident, huh?"

"It's a long story." I hadn't meant to unload this piece of information at all. Maybe if we became friends, I could trust him enough. I'd always wanted another person's perspective on the whole thing, but I never wanted anyone thinking I was crazy. "Your parents okay with you being overseas?"

"Mom didn't want me to come here, but she understood the honor. And my desire. It'll be hard on her though. I'm an only child, and my dad died two years ago."

"Oh shit. I'm sorry."

He shrugged. "Iraq. His helicopter was shot down outside Mosul."

"Why didn't your mom relocate here?"

He looked horrified at the idea. "Your mom must not be overbearing."

"Not really. I've got an older sister who needs much more attention that I do."

"With only me, her love is incredibly focused, like a laser beam. I don't want to be in her line of fire." He shivered. "Besides, it's only four years. And I'll visit."

My parents and I hadn't really discussed any visits home. Not seriously. The plane tickets here had cost most of my parents' savings. Going home for vacation seemed counterproductive. For summers, I'd have to, but not likely for the shorter breaks.

"Did she fly over here with you?"

His body convulsed again, and he almost dropped his muffin. "No, thank God."

I laughed. "You want to meet after dinner to throw around your football?"

"Yeah, that'd be great."

I glanced around the emptying hall. "Are we allowed we go now?"

"Looks like it."

I took my plate with mostly untouched food and put it in the trash can.

Omar did the same, though he'd eaten much more than me. "I'm heading back to the dorm. You going that way?"

"Yeah."

We set off together toward the doors. It was almost noon, but the sun was much lower in the southern sky than I was used to. It was just as bright, but different. Another reminder I wasn't home.

"You want to exchange numbers?" I asked Omar as we rounded the corner of Regalia Hall.

"Yeah. I'll text you when I'm heading down to dinner. We can meet in the cafeteria."

Eagerly, I pulled my phone from my blazer's interior pocket. I opened up a new contact and handed it over. He did the same with his.

I typed my name and then had to ponder for a moment before I remembered my new number. Changing it had been a hassle, but necessary since I planned to be here four years. I gave it back, then accepted mine with a grin.

"Cool," I said. "I think my new plan has unlimited texting."

"Mine does. Mom's already texted me a hundred times."

My parents had called at some point during the night—when I'd been passed out drunk. I had to call them back, but I'd have to wait until they were awake. This time difference was weird. I was six hours in their future.

At the dorm, we split up. Omar's room was on the first floor, so I waved as I approached the stairwell. Walking down the hall, I wondered if Terrence would be back from his meet and greet yet. My heart ached to see him again.

When I got to our door, I knocked before turning the knob. Terrence was in, but to my surprise, so were four other people. They barely fit into our small room.

"Hi, Collin," Terrence greeted. He sat on his bed, in between two women. On my bed were two men.

I shut the door behind me. "Hi."

Terrence nodded his head to the side. "This is Fresha and Mallory." He gestured to the other two. "That's Ham and Kenneth. They were just leaving, weren't you guys?"

They stood as one, as if Terrence's words had been a command.

"See ya," the tallest guy said as they walked to the door.

They left before I could say anything.

"How was meet and greet?" Terrence said. I'd watched his friends leave the room, so I turned to face him. He was standing close, the cinnamon scent of him assaulting my nostrils. I almost retreated from his nearness before remembering that was my goal. I relaxed in his radiating warmth.

I smiled. "Good. I met the other freshmen. One's from Georgia. About two hours away from where I live."

He reached out and gripped my forearm. "Friends already? Should I be jealous?" There was a twinkle in his eyes.

I regarded him seriously. "You have nothing to worry about."

He stepped even closer. "Don't I? What about this man from Colorado?"

Why was he bringing this up now? Why this sudden flirtation? The attitude was welcomed, but the little I'd gathered about his personality was he didn't do anything spontaneously. This was planned, which meant he had a purpose. Using me.

Did I care? No, because he was smiling and drawing nearer.

"What about him?"

"Should I be jealous?"

"Of course not."

He stood right in front of me, a bare inch between our bodies. "Good."

I leaned forward and closed the distance separating us. His lips responded. The taste of him, of strong, heady spices, filled my mouth. I groaned as it all overwhelmed me.

He pulled away, and my eyes slowly opened. He wore a grin, still playful and light.

"What was that for?" I asked.

"Nothing."

My hand trailed down his arm, and I twined our fingers together. His skin was incredibly hot—like a fever raged within him. My grip tightened.

Suddenly, he drew back. "Ow."

I looked at his hand and saw a speck of blood dripping from a tiny prick in the pad of his thumb.

"You okay?"

He stuck his digit into his mouth, almost coyly. "Papercut. You bumped it and reopened the wound."

"I'm sorry."

He waved away my concern, then walked back to his bed. "No problem. It'll stop."

I ached to have him beside me again. I almost followed, wanting to keep in contact, but I refrained. Instead, I went to my desk and plugged in my cell phone.

"How was your meet and greet?" I asked. "Did you meet those guys there?"

"I met Fresha last month when Mom moved me in. Her parents dropped her off early too. Ham and Kenneth have a room down the hall. Mallory I met today. She's very ambitious."

"Well, your program is competitive, right? It makes sense to be ambitious."

"I think she'll be useful."

I glanced over at him, and he shot me a smirk. Was he still playing? Yes. I could tell by the curve of his lips. "Do I need to be jealous?"

He laughed, but didn't reject the statement like I had.

He would betray me. Meaning he'd sleep with someone else? Was that the worst of his crimes against me?

I pushed it from my mind. Even if I knew how, I couldn't prevent it.

"I need to call my parents." I glanced at my clock and then mentally subtracted six hours. "They should be awake by now."

I sat at my desk so I could keep my phone plugged in. This battery wasn't as good as the one in my old phone. I tapped on the picture of my mom in my contact list and waited for it to ring. She answered almost immediately.

"Hey, Collin! We were waiting for you to call us back."

"Didn't want to wake you."

"It's been hard for us to get back on Florida time, after all the time-zone hopping. I've been up since four."

"You should have called me then."

"Didn't want to interrupt your meet and greet. How'd it go?"

I ran through the details of my classmates and the Regalia building. She listened intently and asked all the right questions. She was happy that Omar was a neighbor, and she insisted I ask for his mom's number so she could connect with her. That seemed weird to me, but I told her I'd try.

She caught me up on Mindy and Rocket, our cocker spaniel. But obviously things hadn't changed in the three days I'd been gone. Nothing moved that fast in Cross City.

"Make sure you call me tomorrow after class."

"I will, Mom."

"Talk to you later, sweetie. We love you."

I glanced at Terrence, a bit embarrassed. "Love you too."

I hung up, then set my phone on my desk.

"What do you want to do the rest of the day?" Terrence asked.

Glad he didn't tease, I said, "Anything but go to the bar."

"You didn't enjoy that yesterday?"

"I don't think my stomach could handle it again so soon. Oh, and I told Omar we'd play football after dinner."

"We, you and him? Or we, you and me?"

Again, there was a light in his eyes, and a flirtatious tone laced his words. What the hell was he doing?

"You interested in American football?"

His nose wrinkled. "*American*? Not really."

"Then you don't have to come."

"But am I invited?"

"Of course you are."

He nodded. "You'll have to show me how to play."

Chapter Eight

The next morning, my muscles groaned as I rolled out of bed. I slid my finger along my phone's screen to silence the alarm, then moaned in pain. Throwing around the football last night had morphed into an impromptu game, complete with tackles when others had joined. I hadn't complained when Terrence threw me to the ground and straddled over my hips, but I was paying for it now.

Across the room, Terrence was also climbing out from his covers. Once again, he stretched, and his pajama shirt lifted slightly, showing the pale skin of his stomach. It had to be intentional.

"Morning," I said.

"Morning. Fight you for the shower?"

"You go first."

"Sure?"

I nodded. "But hurry or I'll fall back asleep."

"You can climb in with me."

I met his gaze, my heart suddenly beating furiously. He smiled.

I didn't return his grin. "Don't tease me. What if I said yes?"

"Who said I was teasing?"

"You want to take a platonic, joint shower?"

He walked to me, his lips still curved. "Why don't we start there and see where it leads?"

Then he kissed me. Electricity shot through my body. I reached out and grabbed his shirt in my fists and pulled him against me. He made a noise but didn't try to get away.

I moved my mouth hungrily against his. I'd been so starved for his affection, always wondering if I'd feel this intimacy with him. How fucked up my adolescence was, knowing he was out there somewhere but unable to be with me. So many avenues of exploration had been cut off to me, sexual and otherwise due to my obsession with my red-eyed man. Now the paths aligned, and I couldn't heed the yield signs all around.

I took a step backward and bumped the edge of my bed. I toppled onto it, dragging him with me. We landed in a heap, him atop me, our kiss never stilling.

God, this is too good. This is everything I ever wanted.

My morning stiffness was already evolving into an erection. I could feel a similar reaction from him, digging into my thigh. This was all happening too fast, or not fast enough. I couldn't tell. My mind was a haze of heat and cinnamon.

Terrence broke our kiss and said against my lips, "Come with me to the shower."

I struggled to think, to focus on the facts: namely, that it was the first day of school, and we'd be late if this continued. "We don't have time."

"Fuck it." He punctuated his point with another round of frenzied kisses.

I wanted to, more than anything in my life. *Why am I resisting? He's willing. I'm more than willing.*

"Fuck it," I repeated. "Let's go."

He moaned and got off me. I stood, awkwardly trying to hide the tent in my pants. Not that it mattered, as I immediately began to take off my clothes. Terrence stood less than a foot away and removed his own pajamas. I got distracted as I watched him reveal more and more of his pale skin.

"Quick," he prompted.

I gave a start, then resumed my task.

He finished first, which left me grateful. I had been filled with doubt, thinking this was a joke, and he'd eventually stop and laugh at me. With him nude and erect in front of me, those doubts vanished.

He took a half step toward me. "Need help?"

"No, go start the water. I'm right behind you."

He shot me a smirk, then went to the bathroom. I was distracted again as I stared at his ass. Once he disappeared from my sight, I pulled off my pants and boxer briefs, then hurried after him.

The bathroom was wide in length, but short in width. The single sink in front of the door hardly gave us enough space for both our toiletries. The toilet on the right and the shower stall on the left completed the room. Not easy for two grown men to navigate together. Still, we persisted. Me, fueled on by my years of desire, him, likely just by hormones. Because he *didn't* love me yet. I had no idea why this was occurring.

Terrence tested the water's heat with his hand, then climbed inside. I joined him. The smallish rectangle barely held both of us. The tight quarters forced us close, not that I minded.

He had the foresight to realize we did need to get clean, so he grabbed the bar of soap and wetted it under the showerhead. He lathered his body as I watched, salivating. The bubbles slid tantalizingly along his skin. When I reached out to touch him, he stopped me.

"Business first."

He gripped my shoulders and shifted us so we switched positions, me under the water's flow. I expected him to hand me the soap. Instead, *he* ran the bar over my chest. Despite the heat of the water and his body, I shivered as it brushed across my nipples.

I couldn't stand it anymore. I pressed him up against the slick wall. I attacked his mouth and delighted in the feeling of his eager response. My tongue licked at his lips, begging entrance. He obliged and his spicy taste increased. Our tongues mingled, and my brain's fuzziness increased. My entire awareness zoomed into a single focal point of our bodies' alignment.

The soap made us slide against each other. My arms gripped his shoulders, pinning him in place. The suds migrated south, and so did Terrence's hands. They started on my hips, guiding my grind into him, but they eventually roamed farther down. His knuckles brushed against my cock, and I took a labored breath.

"Good?" he asked.

"Yes, Terrence." I savored the taste of his name on my tongue. How satisfying to know it now.

"What else?" His fingers shifted to grip my cock. Aided by the suds, his palm slid up and down easily.

My eyes shut from the intensity of the pleasure. It was better than I ever imagined.

"What else?" he prompted again.

"Can I touch you too?"

His grip on me tightened. "I'd like that."

I pressed our lips together as my hand sought his erection. The heat of it was unreal, and my mind thought of how good it would feel in my mouth, or pressing into my asshole. For now, this was perfection.

He gasped against my lips, and I echoed with one of my own. Our hands began to move, and I matched my rhythm to his. We fell into sync, sliding in unison.

"Oh God," I mumbled. "Terrence."

"Faster?"

In answer, I sped up my hand. He mimicked my pace.

I leaned forward and buried my face in his neck. The soap dampened the scent of him, but it still lingered. I inhaled deeply, wanting to drown in his smell.

"Gonna come," he said.

I grunted in reply.

His body tensed, and he uttered my name like a curse. Semen shot from his cock, coating my fingers. I followed a second behind, squeezing my eyes shut in the bliss of my orgasm. I still kept my hand moving, though slower now.

I breathed heavily against his neck, spent and satisfied. My hand stilled and just held him, and he did the same to me. It had been the most amazing experience of my life. It left my whole body shaking and filled with energy.

Shifting, I moved my lips to his. We kissed gently now, our bodies pressed close.

"We need to hurry," he said into my mouth. "You don't want to be late your first day."

I was beyond caring at that point. My whole world had just turned upside down. Trivial things like school were pushed to the periphery of my attention.

I raised my hand to his face and ran my knuckles along his cheek. His smile held a bit of mischief.

"Why did you do this?" I asked.

His smile slipped. "What?" He moved out of my embrace and into the stream of water. He let it fall over his head and wet his hair. He added shampoo to his hand and lathered it into his locks.

Despite the sudden ache in my stomach, I did the same. "You're pushing this along too fast."

"Me? You're agreeing to everything I suggest."

I growled softly. "You're not making sense. I've got my reasons for liking you—"

"This guy from Colorado?" he said with a barely suppressed sneer. "Using me as a substitute."

I shook my head. "No, that's not what this is. I don't... I don't love him anymore. Or rather, I love him in a different way."

"You're not making sense," he retorted, then put his face under the water. When he emerged, he eyed me up and down. "You think I'd do this with anyone?"

His betrayal was what caused these thoughts in me. But he hadn't done it yet. How could I be mad at something that was in our future?

I sighed. "I don't know. Terrence, this is getting confusing. I need to think, and I can't do it when you're next to me."

He grinned again and slid closer to me, his anger apparently gone. "Maybe we should share a bed tonight? Wouldn't that be nice?"

Frowning, I still let him kiss me. Then he drew back and rinsed himself. "I'll get out of here and let you finish. We won't have time for breakfast, but we shouldn't be late for class."

He climbed from the stall, leaving me alone. I rinsed, too, running my hands through my hair. My body still felt on fire from his attention. At the same time, my heart ached from his absence.

I turned off the water and opened the glass door. My towel was hanging on a peg on the wall, and I quickly used it to dry myself off. Terrence was at the sink, brushing his teeth. The room was too small for us both to do that, so I went out into our bedroom and dressed. When he emerged, we switched places, and I finished my morning routine.

I'd set my alarm for six thirty, but all that petting had eaten a huge chunk of our time. It was already quarter past seven. My first class started at seven thirty. If this became a habit, we'd have to wake up earlier.

I grabbed my messenger bag with my sketch pad, notebooks, pencils, and laptop inside. I wasn't sure which method would be best for taking notes, so I brought along everything today.

Terrence slipped on his shoes at the door. "All set?"

I nodded and put on my loafers.

We headed out into the hallway. It was empty. Everyone would be down at breakfast by now. My stomach rumbled, but I didn't regret our actions. I'd choose Terrence over food anytime.

We took the stairs to the lobby. Here were a few stragglers, which made me feel better. At least we weren't the only ones who were running late.

The morning air was chilly, and I was thankful for the blazer's warmth. If it was like this in September, how cold would it be in December? I shivered at the thought.

"You okay?" Terrence asked.

"Fine. I guess I'll see you at lunch?"

He smiled. "Oh no. I'm going to meet you after your first class is done. I can't wait to see your face."

"I hope I don't disappoint."

Laughing, he nudged me with his shoulder. "You'll understand later. You'd do the same in my position."

I shook my head. When we reached the corner of Regalia, Terrence headed to Hayden Hall for a math class. We'd compared our schedules the night before. The odd thing was that Terrence's courses were normal sounding: Business Ethics, College Algebra, Marketing 101. Mine were strange, with names like Methods, Tomes, and Theory. Theory was my first class, and Dean Helmer was listed as the professor.

"I guess I'll see you," I said.

"Good luck," he replied ominously.

I wanted to kiss him, but he turned and left before I could grab him. I watched him walk away, my heart pounding a quick beat.

"Collin!"

I spun at the voice, recognizing it as Omar's. He jogged up behind me, apparently also running late. "Hey. Didn't want to interrupt your time with your roommate." He nodded his head the way Terrence had gone.

"Nothing to interrupt." He raised his eyebrow questioningly, but I pressed on before he could say his thoughts aloud. "So, you ready for class?"

"Yeah, but let's hurry so we get good seats."

Chapter Nine

We walked into Regalia, the mosaic tiles drawing my attention down. A few other students milled about. Most were heading to the large lecture hall to the left of the room. I saw Tabitha and Laura going that way too.

"Do we all have our first class together?" I asked Omar. He obviously knew more about this than I did.

He nodded. "Theory class touches on different topics, so most of the time we'll be in a big group. The lessons apply to every level."

"I see."

We followed the crowd into the lecture hall. It was a pretty normal classroom, with three rows of stadium seats facing a raised platform on the lowest level. The twenty of us could easily fit into the first row, which implied that Marke Staple used to have more students in the literature program. Why had they downsized?

Omar entered the second row and sidled down the aisle until he got to Tabitha and Laura. He sat and I took the seat next to him.

I leaned forward and waved to the women. "Hi."

They both waved back.

Omar turned to me. "So, how are things with your roommate? He seemed really nice yesterday when we played football."

I dropped my voice to a whisper. "We jerked each other off in the shower this morning."

Omar blinked a few times—I knew I gave way too much information, but I had to tell someone. After a moment of silence, Omar smiled. "Well that's good. Means he must like you too. Right?"

I shook my head. "It's not that easy."

"You'll have to explain to me why. He seemed really into you last night. He touched you more than he had to."

"Territorial," I answered. "I think he wants to claim me."

His brown eyes narrowed. "That's usually not a good thing in a relationship, Collin."

"I know. A lot of things about us are unconventional."

"Don't let him take advantage of you."

I nodded. He was right, but at the same time, I knew I'd give Terrence anything he asked of me. Maybe that was his betrayal?

"Good morning, students," Dean Helmer called out as he walked down the stairs to the bottom stage. He held a briefcase in one hand and plopped it down on the lectern. "I see the last of us are coming in right now." He pulled out a cell phone and glanced at its screen. "Hurry, Miku and Jacques. Take your seats."

I glanced up the walkway and saw the two students drop into the last row.

"Thank you. Now, I'm so excited to start off the school year with new students. Though you likely met them yesterday, I'd like to ask all the freshmen to come forward and introduce themselves."

My stomach dropped like a lead ball. Get up in front of everyone? That was awkward.

Sammuel, in the front row, was the first on his feet. He marched proud and confident to the lowest level of the room. I glanced at Omar. He shrugged, then stood as well. I followed. Tabitha and Laura walked down too.

The five of us stood in a line beside the dean. Sammuel stepped forward first.

"I'm Sammuel Larkspur," he said, smiling at the students and Helmer. "I aim to be the best in the class. My special is ice."

The students still seated murmured appreciatively. I had no idea what he was talking about.

Laura, the tall girl from Canada, spoke next. "I'm Laura Ammar. My special is music." She kept her face lowered as she said that, and I noticed her cheeks were pink.

Next was Tabitha. "I'm Tabitha Fabron. My special is water."

I was up. "I'm Collin Fray."

The class stared at me expectantly.

When I didn't say anything else, Helmer kindly said, "Go on. What's your special?"

"I don't have one."

"Oh, so you're an Omnium Artium," he said with a chuckle. "Don't get too many of those. You may be able to give Sammuel a run for his money, then."

Sammuel eyed me with a calculating expression.

Then, Omar said, "I'm Omar Jones. My special is transformation."

There were several gasps from the students, including the other freshmen. Sammuel's piercing gaze switched from me to Omar. Sammuel didn't seem too happy by that announcement.

"Excellent," Helmer said. "I'm so happy to have new blood and new potential added to our school. We can all learn from each other, so do your best to help out anyone who needs it. It's never too late to add more to your repertoire."

We returned to our seats.

Helmer moved behind the podium. "Everyone should have the basics down by now. But, it's never a bad thing to review. Please take out your coins."

The students shuffled in their pockets, or purses, or bags, each pulling out small metal coins. My mind instantly went back to the ski slope to the silver coin Terrence had dropped in the snow. The coin with my face.

A queasy feeling filled my stomach.

Helmer noticed that I didn't have anything in my hands.

"Collin, where's your coin?"

I swallowed the taste of bile rising in my throat. "I don't have one."

The dean tilted his head quizzically. "Even if it's not one minted here, any coin will do."

I shook my head. "I don't have any coins."

Every eye fixed on me now. The dean's smile was wavering, and I could tell he was growing frustrated. "If you're in this program, you should have a coin."

"I, uh, might have a quarter in here."

The class laughed, and Helmer's smile fled. He said grumpily, "Omar, hand Collin your coin. See if it will refresh his memory."

Omar eyed me doubtfully but passed over his coin. It was small and made of a shiny, silver metal. On one side was a building, one I didn't recognize, but the words *Magica Meridiem* were printed under it. I flipped it over and saw what I expected. It was an exact replica of Omar's face. I could see the deep set to his eyes, his broad nose, the slight curve of his lips.

I looked up at the dean, my eyes wide with confusion and alarm.

"What is this coin?" I asked, my voice low and trembling.

The dean stared at me, taking in my pale face, my shaking hands, my quivering voice.

"The coins are the only way to access your magic in modern society."

Magic. Access *my* magic? The idea was ridiculous! I couldn't do magic. It didn't exist in the first place. And yet... I'd seen a man disappear. A man from my future. Time travel had to fall under magic. Or science fiction.

"Collin?" Dean Helmer's voice sounded far away. The room seemed to spin. "Collin?" his voice whispered, echoing off the caverns of my mind.

Everything went black.

Chapter Ten

My eyes fluttered open, and a wave of nausea made me shut them again. I groaned, then thought better about having my mouth open. I clamped my lips together. I was reclining, but not in bed.

"Collin?" Dean Helmer's single word reached my ears as if through water.

I kept my eyes closed tightly and shied away from the memories his voice tried to raise. I did not want to think about magic.

A hand touched my arm, and I flinched.

"Collin?" His voice sounded closer now, normal.

I risked another glance and saw his face, pale and frowning, only a few inches above me.

When he met my eyes, he sighed with relief. "Thank God. You gave us quite a fright."

Laboriously, I turned my head and saw Omar on my other side, crouched, his hand on my forearm. Behind him were eighteen of the literature students, staring at me with wide eyes.

Jesus! I'd fainted in the middle of class and everyone knew! There'd be no living down this shame. Why hadn't I asked to use the bathroom? Or just booked it out of there? Any option would have been better than this!

I tried to sit up and Helmer gently pushed my shoulder. "Stay still a moment longer. I've summoned Vivaan, our campus doctor. She will be here shortly."

"I'm fine," I insisted, but even Omar applied pressure on my arm to keep me down.

"Let's let Vivaan determine that," Helmer said. He glanced up and grimaced when he saw all the students still hovering behind Omar. "I fear the rest of class will be canceled. You're dismissed."

They didn't move a muscle.

Helmer's eyes narrowed. "Come on now. Off with you. Let the man get some air."

They muttered and shuffled. I shut my eyes as they left, trying to drown out the embarrassment that made heat rush to my cheeks.

Omar didn't leave, and Helmer didn't tell him to.

Once all the footsteps faded, I glanced at my professor. "What happened?"

Instead of answering, the dean hesitated. He thinned his lips into a line, as if contemplating. Finally, he said, "I suppose we need to clarify certain things about your scholarship, Collin."

Another spike of anxiety filled me. Were they going to pull me from the program? Did they realize I didn't really belong here? That I wasn't magic?

Helmer continued. "I never even considered that you didn't know about your magical potential. It's not unheard of for one of our students to come from a regular high school, but I've never had a student not realize what they were." He met my eyes, his gaze troubled.

"What I am?"

"A practitioner," he supplied. "A wielder of magic. Someone who can see the arcane lines in the world and manipulate them."

I swallowed, loudly, and shut my eyes against another wave of dizziness. "M-magic?"

Helmer said, "It's understandable your mind can't comprehend something it didn't know existed. It was a lot for your consciousness to absorb."

I *knew* it existed. I'd always known. Every one of my explanations for my experience in Colorado derived from the supernatural. I believed. I just never considered I'd be part of the population myself.

"I can use magic?" I clarified, glancing at the dean again.

"Yes. And according to our records, you're one of the most powerful in the United States."

My eyes widened. "What? How is that even possible?"

The dean grimaced and shrugged. "Governments keep tabs on practitioners, Collin. We have ways of reading a person's magical aptitude. Of course, anyone who has the skill is able to attend a specialized school—"

"A literature program?" I interrupted.

He smiled, as if I was following his line of thought. "Yes, exactly. These programs are available to all practitioners. But at this level, we seek only the most talented. When you applied, your government sent us your aptitude readings, and your scores are very high."

"How can they have a reading on me if I've never performed magic?"

"Magical ability is innate. The power you were born with stays with you until you die. Your familiarity with magic, your skills, your knowledge of spells, those can be increased as you practice and study. But there is no changing your initial spark. That magical DNA is measurable to someone who has the right instruments."

I shook my head, then regretted it. My brain felt like it sloshed around inside my skull. "How could other people know I had magic, but I didn't?" I glanced at Omar.

"You attended a magical school in Georgia, right? Magica Meridiem. Why didn't I go there too?"

"I got an acceptance letter when I was eight. Another from Aestus School of Literature in Sedona, Arizona, and Riggen's Academy in Quincy, Massachusetts. I picked Magica Meridiem because it was close to home. It had been Mom's plan all along."

Helmer spoke up. "Are you sure you didn't get acceptance letters, Collin? With your aptitude scores, I'm sure you must have."

"I don't know. My parents never mentioned them to me. But then, they wouldn't have understood why I was suddenly getting letters from weird schools."

"Shall I call them, Collin? Explain the situation and your abilities?"

"No!"

Helmer and Omar both looked shocked by my vehemence.

"No," I repeated, calmer. "I, uh, I'm not sure they'll believe you. If you call them and tell them all this, they'll think you're crazy. They'll be on the first plane back here to take me home. I don't want that."

The sudden sound of footsteps announced the arrival of the doctor. She was middle-aged, with her dark hair pulled back into a braid. Her green eyes bore into mine as she pushed Helmer aside to kneel next to me.

"What seems to be the issue, Mr. Frey?" she asked, her voice professional but soft.

"He fainted, Vivaan. The strain…"

She nodded, then lifted my palm into her right hand. With her left, she pinched a metal coin between her fingers. A cold chill entered through my veins, spreading out from the touch of her skin on mine. The invading tingle circled my entire body. I shivered uncontrollably as it lingered. Finally, it reached its origin and disappeared completely. Dr. Vivaan removed her hand.

"Fit as a fiddle, Dean Helmer. The fainting spell did no lasting harm. The knock to his head is better."

I blinked in surprise, realizing my head *did* feel better. I sat up, no longer woozy.

She reached out her hand to steady me, but I didn't need it. I got to my feet, hungry, but fine.

"Thank you, Doctor," I said. "I feel much better."

"You need to keep up your strength," she said. "Don't skip breakfast again tomorrow. You should have enough time to get a bite to eat now, before your next class starts."

"An excellent idea," Helmer said. He patted my shoulder and placed his other on Omar. "Omar, would you mind escorting Collin to the cafe? Then make sure you're both back here for Tomes."

"Yes, sir," Omar answered.

We started toward the door.

"And, Collin," Helmer said.

I turned to look at him over my shoulder.

"If you need to talk to our school therapist, please let me know. Talking may help."

Dr. Vivaan raised her eyebrow, and I didn't doubt Helmer would share the gossip as soon as we were out of earshot.

We exited the room and headed toward the building's main doors.

"You don't need to walk me," I told Omar, embarrassed. "I really do feel fine. Dr. Vivaan's...whatever she did...worked."

"A healing spell. My mom's an RN—a normal one, at a normal hospital—but she's able to use magic occasionally. Magic can only use the body's existing components. It can't cure cancer, or grow back limbs. Your fall couldn't have been too bad."

I was glad he'd clarified magic's limitations, because my first thought was how cruel the magical community had to be to deny regular people aid for horrible diseases.

"I always came home bruised from football practice. Mom could heal those." He fell silent as we passed through the doorway and into the sunlight. "So, uh, you've got questions, right?"

I sighed. "I don't even know where to begin. If I've got magic, does that mean my parents do too?"

"Usually. About 75 percent of the population can use magic. It's common. Though the skill those people possess is small. If they activate their magic, it's only for little things. A cut healing quicker. Something falling off a bookshelf. Loud noises at the end of a hallway."

"Supernatural phenomenon is really people's magical abilities coming out?"

"Pretty much. Reports of a ghost or possessions are untamed magic running free."

"Then why don't more people know about magic? Why let their powers go unused?"

"This is Theory 101, Collin. If people even suspected magic was real, they'd want magical solutions to all their problems. And I'm sure you've already guessed that magic can't do that. It's pretty limited."

"Then why learn at all?"

He shrugged his broad shoulders. "It has its uses. Most who become skilled practitioners try for places in the government."

"Lisbeth said that yesterday too."

"The senior? Yeah, she does have her sights focused on that. Wants to follow in her father's footsteps. He's one of the lead practitioners here in the British government."

I looked at Omar questioningly. "How do you know that?" I was suddenly reminded of how much he knew of the student body yesterday at our meet and greet.

Surprisingly, his dark cheeks turned darker. "I follow her on social media. And all the other literature students who accepted my request. I don't like being in the dark around other practitioners. I like to know who I'm up against."

"You make it sound like it's a fight."

He shook his head. "Not a fight, but definitely a competition. You heard Sammuel. He aims to be the best in our year. I'm not going to sit by and let that happen."

I understood competitiveness, even if I didn't have a spark of it myself, currently. Ambition, the desire to be the best you can be, had to be a trait the government wanted. It made sense the school would encourage that battle for superiority.

"But what if you don't want to work in the government?" It sounded boring to me.

"You can teach. There are many schools with literature programs."

I wrinkled my nose. "What else?"

"You can be anything you want, Collin. You don't have to use your powers for a job. Be a postal worker. Be an architect. Be a painter, or a writer, or a stockbroker."

I laughed. "For that, I should transfer to the business program."

He shared my grin.

The cafe was empty when we entered. The workers still had it set up for breakfast, as there was enough time between the first and second class to grab a snack. Omar told me he'd eaten already, so he only ordered a coffee. I helped myself to a plate of biscuits and gravy. We sat at a table beside the window.

After he took a sip of his drink, Omar regarded me. "Collin, if you didn't realize you had magic potential, why did you come to this school?"

I frowned down at my food. How much to say? Could I confess it all? He surely wouldn't think me crazy, now that I knew how deep this rabbit hole went.

"Can you keep a secret?"

He perked up, leaning forward across the table. "Yeah."

"I had a supernatural experience when I was twelve."

He nodded eagerly.

"My parents took me to a ski lodge over Christmas. Our last night there, I went up the slope by myself. I found a coin in the snow. A coin with my face on it."

Omar's brows lowered. "But you didn't go to a magical school. How could you have a coin?"

I shook my head. "It wasn't my coin. It was my face, but older. How I look now. And the back was stamped *Marke Staple*. I think it was from my future."

Omar's eyes flew open, and he leaned back. "Woah. Even in our circles, most believe time travel isn't possible."

"There's more."

Omar nodded for me to continue.

"After I found the coin, I heard a British voice behind me." I glanced around the room—no one else had come in, but I still lowered my voice. "A man came out of the trees, not dressed for the snowy weather. He looked at me, and his eyes were red. Like, bright red. A shade I never knew a human's eyes could get."

"Contact lenses?"

I shook my head fervently. "No way. This man—he was sobbing, crying so hard. The lenses would have moved."

"Why was he crying?"

I swallowed. "He came toward me and said, 'Collin, is it really you?'"

Omar rubbed at his arms. "That gave me chills. For real? He knew who you were?"

"Yeah. I never saw him before, but he knew who I was. He...he apologized for hurting me."

"Did he say how?"

"No. He just begged me to forgive him. And then he picked up the coin with my face on it, pinched it, and disappeared."

There was silence for a moment; then Omar sighed. "That's deep, man."

"You don't know the half. I memorized his face, Omar. I devoted all of my time from then till now thinking of him." I reached into my bag and pulled out my sketchbook. I flipped to a drawing of the red-eyed man I'd done two years ago. I held the pad out to Omar.

He raised his eyebrow but took it. When he gazed down at the drawing, his jaw dropped. "Collin, this looks identical to your roommate."

"When I met him two days ago, I nearly had a heart attack. He's the same person. He has to be."

"But his eyes aren't red."

"Not yet."

Omar regarded me over the top of my book. "This is weird, Collin."

"Tell me about it." I accepted my sketchpad back.

"And you love him, based on that one encounter?"

"I think I do. He was so raw, Omar. So open. So tormented and ashamed. I know he regrets what he does. I know he's not really a bad man. He just has to make that wrong choice before he realizes it."

Raising his hand to his forehead, Omar rubbed at his skin. "This is crazy. Are you sure Terrence doesn't have a twin?"

"Even the scar on his neck is the same." I flipped to a different drawing, which highlighted the scar, and showed it to Omar. "You saw it, right? When we played football?"

Omar nodded. "It looks the same to me." He took a deep breath. "You know, just because you believe he's going to be redeemed doesn't make it guaranteed. You need to watch yourself with this guy."

"I don't think I can. I'm in over my head already."

Omar's lips thinned to a line. "Maybe you need to switch roommates."

"No! I can't. Not now. Not ever. I need him, Omar." I lowered my chin and finished in a whisper. "I truly do."

"Well, I don't want to be the one who stands in the way of romance, or whatnot. But I'm going to keep an eye on him. Someone's gotta have your back."

I looked up. "You'd do that? For *me*?"

His grin was shy. "Sure, that's what friends are for. Now, do you want to give me your social media handles? I'll add you."

Chapter Eleven

Omar and I sat in the cafe until break time. Then we got refills—sodas, this time—and headed back toward Regalia Hall. There were thirty minutes between classes, but I didn't want to be in the cafe once everyone started showing up. Bad enough I'd fainted in front of my classmates. No doubt my episode would be spread to the business students too.

Sure enough, Terrence came running up to me as soon as we got out the door.

He glanced me up and down and gave Omar a sidelong look. "Hey, Collin. What are you doing in the cafe?"

Heat touched my cheeks. "I passed out in Theory class."

I expected Terrence to grin, to gloat, to laugh at my expense. Instead, he reached out a hand and gripped my forearm. "Are you okay?" He leaned close to me and inspected my face. "Did Dr. Vivaan look you over?"

I nodded. "She scolded me for not eating breakfast."

A smile twitched at Terrence's lips. "Good advice." Then he sobered. "Are you feeling better now?"

"Yeah. I'm fine. It was just a bit of a shock."

"I didn't realize you'd take it so poorly. I'm sorry I didn't explain it all to you sooner."

Omar glared. "You knew he didn't understand about the literature program?"

Terrence met Omar's gaze and tilted his head. "Yeah, he kept going on and on about Faulkner when went to the pub the other day." Then he looked at me, his eyes strangely fiery. "That was right before you kissed me, right?"

Oh, God. He's getting jealous again. No—territorial. He doesn't like the idea of Omar being a romantic rival. I'd told him I had no interest in Omar, but he had to make sure.

Omar pressed on, unperturbed by Terrence's change in topic. "Why wouldn't you mention it if you knew? You think it's entertaining to be that overwhelmed? To be stared at and laughed at by your classmates?"

I grimaced. They'd been laughing?

Terrence raised his hands and took a step backward. "Oi, I was just trying to have a bit of fun. How was I supposed to know he'd react that way?"

Omar opened his mouth, but I held up my palms between the two of them. "Don't worry about it. Both of you. Like I said, I'm fine." I started walking toward Regalia and they fell in on either side of me.

"So, what'd you learn?" Terrence asked.

I chuckled, but it held little mirth. "That I can use magic. That I've been able to do it all my life, but no one told me. That I could have been attending a specialized school all this time, but haven't. Jesus. I'm so far behind, I'll never catch up."

"Don't worry about that, man," Omar said. "We all come from different places in our skills and formal learning. You can't compare yourself to others."

"I agree," Terrence said. "It's not so difficult to get the hang of it. Once you tap into your blood."

"Blood?" I asked.

Omar nodded. "That's where most magic lives. It's innate in our blood cells. Or a special cell, that exists alongside our blood cells. It's invisible to the human eye, but I've read research papers claiming you can see them through magical means."

Terrence picked up where he left off. "For millennia, magic users tried to harvest other people's blood. They slaughtered thousands and thousands of people, harvesting the tiny magic within their bloodstreams. It took them ages to discover that a practitioner can get a hundred times more power using their own blood."

Omar said, "They didn't want to risk themselves, so they never tried their own blood as a source of power. It was around the 1400s when they started mixing their own blood with metal alloys. They've refined it over time, and it's now our current system."

I felt queasy thinking about using blood in such a way. "I have to mix my blood with metal?"

"There's a mint—" Terrence began, just as Omar said, "The Gyranium is used—"

They both stopped talking and stared at one another.

"How do you know so much?" Omar asked. "You're not in our program."

Terrence's back straightened. "Just cause I'm not in the program doesn't mean I'm not a practitioner. Didn't Collin tell you the dean is my father?"

That gave Omar pause. I guess I hadn't mentioned it.

Omar continued. "Why aren't you in the program, then? Skill level? Or power level?"

Terrence's face took on a sickly pallor. "Neither. I'm much more powerful and much more skilled than anyone on this campus. Including Helmer. People fear what's superior to them, and my father is no different. He cut me off from magic, forbade me from being in the program. But—" Terrence cut off, clamping his teeth together with an audible snap.

"Terrence," I began, but he glared at me.

"I'm leaving. I'll see you later." He turned and headed toward Hayden Hall.

"I'm sorry," Omar said immediately. "I shouldn't have said that."

I shook my head. "You didn't know that. I didn't know that. It seems a natural question to ask." I eyed Omar. "Thanks for feeling like you have to defend me. But it's okay. Terrence was building this up for days. He just wanted a laugh."

"I don't think I like him."

"You will. Give him time."

Omar chuckled, but it lacked any sense of humor. "Wait until he betrays you? What if he hurts you beyond repairing?"

"He won't. Believe me. I'll be strong enough to handle this. I've trained for it for so long."

Omar dipped his head. "I do trust you, Collin. But I am going to keep my eye on him."

"I'm sure he'll keep an eye on you too."

"You seem a nice enough guy, Collin, but I'm not gay."

I laughed. "I know that. I'm not going to hit on you."

"That's not what I'm worried about."

"Come on, let's go to class."

We headed back to Regalia.

"What's Tomes?" I asked as we entered the building. "I mean, I know it's books, but is it like magical books?"

"I'm sure there'll be magical books in the library. On history, lore, creatures—"

"Creatures? That means I can research more of what red eyes could mean?"

"Yeah. That's usually what Tomes is. Some teachers give specific topics, but I have already heard Professor Lorel is pretty lax. As long as you're doing your work, it doesn't matter the topic."

In the grand entrance hall, a few students stood around. I spotted Sammuel beside a fluted column surrounded by several others. They were talking animatedly, but their words cut off as they saw us. Saw me.

"Hey," Omar said softly, drawing my attention away from the others. "Don't let them get to you. Remember what I said about competition. They're gonna underestimate you now. Surprise them."

I swallowed, then nodded. He was right. I could use this to my advantage. Maybe.

Surprisingly, Sammuel left the group and fell in beside Omar and me.

"Feeling better?" he asked.

"A little," I answered.

"So you're not really an Omnium Artium."

I glowered. "I don't even know what that is."

Omar said, "It means you're good at everything."

"Helmer said they're rare, right?" I asked.

Omar nodded. "It's about the rarest special you can get."

"Then I'm sure I don't have it."

Sammuel shrugged with a self-satisfied grin.

Omar frowned. "You could be," he said. "You're here for a reason, Collin. The school's stats on your potential are accurate, even if you've never used magic before."

With a grunt, Sammuel's smile became a tad less sure.

Chapter Twelve

I was glad someone knew the way to the library, where our Tomes class met. Omar and Sammuel chatted amiably, keeping to safe topics—not my abnormalities. I didn't join in. Too many thoughts occupied my mind.

Why had I been so sure all my problems would vanish the moment I found the red-eyed man? I cursed my lack of foresight. I'd spent years studying to earn this scholarship, but now that I was here I had no idea how to complete this program. I kept telling myself to get over here to Marke Staple. Such a childish, foolish idea.

And Terrence. What was I going to do about him? Besides love him. I'd accomplished that already. Another stupid decision.

We went down a side hallway, my eyes glazing over the various paintings on the wall, the fine vases or marble statues placed just so along a side table. There would be time to explore the physical world later. For now, I had to travel through my own mind, like a maze—an unending corridor with dead ends likely on all sides.

At the end of the hallway, Omar pushed open a set of double doors. Sammuel followed him in, leaving me to bring up the rear. Despite my own troubles weighing heavily on my thoughts, I gaped when I stepped into the library.

It was four stories tall with shelves and books reaching to the rafters. Millions upon millions of tomes had to be displayed here. The center of the room opened in a square, which repeated on each of the four levels, letting sunlight from the domed ceiling trickle down. A counter stood right in front of me with a dozen tables and chairs spaced around it. But every other inch was dedicated to hosting books.

"This is amazing," I said, my voice barely above a whisper. "And they're all magic?"

Omar stood beside me—Sammuel had already wandered in among the shelves. "All of them. Oh, they likely have some fiction books in here, but they'll be written by practitioners."

"Amazing," I repeated.

"This is my favorite place," said Laura, stepping up beside Omar. "I'm tempted to stay over the holidays just so I can spend my time here."

"My school back home's got a decent library," Omar said. "I can still get books from them even though I'm no longer a student."

Laura shrugged. "Mine's okay too. But not like this."

I raised my eyebrow. "Can't you check books out from here and take them home for the holiday? A library that won't lend books doesn't seem like a good idea."

Omar said, "You can check them out, but they can't leave campus. Can you imagine what a normal person would do if they got ahold of a magical book?"

My confusion deepened. "But we have a couple hundred normal people attending school here."

Omar and Laura both snorted, and I could tell they were trying not to laugh.

I wrinkled my nose, but I couldn't blame them. Maybe I needed to keep my mouth shut instead of asking questions.

"Sorry," Omar said, clearing his throat. Laura repeated the apology. Then Omar explained, "The students in the business program aren't normal, Collin. They're like Terrence. Aware of magic. Most will be practitioners themselves, but not good enough to be in the literature program."

I shook my head. This new world I was a member of made no sense.

Sammuel made his way back over to us, and Tabitha entered and joined us as well. We stood there, silently, waiting for our professor to show up.

Eventually she did, though not in the way I expected. I pulled my phone out for the fifth time to check the clock—class should have started five minutes ago—when a loud voice called from the second floor. At the edge of the open area, a woman leaned against the railing. Her short blonde hair peeked out from a scarf, and even from this distance her green eyes cut like knives.

"Up here!" she bellowed, her voice echoing off the walls and amplifying. "You five are late!" Then she disappeared to the back of the building.

"The hell?" I asked softly. "We've been here for fifteen minutes. We're not late."

Laura motioned her head to the right. "The stairs are this way."

We fell in behind Laura. The stairwell disappeared into the wall, but books still lined both sides of the enclosed space. I gazed at the titles as I passed. A few of them were written in languages I couldn't read, but I saw *The Lights from Above*, *Preventing Curses*, and *1001 Uses for Lizard Tails*.

On the second floor, Laura led the way to a small section in the back where four tables sat in a row. Our professor, Mirah Lorel, stood in front of the tables, her lips thinned to a line.

"For future reference," she said as we approached, "class sessions meet here. Once you're signed in, you can commence your research."

"We didn't know that, Professor," I said gingerly. "Today's our first day."

"Collin, yeah?" she asked, eyeing me. "That's why I said 'future reference.'"

I swallowed, suddenly nervous with her gaze on me. "But you said we were late."

She pulled up the sleeve of her green blouse and looked at her watch. "You are."

"But—"

Tabitha cut me off. "Where do we sign in, Professor?"

Still keeping her focus on me, Professor Lorel gestured, and a piece of paper and a pen suddenly appeared on the desk. My mouth fell open. A small smile played at her lips, and I saw a look similar to what usually lurked in Terrence's eyes, the sign of a person who enjoyed putting people off-balance.

The others paid no mind and hurriedly scrawled their names on the sheet. I was last. I lifted the pen in my hand, feeling its weight. It was real. No different from any other pen. Where had it come from? Had she summoned an actual pen from another location? Had she created it instantly on the spot?

"I think I'm going to have fun this year," she said softly. "The staff will enjoy you, Collin. Something out of the ordinary will be entertaining. Break up the monotony."

I signed my name below Omar's and set the pen down. "If you say so, Professor."

"I'm sure you need instructions on how this class will work. Am I right?"

"We pick a topic and research it. Pretty easy."

Her grin was wider now and much more mischievous. "Easy, you say. I'm glad you feel that way now. You might not in a few months. Yes, you pick your topic. But I demand results. None of this hogwash of dilly-dallying or wasting time. You have a week to select your topic; then we'll discuss your purpose and set up a time frame. Stick to the time frame, and you pass. Fall behind..." She spread her hands.

"Got it." I started to walk away to follow Omar to a different level, but her hand stopped me.

"You have a topic in mind?"

"Yes, I want to look into mythical creatures."

"Mythical? Meaning nonexistent? We have nothing of the sort in this library."

"No, I mean, what regular humans would consider mythical. Dragons, or vampires, or werewolves."

"Magical creatures is the term you're searching for. Those books will be on the top floor, in the back left corner." She waved her fingers over her shoulder. "Try there first."

"Thanks, Professor."

I headed away from her, the way Omar had gone. As I hoped, there were identical stairwells along each of the library's walls. I went up two more floors, hearing Tabitha's and Laura's soft voices as I passed the third. At the top, it was quiet.

Before I started my search for the books, I investigated the library. It smelled musty and old, but so good. The way libraries should. Besides the natural light filtering in through the skylight above, several sconces hung on the outside walls. And a few sat on the ends of bookshelves. The ample illumination gave the space a comfortable feel, not the lingering dread one would expect from a magical—probably haunted—library.

I went down a random aisle and trailed my fingers along the spines of the books. Their covers crackled under the slight pressure of my fingertip. I stopped and pulled one off the shelf, cradling it carefully in my palm. I lifted it to my nose and breathed in deeply.

"What are you doing?" Sammuel asked.

I jumped and hastily put the book back on the shelf. "Nothing."

He raised his eyebrow skeptically. I'd answered too quickly.

"I like it in here," I said, almost defensively. "The books, the lights, the quiet."

Slowly, he nodded. "Everyone does. Only the best of the best get into this program. We all love it in here. I've heard it can get crowded on school holidays."

I blinked in surprise. Was Sammuel going to be nice all of a sudden? No, he probably thought of me as below his notice, like Omar had said. He didn't take me seriously, so there was no need to be arrogant.

"How are the books arranged? Dewey Decimal system?"

Sammuel laughed quietly. "Not quite. They're all by subject, but not the way regular people would sort them."

"How do I find what I'm looking for? Professor Lorel said the magical creatures books are back this way, but what if I want something specific?"

"You can use your coin to ask the catalog."

I barely kept the glare off my face. "I don't have a coin," I said, tightly.

"Oh right," he answered, as if he'd forgotten that piece of information. I knew he hadn't. He wasn't the type to forget anything that could give him an advantage.

Like Terrence. Maybe magic makes people act this way. Terrence claimed he was powerful, but unable to practice because of his father. I didn't want it to turn me into an asshole.

"Well," Sammuel continued. "When you do get your coins, it's simple to ask the catalog." He gestured, and I followed him to the opening at the center of the room. Beside the south railing was a large box. We went toward it, circling around the large, open square that looked down onto the lower floor.

At the box, Sammuel pulled his coin out of his pocket. I saw the name *Hollywells School of Literature*, and a building that appeared to be underwater. He pinched the coin between his fingers, then said softly, "Catalog, please show me books about mermaids."

The box shook, and an intensely bright light shot out of it. The light fell to the floor and darted down the center aisle and turned at the third bookshelf.

"Amazing," I said, eyes following the line on the floor.

"It'll stay activated until you turn it off. Or someone else uses it." He pinched his coin again, and the line disappeared.

"Thank you."

He shrugged and started to turn away.

"What are you going to research?" I asked.

"Fire spells." Then he headed in the opposite direction from where the light had gone.

Fire? His special was ice, so maybe he wanted to train on its opposite. *I* needed to study specials, to find out what mine could possibly be. For now, though, the thought of the red-eyed man remained foremost in my mind.

I went to the back corner, like Professor Lorel had said.

Without any real guidance, I flipped through a dozen books on creatures. There were ones I already knew had red eyes: hellhounds, the Mothman, the Flatwoods Monster, Skinwalkers, demons, dragons, roggemoeder, banshees, Ijiraat, the black Cadejo, Chupacabra, and even the Egyptian god, Set.

All of which were not-so-nice legends.

I found a book on dragons and one on banshees, so I took them with me back to the second floor. Professor Lorel eyed them, but said nothing as I presented them to her. She jotted down the titles on a piece of paper.

"And what's your topic?" she asked.

"Uh, I'll need to read up on them more before I decide."

She nodded. "You have two weeks to get a rough draft. Fifteen pages. At least three sources, all from print, no electronic."

"Sure, Professor."

I took my books to the bottom level and sat in a hard wooden chair beside a table. I flipped through the one on dragons. I knew a bunch of the lore already, but this book included facts. Asian dragons, European dragons, American dragons, even dragons from other dimensions.

Could that be what happened to Terrence? Did he run afoul of a dragon? It didn't seem likely.

The hour-long class ended, and I waited for Omar to join me at the library's exit. Sammuel left with Tabitha and Laura on either side. They were talking quietly about a spell.

"See you in Latin," I said to them. They all waved distractedly and didn't cease their conversation.

When Omar joined me, I sighed. "You know, you can hurry and join them." I nodded my head to the three. "You don't have to hang out with me if I'm going to make you ostracized too."

"Don't worry about it, Collin. They'll warm up to you. Besides, I think you need a friend more than them. Wanna go get lunch?"

A surge of affection filled me. "Yeah."

Chapter Thirteen

Terrence didn't show up for lunch. Any time the door in the cafe opened, I looked over my shoulder, hoping it was him. It never was.

A few of the American students stopped by and asked Omar when the next football game was going to be. He pulled out his phone and traded contacts with each of them. He said he'd group chat everyone, and they could decide when to play.

"You sure are a social butterfly," I said as we stood to leave.

Omar shrugged as he threw his messenger bag over his shoulder. "It helps my anxiety."

"Huh? Isn't it the opposite? Like more people equals more stress?"

"Not for me. When Dad died, I isolated myself. Mom made me see a therapist, and she suggested I do the opposite; I needed a larger support circle. She was right. I feel better when I have friends to talk with."

A sharp pain filled my heart. To imagine losing my own father hurt. "I'm sorry."

He offered me a half smile. "Don't worry about it. Different things work for different people. Mom's coping skills are not even close to mine."

"Let me know if there's anything I can do to help."

"You're already doing it. It's nice to have someone from home. Makes me feel less cut off."

I nodded. "Me too. I didn't realize I'd miss Florida so much. Or my family. I was so set on getting here, on finding Terrence, I never gave a thought to the consequences."

"You regret your choice?"

"No," I said without hesitation. "I know I'm supposed to be here."

"You religious, Collin?"

"Not really. I mean, we got to church occasionally. Why? You thinking this is God's will?"

He lifted his shoulders. "Fate. Destiny. They all mean the same thing. Even in magical circles, we have a saying that goes, 'From birth to death and rebirth, the circle of life is all.'"

I laughed. "Quoting *The Lion King*?"

"You think Walt Disney wasn't a practitioner?"

My chuckles cut off. This world still baffled me.

We went back to Regalia Hall. As we crossed the grassy knoll, my gaze swept across the sea of students looking for Terrence. I couldn't spot him among so many. Plus, he was obviously avoiding me.

A sudden thought struck me. I had his phone number. I could text him. See where he was. See if he'd talk to me.

I pulled out my phone and opened my messages. I'd only texted Mom and Dad on this new phone so far. I added a new conversation and typed in Terrence's name.

Didn't see you at lunch. Will I see you at dinner?

I sent it before I could talk myself out of it.

Omar eyed me, but didn't say anything as we entered Regalia.

Our next class, Latin, was with all the grade levels again. Omar and I filed into the classroom behind a few juniors. The room had five tables, and the students seemed to segregate by grade. Laura was already seated at one table, so Omar and I joined her.

I glanced around the room. Lisbeth and Mary, as well as the three other seniors, sat at the farthest table. Those were the only other students I knew. Maybe Omar was right, trying to expand his circle. I'd be more successful if I had many people to depend on.

Eventually, the last student entered and took their seat. I glanced around the room, looking for the professor, Elai Jenkins. He wasn't here. Then I saw a young man, more a boy, probably only sixteen years old, sitting by himself at one of the tables. What was he doing in here? Was he lost?

The kid stood and straightened his button-up shirt. He didn't lift his chin, so he stared at the floor beside his feet. "Hello, students. Welcome to Latin."

I made a gurgle that drew the eyes of my classmates. I quickly shut my mouth, but I couldn't get my eyes to stop bulging. He was the professor? He was younger than me!

Professor Jenkins had paused at my noise, and he started to move his head in my direction. Before he met my gaze, he dropped his chin and his eyes looked back to the floor. "And a special welcome to you freshmen. I understand your circumstances are a bit unorthodox, Collin. But we'll figure something out." He cleared his throat. "Now, let's get started, shall we? Typically, we won't have everyone together for Latin. It makes no sense for beginners to be practicing with the experts. However, Dean Helmer mandated we have the first week with all levels to review some basics.

"For those of you who are new"—he half glanced at me again—"you may want to take notes, as this is the core on which all verbal spells are based."

I dug in my bag for paper and a pencil. Once I had it all set, he nodded.

"Good. So, you all remember that spells are mostly made up of Latin terms, but with key variations."

I wrote what he said, word for word. It made absolutely no sense, but I hoped it would, eventually.

"Spells are a code, of sorts, a summoning and directing of power. So, the Latin terms, with other terms mixed in, give them guidance. They can be viewed as coordinates. Of course, it goes without saying that not all spells conform to this—there are always exceptions. But, a vast majority of the verbal-attack spells used in dueling follow this formula."

He moved his head slowly as he spoke, but his gaze still stayed on the floor.

"The spell needs to be as specific as possible to be as effective as possible. Vague directions or incorrect pronunciation can result in dire consequences. To start a spell, you need to state the type of spell first, be it *aeris* or *ignis*—which are air and fire respectively." I was sure he added that for my benefit.

"Next, we tack on the size of the spell, or the intensity. You can call a spell that will stretch kilometer wide, if you can name it correctly, or you can pinpoint it to a millimeter destination. This is one of the advantages to verbal spells versus elemental spells; they are a lot more precise.

"For intensity, it's typically high, medium, or low— *altus*, *mediocris*, *humilis*—and for size, we go for small, medium, or large—*parvus*, *modus*, and *magnus*. It's important to remember which is size and which is intensity. You can add both for extreme results, if desired."

I scribbled as fast as I could, but the man wasn't saying anything I could understand. The other students looked bored out of their minds for having to sit through review. I'd have to attend remedial classes; I would never be allowed into lessons taught at a normal level. All of this was way over my head.

Jenkins continued. "When using location, you must be precise, as I said earlier. All words of distance are perceived from your body—you are the epicenter, so it's from your position the spell radiates. You could use any way of calling out the destination that makes sense to you, like 'Three feet to the left,' or 'Seven meters north.' But you need to be specific. You can't just say, 'Over there' or 'By my attacker.' It's all about the physical location. Typically, these need to be said in Latin as well, and are at the very end of the spell."

He cleared his throat. "So when we put it all together it'll sound something like this. *Aeris humilis duo pes primor.*"

About a foot in front of the professor, a burst of wind appeared, contained and swirling within a few inches of space.

"*Perago,*" he said, and the spell vanished.

My mouth fell open, but none of the other students were even looking.

"Of course," he continued, "the verbal status of the spell has many drawbacks. First is that there is a chance your opponent can hear you. Since the words need to be spoken clearly and not muttered, there is always the chance this can happen. Also, while you're completing your spell, your opponent may hit you with one of their own, throwing you off-balance. This can make your location change in relation to them, sending your spell somewhere you don't intend, or it could make you cast a wrong spell."

My hand shot into the air, and Jenkins seemed perplexed, like he had no idea what to do when someone had a question. He muttered a few unintelligible words—maybe Latin—but finally managed to say, "Y-yes, Collin?"

"You said there's a difference between verbal and nonverbal spells, right? I've only seen nonverbal spells before. According to what you just said, nonverbal gives the caster a disadvantage. So, why even do it this way?"

He stood silent for a moment, processing my words. He started to raise his eyes, but halted before reaching my face. "Well, Collin, verbal spells are usually only used in dueling. It is one of the magical community's greatest pastimes. Ah, since you're relatively new to the community, it's understandable you don't know about dueling. There are national, regional, international competitions, as well as pro teams that compete."

One of the seniors next to Lisbeth said loudly, "It's like a sport. Our team just beat yours last week."

The classroom dissolved into excited talking, and angry mutters. Omar glared at Sammuel and said, "Only because the Knights cheated."

"The Rooks are a bunch of know-nothing amateurs," Sammuel retorted.

I blinked in surprise, baffled by Omar's sudden aggression. He'd been so calm about everything up till this point. Why had these duels set him off?

"Quiet down, class," Jenkins said, but softly. Eventually they did still, but not because of anything the professor did. "As I was saying, it all has to do with dueling. Marke Staple has a dueling team that is pretty highly regarded within the European college circuit."

He dipped his head toward me. "In dueling, you earn points based on how well you perform spells and how well you counter the opposing team's attacks."

I raised my hand again.

Beads of sweat began to form on Jenkins's brow. "Another question, Collin?"

"Yes, Professor. You said the spells are all in Latin. Why can't we just speak in our native languages?"

He relaxed, slightly. "This is more a topic for Theory, Collin. But the way I view it is like this: when our ancestors first discovered magic, and its use became widespread, Latin was the language they clung to. They embedded so much magical force into the words that they still hold power today. Other languages do have magical words as well, which is why I said *most* of your words will be Latin. Any word of power will work."

He turned his head, taking in the students. "Okay, split into groups of two or three and practice nonthreatening spells."

Instead of joining a group, I got out of my chair and hurried toward Jenkins.

"Professor?"

He turned toward me and jumped.

This close, I could make out more of his features. He was young. He couldn't be a day older than sixteen. His hair, red-gold, shined beneath the fluorescent lights. A sprinkle of light freckles dotted his nose. His eyes appeared to be light brown, but the color was hard to make out, since he refused to meet my gaze.

"Yes, Collin?"

"I don't know any Latin words."

"You may want to invest in a tutor. I can get you started on the basics, the words you should have learned in primary school. You may even consider joining the dueling team. It would accelerate your learning and your practice."

"Uh, I'll think about it. But, are you sure I should be in this class with the other students?"

"Oh yes, Collin. Many of them don't take Latin seriously, so they won't have many spells memorized. You're not as far behind them as you fear. Catching up is feasible, with dedication on your end."

"Oh, good. I was a little worried I'd fail out on my first day of class."

A small smile touched Jenkins's lips. "Don't think like that. Marke Staple is a fair school, judging each student on their own potential, not comparing them to their classmates'. We'll push you, but only within what you can handle."

I sighed in relief. "Thanks, Professor."

He nodded. "Here, let me get you a book that might help." He went back to his table and picked a brown satchel off the floor. He dug into it, his arms dipping in much deeper than the small bag appeared. Finally, he pulled out a book, then returned to my side.

I took the book as he handed it to me. Heat touched my cheeks as I gazed at the cover. It was like a picture book, all done up in bright colors with cute puppies and kittens.

"What is this?"

"It's an introduction to Latin. As I said, you should have learned this in primary. But you can learn it now."

"Don't you have a more advanced one I can try?"

He shook his head. "Start with the basics. Now, go have a seat and read the first page. Try the spell and see if you can get it to work. They're simple and harmless, so don't be afraid."

"I don't need a coin for this?"

"Oh, no. Coins—or more accurately, the blood within the coins—access elemental magic, an essence that's in all things. Energy, you could say. Chi. Soul. Spirit. Any sort of word like that fits. With blood, we can touch those threads of energy like they're strings on a guitar. Pluck them. Manipulate them. Move them. Shift them. All sorts of things.

"But when we use magic within words, we tap into something completely different. This is elemental magic versus lingual magic. Oh, there are a few other branches as well. Vortexes, for example."

"Vortexes?"

Jenkins finally looked up at me, his brown eyes sparkling. "You don't know about the vortexes? They have a fine institute in Sedona, Arizona, that specializes in studying and using the vortexes."

His obvious enthusiasm threw me off, as did the passionate light burning in his eyes. I recalled Omar mentioning a school in Sedona, but I couldn't remember the name. "I've never been to Arizona."

"It's amazing. There is another large vortex in Egypt. At the Pyramid of Giza, to be exact. Some records indicate it may be the oldest vortex on the planet."

"Is that so?" I asked politely.

For the next hour, Jenkins talked my ear off. He explained about the vortexes—whirlwinds of condensed magical power—and listed all sorts of theories leading practitioners had suggested concerning their purpose. I kept nodding through it all. Some of what Jenkins said made absolutely no sense to me. When he began talking of terraformers and extraterrestrials, I fixed my grin in place to keep my brow from wrinkling.

Jenkins was crazy. How did this young, insane child become a professor at a prestigious university?

"Professor?" someone asked loudly.

Jenkins glanced away from me, toward the student, but not at them. "Yes?"

"Class is over."

Spinning, Jenkins looked at the clock on the back wall. Technically, class had ended five minutes ago. I glanced around the room and saw that nearly half the seats were empty.

"Oh," Jenkins said; then he turned back to me. "I'm sorry, Collin. I do tend to babble on sometimes. Class is dismissed, of course. And make sure you study that book tonight. We can try a few spells tomorrow."

"Sure, Professor. Thanks." I walked to my seat to grab my things, my legs aching slightly. Standing still for so long had put a cramp in my calf muscle.

At our table, Omar and the others were gathering their belongings. I was kind of glad they hadn't left. Jenkins may be crazy, but he didn't deserve the rude behavior from the students. I fell in with the group, and we left the classroom.

As soon as we were out of earshot, Sammuel threw his arm over my shoulder. I flinched at the unexpected move.

"Thanks, man," Sammuel said, the smile plain in his voice. "I've heard Jenkins can be a nightmare. You distracted him the whole time; it was amazing!"

"A nightmare?" I asked. "Why? He seemed nice enough."

Tabitha groaned. "When my mother dropped me off, she insisted on meeting all the teachers. We couldn't get away from Jenkins because he kept talking about the

Pillars at Maison de Verre. They're ancient artifacts from a magical community, so no one understands their true purpose. Usually pretty interesting, but the way Jenkins went on and on... It was terrible. Mother regretted her decision by the end."

Omar gave a snort of a laugh. "They say his theories are over the top, even for a practitioner."

I bit my lip. I had thought him crazy—especially when he started talking about aliens—but he'd been harmless. And his passion for the topic had been obvious. Endearing, even.

"Don't laugh at him," Laura said softly. "You do realize he's smarter than all five of us combined?"

Sammuel squawked in indignation. "No way is he smarter than me."

Laura rolled her eyes, though only one was visible, the other hidden behind her dark hair. "Yeah, because you're a professor at a university at the age of eighteen. On top of that, he's been teaching here for three years. Can you do that math?"

With his arm still draped over me, Sammuel glared at her. When he opened his mouth for a comeback, I cleared my throat. "Can someone explain to me the difference between elemental magic and linguistic magic?"

"*Lingual* magic," Sammuel corrected. "Words have power. What's hard to understand about that?"

"But how can blood be needed to use some kinds and only words for others?"

Tabitha moved in closer to me. "It's the difference between the physical and the mental. In elemental magic, you are physically touching the noosphere—"

"We call it the otherworld," Sammuel said.

"Ether," Omar added.

"Regardless," Tabitha said in a clipped voice, likely annoyed at being interrupted. "It is the world of energy—"

"Chi," Laura cut in.

Tabitha growled, but Laura shot her a grin, and Tabitha's cheeks turned pink. She cleared her throat. "A spirit world. You're pushing and pulling and manipulating things on another plane. With lingual magic, you're tapping into a thought. It's nothing physical."

I furrowed my brows, my understanding even more confused than before. "But Jenkins summoned a small tornado. It was physical."

All four of them groaned.

"We'll have Professor Watanabe explain," Tabitha said. "She'll do it better."

Chapter Fourteen

We hung out in the entrance hall. I sat on the floor beside Tabitha. Omar and Sammuel leaned against the pillar. Laura hovered along the side of the wall, eyeing a painting, but still adding to the discussion.

A sense of peace filled me. Unintentionally distracting Jenkins had made me a hero in their eyes. If that was all it took, I could monopolize the professor's time tomorrow too. I had a lot of catching up to do, so having his undivided attention would help.

"They're having a gala next month," Tabitha said. "A sort of formal get-together. Students are invited, as well as important practitioners from this area. It's a great place to network."

"Plus there's a dance," Sammuel added. He shot Tabitha a grin. "Wanna go as my date?"

Her lips thinned to a line. "No, but thank you for asking."

Sammuel slumped, but he didn't look as if he'd expected a different answer.

"Do we have to go?" I asked. I imagined myself forced into a fancy tuxedo. I'd never worn one before. Would it make me look dashing? Would Terrence like it?

"It's not mandatory," Omar said. "But it's encouraged. There's really no reason *not* to attend."

"Afraid you can't get someone to go with you?" Sammuel asked.

Omar snorted. When the others turned to him, he shrugged and said, "Collin already has a boyfriend."

My cheeks heated when their gazes returned to me.

"Really?" Tabitha asked excitedly. She leaned in closer. "What's he like? Is he a literature student?"

I shot Omar a look, but he failed to understand its meaning. "He's not in the literature program, and he's... uh..." *Using me for my magic.*

Sammuel laughed. "Sounds like true love."

"He's gorgeous," I said, defensively. "Smart. Driven. Ambitious."

"A practitioner?" Laura asked, glancing at me over her shoulder.

I hesitated. "Yeah, I guess he is."

Sammuel smirked. "Not good enough to make the cut, huh? Is he jealous of you? Especially since you don't even know *how* to do magic."

Tabitha sighed. "You're an ass, Sammuel. Do you always say what's on your mind without thought? Do you lack a filter, like Professor Jenkins?"

Instead of getting angry, like I expected, Sammuel grinned wolfishly. "I find it easier to be an ass. It saves me time and effort."

I glanced at my cell phone. Terrence hadn't texted me back yet. But the digital clock said it was time to get going.

"Shall we head to class?" I asked, already getting to my feet.

We moved as a group down the hallway. Tabitha drew Laura into a quiet discussion, while Omar and Sammuel talked about the gala some more. I smiled to myself. Sure, we all weren't best friends, but at least we were talking, and I was included. Suddenly, I didn't feel so alone, even with Terrence mad at me.

At the end of the corridor, we took the stairs to the top level. Our Methods class was in the second room on the right. Omar pushed the door in and held it for us as we entered. Like the classroom this morning, it was a mini amphitheater. Two aisles sloped down to a small stage at the bottom. At least fifty chairs surrounded the lectern. And here we were, five students. Why?

I followed at the back of the group, Sammuel in the lead. He took us to the front row, center, and sat.

I finally voiced my concerns aloud. "Why are we meeting in such a large room for such a small class size? It seems a waste."

Omar shrugged. "Most literature programs downsized around the 1900s. Too many people were using powers, and even with coins, it was chaotic. I think the largest school is in Japan, the Fujioka Academy. And they only have about fifty students total. Not that much bigger than our program."

I shook my head. "But you said 75 percent of the population can access magic. Why not let them try?"

This time, Laura spoke. "Yes, it's true many may be able to access their aura, but most are only powerful enough to light a lamp. It's not worth the time required to train them when they won't amount to anything."

"Maybe," I allowed. I thought of my parents. If they knew they could use magic, wouldn't it have helped our lives? Dad could have summoned waves at Horseshoe Beach. Mom could have helped her backyard garden grow bigger or faster. Even Mindy might have saved some money if she could use magic to dye her hair bright colors.

And I was powerful enough to be worth it, huh?

"This doesn't make any sense."

Omar opened his mouth, but at that moment, the door to the classroom opened, and the professor walked in. She was young—though not as youthful as Jenkins—with her black hair pulled up into a bun on the top of her head. She wore a red pencil skirt and a cream-colored blouse. The heels on her shoes were five inches long and as thin as my pinky finger. She clutched a leather briefcase in one hand.

She stepped onto the raised floor at the bottom of the room. "Good afternoon," she greeted with an Asian accent. "I understand we had some excitement this morning? Collin, are you feeling better?" She smiled at me, and I wondered how she knew who I was.

"Yes, Professor."

"Fantastic. Let's try to forget about that and focus on this class only. I'm Yuu Watanabe, your Methods teacher."

I nodded to her.

Her eyes left mine and traveled to my classmates. She smiled at them and then named each one. Tabitha had said she and her mother met the teachers before, but how did Watanabe know the rest of us?

"Let's begin with a refresher for those of you who may be unfamiliar." She looked at each of us in turn, but lingered on me. "Methods class is largely devoted to developing the style and efficiency of your spell casting, as well as exploring various ways to interact with magic."

She reached inside her briefcase and pulled out a coin. "Coins are the simplest way to access our magic, but we have other methods available to us. Anyone care to share what other objects they've used?"

Laura's hand shot into the air.

Professor Watanabe nodded to her.

"When I was little, my mother taught me with wands."

"Yes, that's an old staple in magical practice. It's especially easy for beginners. But what are the drawbacks?"

"They're conspicuous," I said, surprising even myself. I stumbled a bit when they all looked at me, but I pressed on. "I mean, if you wave a wand around, people will think you're crazy."

"Yes," said the professor. "It's way too obvious. But what else?"

Tabitha raised her hand. "The wood's not able to absorb much energy."

"Correct." Watanabe held up her coin. "The metals inside my coin work twofold. They absorb my magical charge—wands have a tendency to explode if the spell is too powerful—and the metal amplifies the magic. Watch."

She took the coin between her thumb and forefinger, then pinched it.

A small flame appeared in the air between us and the professor. It shimmered slightly, then gained intensity, roaring into a column of fire.

I shied away from its sudden heat.

"Now, watch that same spell with a wand."

She extracted a wand from her briefcase. I bit back a laugh when I saw it. It looked like a chopstick.

Watanabe grinned and wiggled the wand at us. "Not so conspicuous, huh?"

She held the wand, pointing it at the air in front of us. She flicked it sharply, and another tiny flame appeared. It wavered, grew to the size of a basketball, then evaporated. I barely felt the heat from that one.

"Naturally," the professor continued, "fire isn't my special. I used one of my weakest spells. But that was the extent of what I could do with a wand. If I had pushed any harder, the wand would have broken."

I put my hand up into the air.

"Yes, Collin?"

"Does the wand use blood, too, like the coin?"

"Yes. Blood is the root of all elemental magic. When you construct a wand, the core needs to be dipped in your blood. It is the only way to activate any magic."

"Does other blood work? Like animal blood?"

"Yes, it would work, but the spells would be very weak and ineffective. Using someone else's blood is also ineffective. Throughout history, practitioners enacted so much bloodshed, took so many lives, in an attempt to cast spells. They didn't want to risk opening their own veins for the power and resorted to stealing from others."

I shivered at the gruesome history. Hopefully, the magical world was more civilized now. But her explanation raised another thought. "So, if I used *your* coin, I could access *your* magic?"

"This is something we should talk about in Theory, Collin," she said kindly. "It's something leading practitioners argue about. Some say that you access the blood inside the coin, someone else's blood. But others contest that, while it is foreign blood that activates it, it is the caster's blood that fires it."

"Would my spell with your coin be as powerful as my spell with my own coin?"

She laughed, and it made her dark eyes crinkle at the corners. "I love your enthusiasm, Collin. Again, there's many points of view on this subject."

"Seems like it would be easy to test."

She nodded. "You'd think. But each Gyranium is slightly different. Every school mixes their alloys in various ways. Each coin might be altered from the others in the batch. It's not as easy to measure as you're assuming."

"The metals play that big a part?"

"Yes. As I showed with the wand, other vessels are unable to hold so much magical pressure. Coins hold it, and in most cases expand it. Conduct it."

I slowly dipped my head in understanding. This was starting to make sense.

Seeing I was through, she turned to the others. "What other conveyances can we use to access magic?"

Sammuel raised his hand this time. "Dolls."

The professor nodded. "Popularly known as voodoo; yes, dolls can be containers for magic. And the inconveniences associated with the dolls?"

"The magic is very limited," Sammuel answered. "They serve only one specific function. It's too difficult to write more than one spell on them."

"Correct. Anything else?"

"Runes," said Omar.

"Yes," said the professor. "Runes have power within them, and when written by a practitioner, they can produce effects. But they are usually used as wards only, for protection. Using runes to cast an offensive spell is very difficult."

"Are runes a part of linguistic magic?" I asked.

"Lingual magic?" Watanabe said. "No. Runes fall under script magic. Like voodoo dolls, or wards, or hexes."

I blinked several times. "So there's elemental magic, which is described as physical. Lingual magic, which is based on speech. And script magic, which needs to be written out?"

Watanabe chuckled. "There are several others, like brews or potions, mixing magically potent ingredients for a desired effect. Or borba magija, a type of magic only accessible through certain body positions." She glanced at the others. "Any other ideas?"

"What about things like crystal balls?" I asked.

My classmates laughed.

Professor Watanabe smiled. "This is something else, entirely, Collin. Items can be made into amulets, or into far-gazers—like a crystal ball—but they don't carry magic themselves. They are simply aligned with the magic user, and they work only for that person. A wand, or a coin, can be used by anyone who has the knowledge. Do you see the difference?"

"Not really."

Sympathy and understanding showed on her face. "You will. Don't worry. Magic is complex, which is why so many of us dedicate our lives to studying and learning. But once you have the basics, the rest will flow simply enough."

The knot in my stomach lessened. At least she was saying I had some hope of catching on. I'd half expected all my teachers to give me up for lost.

"So," the professor continued, "we've established the coin is the easiest, safest, most practical way in which to access our magic. Within the next few days, new coins will be minted for you. The location where the coin is minted doesn't matter, though the school will be branded onto the back of your coin. This is helpful in cases of lost coins, or in rogue practitioners. We can use their coins as a guide to find them."

She motioned with her hands, beckoning us down to her level. I followed Omar out of the row and down the sloped aisle. We formed a semicircle around Watanabe.

Her eyes studied each of us as she spoke. "I want everyone to try one spell so I can gauge your level. Please pick something on the weak side. I don't want to deal with holes in the walls or ceiling. Collin, just observe. Then I will walk you through using your blood."

I swallowed hard, imagining cutting my skin to access my magic. I wasn't typically squeamish, but this nauseated me for some reason.

Of course, Sammuel was first. He produced a fireball after rubbing his finger along his coin. He tossed the ball into the air, twirled it on his finger, and then made it disappear in a shower of sparks. It had looked a hundred times more impressive than Watanabe's fire.

"Excellent!" Watanabe praised. "I can see that your reputation is not exaggerated."

Omar went next. He created an illusion. It appeared suddenly, a black bat that swooped around the room performing aerial acrobatics. If I hadn't seen it materialize from nothing, I would have assumed it was a real animal. It vanished in a puff of smoke.

"Impressive," the professor told him, with a nod. "Next?"

Laura pinched her coin and droplets of water began to fall from the ceiling. They grouped together, drawn by some strange gravity, and formed into a giant sphere. Then, it broke into two spheres, four, and then eight, doubling itself into smaller and smaller sections. Finally, she waved a hand, and each tiny pinprick of water turned a different color. It looked like an exploded rainbow. It was the most beautiful thing I had ever seen. Laura threw her hand downward, and the droplets sank into the ground, barely leaving a damp spot on the carpet.

"Wonderful, Laura!" Watanabe said.

"Incredible," I added.

I think Laura blushed, but it was hard to tell with all her hair covering her face.

Tabitha wore a slight frown. Maybe she didn't have anything that could compete with Laura's performance. She held her coin between her fingers; her tongue licked her lips and her eyes narrowed. She slammed her hand onto the desk behind us. The sound ricocheted off the walls, amplifying. Under her hand, the desk began to freeze. At first, it looked like normal frost, but then it grew and mutated. Tendrils of it snaked out around the desk, pushing higher toward the ceiling. The tendrils took on geometric shapes, hexagons and octagons and triangles building atop one another, stretching ever higher.

She pulled her hand away, and the structure stood over ten feet tall, an elegant building of frost.

Sammuel scoffed slightly, and I remembered he'd said ice was his special.

"Very good," said the professor.

Tabitha pinched her coin again, and the ice castle melted and vanished in the blink of an eye.

Watanabe regarded me. "Now, Collin, magic potential is something innate, something you can't change no matter how much you try. However, tapping into that potential is as easy as you want it to be. Some people can build up blocks—more out of their fear than anything else—but most of the time, once you realize you have the power, you can access it and direct it at will.

"The first thing you need to do is breathe."

I laughed nervously, realizing I was holding my breath.

She grinned. "Next, concentrate. The easiest spells to produce are ones that affect things around you, like the air. We teach that first because it's easy to manipulate, and it's also one of the most useful spells you'll ever learn."

"Just using air?" I asked, skeptically. "How is that useful?"

A book, apparently forgotten on a desk a few rows back, began to float from across the room. It landed in Watanabe's outstretched hand.

I shut my mouth, which had fallen open at her display. "Every theory about telekinesis is just a practitioner using air?"

"Yes," she replied simply, setting the book on the lectern. "When you come into contact with your magic, you are able to reach out with it, seeking things to manipulate. After a while, this will become second nature, and you won't even have to think about it. But right now, I want you to only think of the air. Don't let anything else distract you."

"Okay."

"When the magic inside you responds, focus on this book." She patted the cover under her fingers. "Try to lift it. Don't be upset if you don't succeed. It can be difficult your first time. And also, your magic will be a bit...hyper...since it doesn't have metal to tame it. Just take it slow and steady."

"I-I'm not sure if I'm ready."

"Nothing you do can hurt you. You don't have the strength for that yet. Just relax and focus."

I nodded.

The professor produced a knife from her briefcase, hidden in a leather sheath. She pulled the knife from its cover and handed it to me, hilt first.

"Just a little cut will do," she instructed.

"Where?"

"Doesn't matter."

I held the knife if my right hand, and it shook violently. Very carefully, I placed the blade's tip along my left palm. It made a hole in my skin about a millimeter in length—it didn't even hurt. But a tiny bubble of blood welled up from the spot.

I focused on the blood, and suddenly, my vision swam. The lights seemed to have dimmed, and items around the room glowed with an unearthly illumination. Watanabe had a faint blue outline around her body. I looked at my classmates; they shone in similar shades. The air around me seemed to shimmer, too, and I realized that was the magical current I could access. The chi, or energy, or ether. I could take ahold of those currents and use them as I saw fit.

Straining, with a part of my body I couldn't even describe, let alone pinpoint, I grabbed at the air around the book on the desk. The tiny currents hummed and vibrated as my blood commanded them to react. They formed together in the same way Laura's water had, and they turned a vivid shade of red. Once they appeared solid to my eyes, I lifted my hand up, and the book jumped an inch from the table.

I gasped, lost my concentration, and the book landed with a slight *thunk*.

The world returned to normal: all the currents disappeared.

Watanabe patted my shoulder. "An excellent first attempt, Collin. How do you feel?"

"Weird," I answered.

She laughed. "I'm glad you didn't cut yourself more, then. When using blood magic, raw like this, the more blood, the stronger your grasp becomes. For now, I suggest doing only tiny pricks like you did. Does that make sense?"

Sammuel whispered, "Who's got a tiny prick?"

I ignored him. "Yes, Professor."

"Good. Now, you go sit and rest. Everyone else, I want you to run through it again, but try a different spell this time. Collin, you'll still be working with air."

I sat as instructed and watched my classmates work.

Chapter Fifteen

I was able to pick up the book three more times before class ended. Even though I wasn't really losing blood, I felt weak and dizzy once class was over.

"You'll have to rest well tonight," Watanabe said. "It's strenuous on the body to use up its energy this way. Eventually, you'll get used to it. Think of it as running a mile. The first time, it wears you out; the more you practice, the quicker you can run it, and you don't lose as much energy."

I nodded, sweat beading my hairline.

The other students had completed feats so beautiful and amazing without breathing heavy. I felt like a loser.

We walked out ahead of the professor.

Omar gave my shoulder a little pat. "You did really great. I couldn't have accomplished that on my first day."

I knew he was trying to be nice, but still the words flowed from my mouth. "And your first day, you were eight. I don't know if that's an accurate comparison."

He grimaced and shrugged. "It's still something."

"It *was* a good lesson," Tabitha said, encouragingly. "You're doing marvelous for a beginner."

"We all have to start somewhere," Laura added. "Sometimes, these things happen for a reason."

"All I know is that I'll beat you," Sammuel said, emphasizing his words with a swaggering gait.

I smiled, eased by their words, even Sammuel's taunt. It wasn't so bad knowing I was last, when I'd at least made it into this competitive program. Maybe I had innate talent, but I also had perseverance and drive. I'd catch up. Maybe not this month, or even this school year, but eventually I would.

It was only four o'clock, too early for dinner, so we walked as a group to the dorms. At the junction where the sidewalk split toward the three different buildings, Tabitha and Laura broke off, heading toward the right. We waved bye to them, then continued on.

"You'll have to teach me the rules," Sammuel said. "I'll throw around the ball a bit."

"Awesome," Omar replied enthusiastically. "I'll add you to the group chat."

"Can't be more difficult than rugby."

"It's not," Omar said. "Not anywhere close."

I raised an eyebrow. "You play rugby too?" I asked Omar.

"We tried it once or twice. Too exhausting."

Sammuel nodded. "Tough game. Not for the weak-minded, either." His face lit up with an authentic smile. "It's a blast though. Primal, even."

"Sounds terrible to me," I said. "I'll stick to regular football."

"*American* football," Sammuel corrected, and his sneer was back.

A pang shot through my heart at his words. He'd uttered it like a curse, the same way Terrence had. Would he still be mad at me for prying?

We entered the dorm lobby. Here, we went our separate ways. Sammuel immediately joined a group around the television. Omar headed for the soda machine.

Which left me to hurry upstairs on my own, eager to find Terrence. I took the stairs two at a time.

I needn't have bothered. The dorm room was empty when I pushed open the door. Would he avoid me the whole night? My stomach roiled, and anxiety filled me. What if he wanted a different roommate now? What if he didn't want to see me again?

Collin? It's you, isn't it? I'm so sorry. You were right, and I'm so sorry I betrayed you.

The words, spoken so long ago, reverberated in my skull, bouncing around within my brain. *He begged* my *forgiveness. He won't be mad forever. Though, apparently, he expects me to be.*

I was contemplating calling my parents when the door opened. Terrence strolled in, his messenger bag over his shoulder. My mouth went dry at the sight of him. He was beautiful, more beautiful than I remembered. More beautiful than I could believe.

Without thought, I stood and went to him. His eyes widened in surprise, but he didn't back away. I pressed our lips together, my eyes fluttering closed as the heat of him enveloped me. The deliciousness of his mouth increased as he worked his lips against mine.

The release I felt threatened to weaken my knees. I hastily pulled away and walked to my bed. I sank to the edge of the mattress, my tongue running over my bottom lip, striving for more of his taste.

Terrence half grinned and said, "Are you okay?"

"I—I missed you, is all."

"Yeah? Then why'd you run all the way over there? You could have kept kissing me."

I swallowed past a lump in my throat. "I feel...funny. Needed to sit."

He laughed and advanced on me. In half a heartbeat, he stood over me, looking down, meeting my needy gaze with one full of promises. "Can I sit?"

At my nod, he took the space beside me. Too close. And not close enough.

"Any more fainting spells?" he asked, reaching out a hand to gently rub the back of my neck. "It can be draining at first, especially since you don't have your coins."

"No more fainting. I, well, I was afraid you were still angry at me."

He sighed, and with his free hand, lifted my palm into his. He entwined our fingers. "I'm not mad. I'm sorry for my attitude earlier. It grates at me to think others see me as less. I had to deal with a lot of it growing up, from Helmer and the rest of my family."

"We never meant to imply—"

He bristled. "What else could you mean when asking if someone lacks the skill to be in the program?"

"We were curious. Especially since you have connections. But it wasn't any of our business. Omar and I are both sorry we even brought it up."

Terrence scoffed. "How do you know how Omar feels? Why are you speaking for him?"

"I just know he's sorry. He's a good person." I paused, then rushed on all in one breath. "So can we put this behind us?"

He nodded, and a slight curve of his lips let me know I'd somehow given him what he wanted. What that was, I had no idea.

"What did you learn today?" he asked, still so close to me.

"Well, Theory didn't go so well. Helmer dismissed the class after I fainted. Tomes was good. I...er...checked out a few books to do a research paper."

Terrence made an interesting noise. "What's your topic?"

"Maybe dragons?"

He wrinkled his nose. "All the information at your fingertips and you choose dragons?"

I adopted a look of defensiveness, lest he begin to question why I wanted to study the mythical—extinct?—creatures. "I never knew dragons existed before. I think it's fascinating."

He shrugged, but I could tell he still dwelled on the issue internally. "What else?"

"Oh, ah...Jenkins talked nonstop about vortexes. And then Watanabe walked me through accessing my magic without coins."

That perked him up. He leaned in even closer. "So you can use it now? Were you successful?"

I nodded. "I could lift a book into the air."

His sudden smile lit up his eyes. "Amazing, Collin! I knew you were a natural! When children begin lessons, it takes them months to be able to physically touch the ether. You've accomplished that in an afternoon."

There was obvious pride in his voice, and it made my heart skip a beat.

"I didn't do anywhere near as well as the others."

Terrence waved his hand, dismissed them. "Don't worry about them. You can only measure your success by you."

I'd heard similar phrases from others since coming here, but hearing it out of Terrence's beautiful lips made it sound better.

"Thanks," I said.

I hoped he meant to kiss me, but instead, he stood from the bed and went to my discarded book bag. "You got homework?"

I groaned softly and stood too. "Yeah, Jenkins gave me a book on Latin. I need to practice."

"I'll help."

"Don't you have other things to work on?"

He shot me a smirk. "Want me to leave you to it?"

My cheeks heated. "No. I mean, if you have your own stuff to do, don't worry about me. But if you've got the time and inclination, I'd love your assistance."

His smile deepened. "I've got more than inclination, Collin. You should know that by now." He handed me the bag. "Let's get started. We've got an hour or two till dinner."

We situated ourselves at my desk, with Terrence's chair pulled up alongside mine. Every breath I took filled my lungs with his scent. Studying like this might not be the best idea.

But then we were looking at Jenkins's book—an actual picture book, with cartoonish drawings and bright colors—and Terrence's explanation clicked inside my brain.

"You'll know most of the basics already. *Ignis.*" He gestured to the picture of a smiling fire. "Think ignite. And *anima*, for soul, spirit, or life. I always think of animal." The picture in the book showed a ghost leaving a body.

I nodded. "*Ignis, aqua, caeli, terra, anima.* Fire, water, air, ground, and spirit. The five main powers in lingual magic."

Terrence's encouraging smile put one on my own lips. "You're doing excellent. Like I said, a natural."

I glowed with self-satisfaction.

Then Terrence's hand was wrapping around mine. "Maybe you've earned a break." The next moment, he moved his lips toward mine. I surged forward, meeting him halfway.

We grappled that way for several minutes, working against one another to get as much skin touching as possible. The feel of him, the taste of him, the smell of him. He ensnared me ever deeper.

Terrence pulled away and regarded me, a light dancing in his eyes. "What if we move this to the bed? Sprawled out is preferable to cramped in the shower."

I gulped. Honestly, having him in the shower this morning was the highlight of my life to date. Of course, I wasn't opposed to a repeat, and having more room wouldn't be a bad thing.

I stood from my chair, gripping his arms to drag him with me. My bed was closest, so I went that way, Terrence following obediently. At the edge, I sat, and Terrence bent over to continue our kisses. The height difference made him lean, and the pressure of his stance sent a thrill through my whole body. I moaned into his mouth, as my fingers trailed up his sleeves to hold onto his biceps.

When he pulled back, his cheeks were pink and his breathing heavy. "Get undressed?"

I nodded, backing away enough to pull my blazer jacket off my arms. My shirt went next, straight over my head to spare the minutes needed to work the buttons. I unbuckled my belt and worked my pants open and off my hips. I slipped my fingers under my boxer briefs, but Terrence stopped me.

He'd been watching me strip with an intent gaze. Now, his eyes trailed over my exposed skin, stopping at the bulge forming in my underwear. He didn't touch me but saw to his own clothing. He removed every stitch, then stood in front of me, nude and perfect.

"Come lie down?" I asked, since he still only stared. I patted the bed beside me.

He grinned, and my heart skipped a beat. "I'll do more than that." He climbed onto the bed, but instead of aligning his body with mine, he hunched over my lower half. "Let's see to this first." His fingers hovered over my growing erection, but didn't come into contact. I could feel the heat of him though.

"Please," I said, not sure what he even had in mind, but wanting it nonetheless.

"Anything for you," he said.

I looked into his eyes and saw the lie within them. It should have made my cock shrivel and my desire flee. He didn't mean a word of what he said. And yet, my body still responded to his nearness.

You don't love me, I wanted to say. *But you will*. And that certainly pushed all hesitance from my mind. My thoughts and body synced with the thought of and Terrence and what he could do to me.

"Touch me," I breathed.

He obliged. He lifted my briefs off and over my hips. Immediately, his hands went to my cock. This morning, in the shower, it had been fast and hot. Now, his palm gripped me gently, and his strokes were slow and rhythmic.

His body leaned over mine. To remedy this, I gripped his free wrist and gave a tug. He willingly dropped beside me, his hand never stilling.

With him settled against me, I reached out my hand to grip him. His cock was warm, like the rest of him, and growing harder by the second. I groaned at the feel of him, marveling at his wonderful heat.

"You like this?" he asked playfully. He was on his side, and his lips went to my ear for a nibble. "Tell me what else."

I loved his breath against my lobe, and the way his teeth worried the skin gently, but with increasing pressure.

"Can I taste you? Suck your cock?"

His bite became harder, as did his erection in my hand. "Yes. I'd like that. Shall we do it together?"

"Together?"

Instead of answering, he pulled away from me. I half reached to keep him in place, but he quickly soothed my disappointment. Flipping around, Terrence aligned his face with my cock. He held on to my hips to turn me. This marvelous setup also placed him right in front of me.

I licked my lips, excited, but hesitant.

"I've never—" I started, but he didn't wait for me to finish.

"I know, and it's fine. Take your time and do what feels good, Collin."

His soft, reassuring tone made my heart swell. Did he love me? His gentleness and compassion suggested he did, but the light in his eyes gave away his lies. I pushed the conflicting thoughts from my mind and focused on him. I wanted this, so I had better get to it.

I swallowed, then gripped his cock. This close, I could smell his musky scent, and it sent a quick pulse of desire through my entire body. With a tight hold, I led the tip to my lips. The skin was smooth and warm. I pressed the ridges against my lips.

Terrence moaned, but so far, he hadn't moved. Was he waiting for me to get comfortable first? If so, I needed to prove I could do this.

My tongue darted out and licked his skin. His cock twitched, and his breath caught with an audible gasp.

He liked that. Emboldened by this response, I tried again. I licked the side, going over the rises and falls of his dick. It was so perfectly shaped and aesthetically enticing. I slipped the whole tip into my mouth.

"Fuck," Terrence muttered, and his hips bucked forward. "Feels good, Collin."

With him completely inside me, I ran my tongue to the side, tracing the edge of the head. A simple move, but Terrence began to shake.

As if unable to hold back any longer, he attacked my cock. I froze under his assault. It was a hundred times more sensual than his hand gripping me. The heat of his mouth a thousand times more arousing.

I cried out softly, the sound muffled by my full mouth. That reminded me of my task, and I resumed my attention on Terrence.

We worked in tandem, giving and getting, slowly building up a joint crescendo. I tried to mimic what he did to me—as he was obviously much more experienced. Either way, he seemed pleased, and it wasn't long at all before I reached my tipping point.

I gripped Terrence's bare legs tight in warning, then tensed. My whole body shook, and my cock pulsed in Terrence's mouth. A heartbeat later, Terrence came too. His semen coated my tongue, filling my senses with a salty-sweet taste. I swallowed the viscous fluid.

Terrence released me from his mouth, though he still kept a firm grip at the base of my shaft. Following his lead, I did the same. His cock was red from my sucking, and a few drops of come still dripped from the slit. I licked away those few beads of moisture and he shivered.

"Collin," he said weakly. "That was amazing. I've never done it like that before."

A sense of happiness filled me at his admission—that it was something new for both of us—but a second thought followed that: What else had he done with others? I couldn't begrudge him his sexual forays, but I did bristle with envy. I wished I could have had sexual encounters before now. I'd missed out on a lot of pleasurable experiences.

But I had them now. That was what I needed to focus on.

Terrence moved away from me and flipped so our bodies aligned again. He snuggled in close. My satisfied cock still twitched weakly as his rubbed against me.

"Did you like it?" he asked. "Maybe it was too overwhelming?"

I shook my head. "Not overwhelming." At least, not in the sense he meant. "I loved it. It...it was amazing, Terrence. I liked the taste of you, the feel of you."

The attraction I felt for him was real. The overwhelming emotion continued to grow with each day and each encounter. This was the beginning of love. I knew it in my heart. And when I loved him, he'd eventually love me in return.

He grinned and pulled me into his neck. The slight sheen of sweat along his skin coated my forehead as I buried my head against him. I could spend forever just like this.

Of course, my parents ruined the moment. My phone buzzed on my desk, sending an annoying reverberation around the room. I knew it was them. They probably couldn't wait to hear about my classes.

"I better answer that, or they'll worry."

Terrence nodded and, after a quick kiss, stood from the bed. He dressed as I answered my phone.

"Hey, sweetie," Mom said cheerily. "What's up?"

"Nothing, Mom. How are you guys?"

"We're just fine. Rocket may have an ear infection, so we're taking her to the vet tomorrow."

"Poor girl. Let me know what they say."

"Sure, kiddo. So, how were classes?"

"Good. They went really well. Uh, my Latin class is pretty tough, but Terrence agreed to help tutor me."

Mom laughed, and for a second it didn't seem like she was across an entire ocean. "I can't believe you're learning Latin. It's so hifalutin." She snorted. "You'll have to teach me some phrases so I can impress people too."

I grinned. She believed the only reason to learn a dead language would be to show off. There was no way I was going to inform her of its actual use at school.

I launched into a vague, but satisfying, story of my day: research project, lecture from the dean, lunch with Omar, and so on.

"We are so proud of you," she said, and I could sense the tears in her eyes. "But don't be afraid to call if you get homesick. We're here for you, even if we are a couple thousand miles away."

"I know, Mom. And thanks."

We said our goodbyes after promises to talk soon.

I hung up the phone and realized I was still naked. Terrence sat on his own bed, chin resting on his palm, balanced on his leg. His eyes studied me.

"You have a healthy relationship with them?" he asked.

I didn't know if rushing to get my clothes on would make me more or less foolish. I decided on the latter and pulled on my boxer briefs, which sat at the foot of my bed. With those firmly covering me, I felt more at ease.

"I guess. I mean, we fight, same as any parent and kid."

"Yeah, but that's normal. It's normal to fight. It's normal to argue. And it's normal to still say 'I love you.'"

I frowned at him, more from concern than anything else. "Do you need to talk about it?"

Terrence blinked several times, then shook his head. "No. Just making an observation. Will you be okay till you see them again next summer?"

"Sure," I lied. "I'll manage."

He laughed, as if catching my fib. "Who knows? Maybe they'll miss you so much they'll visit at Christmas."

"Maybe," I muttered, which meant no way in hell. They'd never be able to afford the airfare so soon.

"Why don't you finish dressing, and we can go eat. I'm starving, and for more than just a little nibble of something yummy." His eyes flashed, and I could see the desire he felt for me *was* real.

I nodded, then pulled on the rest of my clothing.

Chapter Sixteen

The next morning, I woke to a blissful heat against my bare back. The alarm hadn't buzzed yet, so I simply lay there, soaking in Terrence's warmth and the relaxed way his body molded to mine. His chest rose and fell gently, and his arm draped over my side in a perfect imitation of intimacy. I'd never been more content in my life.

My phone screeched, and Terrence jumped from deep sleep.

I rolled over and pressed the kill switch, then settled back into his arms.

"Morning," he mumbled, his lips beginning to nuzzle the back of my neck. "Sleep well?"

"Best night's sleep I've ever had."

He scoffed, and the heat of his breath hit my skin. "Trying to butter me up? Didn't you learn your lesson yesterday? No funny business in the mornings. We'll have to save it for later today." He placed a chaste kiss to my neck, then rolled over me to get out of bed.

I groaned at his departure, but he was right. I needed breakfast or else I could faint again. We did our morning routine, him in the shower first while I brushed my teeth and shaved the little stubble that grew from my chin. Then we switched places. I saw just a hint of his luscious body before he had a towel wrapped around his waist.

"Move it," he said, bumping my hip with his.

I vacated the sink and, after stripping off my clothes, climbed into the shower.

At breakfast, Omar and Laura waved to us as we entered. "Mind if we sit with them?" I asked.

Terrence raised his eyebrow. "What if I said yes?"

"Then we'd sit by ourselves."

He shook his head, a small smile on his lips. "What if I meant I wanted to sit with *my* friends?"

"Oh. That's...that's fine. You can do whatever you want, of course." I was babbling, and I knew it.

Terrence lifted my hand into his and locked our fingers. "Collin, I'm trying to make a joke. What's gotten into you today?"

With our hands joined, he gave me a tug and led me to the table where my classmates sat.

"Morning," Terrence greeted cheerfully. "Lovely day."

Omar side-eyed him, but Laura nodded enthusiastically. "I can't wait till it cools down," she said and fanned herself with her hand. "You're from here, right? Will the weather change soon?"

I stared at her. This was too hot? Already, I thought of keeping an extra jacket to cover my blazer in the evenings. Of course, she was from Canada, which was a far cry from the heat and humidity of Florida.

"Usually by the end of September it's chilly. But it likely won't get as cold as you're hoping. The water keeps the air warm enough to prevent snow most of the time."

Laura pouted. "No skiing, then?"

"There're a couple places close by you can get to. Nothing too spectacular, though."

The two of them fell into an easy conversation about likely spots. With them distracted, I turned to Omar, who was still glaring at Terrence.

"I'm going to grab our breakfasts. Can I get you a refill?" I gestured to his paper coffee cup.

"Yeah, but I'll come with you."

I told Terrence my intentions, and he gave me his order before returning to Laura.

"I see you two made up just fine," Omar said.

My cheeks burned. "Yeah, we did."

"Collin, I know it's none of my business, but you're the one who told me he hurts you. I can't believe you're willing to put up with that."

I furrowed my brow. "That's the whole problem, Omar. He hasn't done anything. Yet. It's a paradox. How can I judge him based on things he hasn't acted on? Haven't you ever read *Minority Report*?"

"I saw the movie."

"Nowhere near the same, but the message still gets through. You can't judge a person for crimes in their future."

"So you think he won't betray you?"

I shook my head. "I've always believed that time is set. Altering it isn't possible. But I also thought magic wasn't real and dragons didn't exist."

Omar's shoulders seemed to lose their rigidity. "I see what you're saying. Either way, you've decided to go down this path?"

My heart ached as I whispered, "Omar, I love him. I've always loved him. I won't ever stop loving him."

"Such a romantic. Listen, if there's any time you need me, just let me know. We'll have a secret code or something. It'll tell me you think the bad thing is coming, and I'll do my best to stop it."

I swallowed past a lump in my throat. Why did he care so much about me? We'd only met a few days ago. Of course, I'd only met Terrence a few days ago, too, and I was already sure of the man he was.

"Thanks," I said. "If I get scared or need your help relating to this, I'll tell you I saw red lightning. Will that work?"

He nodded.

"Good. Now, are you ready to hear the details?"

In a low whisper, I filled Omar in on mine and Terrence's exploits, and he listened with rapt attention. Back home, I'd been the one to nod and smile as my friends shared their sexual forays. It was nice to be able to share. Nice to find someone willing to hear me out.

Just as softly, he asked, "Have you ever thought of... you know...doing anal?"

I nodded emphatically. "I'm sure we'll work up to that eventually. I'm fine with taking it slow right now. He's the first person I've ever been sexually attracted to."

"Are you demisexual?"

I smiled so big, my mouth hurt. "Yes. Not many people can understand that. I had several friends in high school who wanted to experiment, and I just couldn't."

"Your experience with him made that strong connection, huh? And your body responds with him only?"

"Another reason I know he's the same person I met. He has to be."

Omar pinched his lips together. "You know, they say no soul is past redemption. I just wish he'd said how he betrayed you."

I shook my head and chuckled mirthlessly. "I was twelve years old, Omar. Would you tell a twelve-year-old dark secrets?"

"No, I wouldn't. And if he didn't, that's kind of considerate."

"See? He has it in him. But it's buried somewhere deep inside. I'll bring it out. I swear I will."

"I believe you, Collin."

We'd reached the front of the line, and I grabbed a plate for me and Terrence. Omar assisted by holding our coffees, as well as his own refill. When we went back to the table, Laura was laughing delightedly, and Terrence was grinning. She even reached out and patted his hand.

The sight filled me with no jealousy, no envy, no anger. And I was surprised. I trusted him completely. I'd told Omar I did, and now I felt it deep in my bones, a truth that filled my entire being. No matter what he did to me, I'd forgive him.

"Breakfast," I said, setting the plate of pancakes and syrup in front of Terrence.

Laura shifted her smile to me. "Collin, Terrence was just telling me about one of his friends. He says he might be interested in taking me to the gala."

Surprisingly, Omar shifted in his chair, his eyes suddenly downcast. I wasn't the only one to notice.

"Omar?" Laura asked. "What's wrong?"

He cleared his throat, but didn't raise his gaze. "I was kinda hoping you'd go with *me* to the gala."

Omar missed Laura's surprised look, but I saw it clearly.

"Me? Surely Tabitha is a better choice?"

Omar finally looked up. "No, it's you I wanted to ask. If you're willing to go with me."

Laura's smile was warm. "Of course, Omar. That sounds very nice."

He returned her grin. "Great."

Terrence leaned close to me. "And I assumed I'd be your date, but maybe I better confirm myself."

Encouraged by the easygoing light in his eyes, I reached out and held his hand. "I assumed you'd go with me too. No need to even mention it."

His blue eyes flickered with something like desire—or maybe something closer to possessiveness. Either way, my mind filled with images and thoughts of my previous conversation with Omar about experimenting with new sexual things.

I shook my head, dispelling the raging wildfire that threatened to burn me to cinders. Class. Class had to come first.

Terrence seemed to understand the path my brain was taking, and he smirked.

I tried to focus on my pancakes, but the feel of Terrence's gaze on me drained my appetite. I forced some down just to avoid a repeat of yesterday.

"We'd better get going," Omar said with a glance at his cell phone.

After cleaning our plates, we headed for the door. Terrence walked with us all the way to Regalia.

"We'll let you guys say goodbye," Omar said and took Laura with him.

Terrence watched them as they disappeared inside the building. Then he turned to me, his face full of mischief. "I'm a great matchmaker, don't you think?"

I crinkled my eyebrows. "You? Why?" I glanced the way Omar and Laura had gone. "You don't mean with them, do you?"

"Yup. You didn't see the way he looked at her? It's very similar to the way you look at me."

I gulped and felt a nervous flutter in my chest. It wasn't embarrassing to be so infatuated, but I didn't want people to assume I was a fool with a silly crush.

Except, that's exactly what it is. You'd do anything Terrence asked. You're so blinded. You idiot.

The thought didn't stop my gaze from drifting to Terrence's lips and remembering all the kisses he'd ever given me.

He closed the distance between us, his hands gripping my forearms in a tight vise. My eyes shut as his lips pressed to mine. Not deeply, I was thankful—I had no intention of making out where others could see—but still sweet and tempting.

When he pulled back, he smiled. "I'll see you at lunch. Be a good boy."

I swallowed. "You too."

Then he was walking toward his own class. I watched him till he blended in with the crowd. I turned toward Regalia and froze. Helmer stood a few paces behind me, his eyes wide and staring at me.

"Good morning, Dean Helmer," I said, proud that my voice didn't flutter. My whole body went rigid when I spied him, and I hoped he was far enough way to miss my tremors.

He stared a moment longer, then said, "Good morning, Collin. Hurry inside or you'll be late."

"Yes, sir."

I hurried up the sidewalk to the door. Helmer didn't move, just watched me disapprovingly. My pace increased, and I all but ran into the hall, down the side corridor, and into the lecture room. Omar looked up from his seat and waved at me, so I jogged to the chair he saved for me.

"You okay?"

I leaned close to him and whispered, "I think Helmer saw Terrence kiss me."

"So?"

"So, their relationship is strained. He definitely didn't look happy when—" I cut off as Helmer stepped onto the raised platform.

"Good morning," he greeted cheerfully, but when he looked at me, he frowned slightly.

"Yikes," Omar said, catching sight of the dean's glare. "He must be pissed."

The dean broke eye contact with me and surveyed the rest of the room. "For today's lesson, I'm going to give a brief overview of magical history." At the collective groan, he added, "It's important to be familiar with our history; it keeps us from making the same mistakes." Again, he glanced at me and furrowed his brow.

Jesus! Why's he so mad? So what if I kissed Terrence? Why would that upset him so much?

Helmer cleared his throat, then went into lecture mode. "Magic has been around since human life began. Was it born from us, or we from it? Those are some of the questions we delve into in Theory class. A lot of the areas we study aren't concrete, but are still being discovered and researched as we chart them. That's the most exciting part about our magic, the sense of wonder of what we have left to find."

Despite my unsettled stomach at Helmer's obvious displeasure, I was hooked by his simple statement. I stared at him in wide-eyed awe. People always said there was nothing left to discover on our planet, but here, in the field of magic, apparently new things still popped up. What a wonderful experience to be a pioneer in a groundbreaking study.

Helmer continued. "Early on, we've learned that blood is the key to magic. At first, practitioners didn't use their own blood, but blood of slaughtered animals or of murdered enemies. This would give them some power, but not nearly enough. After many years of this archaic magic, they discovered that the blood of a magician, willingly given and still alive, would increase the power by one hundredfold. That's what led to practitioners carrying knives on them to access their blood.

"Then, about a hundred years ago, a Japanese magician by the name of Haruki Toshimoto discovered the Gyranium, a plant-machine hybrid that could lock a person's blood magic into a metal object. This system resulted in a surplus of power and control for all practitioners, worldwide. It made our way of life safer. It's why our numbers have started to slow."

I jotted down notes while he spoke. This was much more interesting than any literature course could have been. The rest of the class, though, stared off into space or doodled on their papers.

My hand shot into the air. When Helmer pointed at me, I said, "Why would advances in magic cause our numbers to drop? It seems the opposite would be true."

Helmer nodded. "Easier access to magic means we must be selective. We can't have untrustworthy people be given infinite power."

I dipped my head, seeing the logic of his argument.

Helmer continued. "With this power, we also have a debt to society, even to humanity. We cannot use this to enslave, as our predecessors did. We've all studied the Mayans and how they used magics to control and torture. We—and I mean every practitioner living—must strive to be above such heinous and hateful crimes. We enforce a code amongst ourselves, and it's wise to remember that we have a duty to protect, not hurt."

I raised my hand again. "I asked Professor Watanabe yesterday, but I'm still curious. What are the practical applications of magic in modern society?"

"An excellent question, Collin. Most wind up working for the government. There are many aspects of what we do that the leaders of the world can use for good. We help maintain peace and can even step in if conflicts escalate. Our magical attacks are much more effective than any wartime weapons."

"So we can join the army?" I asked. The students chuckled, but I was serious.

"Not necessarily. We can't use magic as a weapon for just any reason. The needs must be very, very great. So, joining the army wouldn't amount to much for someone like us."

"Besides the government, what else is there?"

"Teaching, of course. Or research."

"And?"

"Living a normal life," the dean said. "Just because you have this power doesn't mean you need to devote your life to it. Some, not many, who graduate from here, get jobs at banks, or at supermarkets, or start families. The main advantage is getting into government positions, but it's not a requirement."

"We don't have shops in obscure corners of town where we sell potions?" I asked.

"No."

"Why not? If our duty is to help humanity, why not make cures for the sick or end world hunger?"

"And you've come to the staple of Theory class, Collin, the ethics of magic. What if we did step in and help a farmer whose crops aren't growing? They'd be thankful. I'm sure. But what would stop them from being hit by a car the next day? What will their family do? They'd be lining up to see us to complain, to say we didn't save them when we could have. Don't you see? We can't police the natural cycle of life. That's what being human is all about."

I nodded slowly, suddenly understanding how difficult a position that would put magic users in. Omar explained the basics, but Helmer's details framed it in a terrible light. People would look for help in everything; they'd become dependent.

Another thought entered my mind. "If most of the population is able to use magic, there'd be a lot more supply to make up for the demand. We'd be able to educate more people, which would create more jobs within the magical community."

The dean shook his head. "While at least 75 percent of the population can access their magic, only a small fraction of that number could produce anything useful.

"There are several problems related to this. First is the fact of low potential. Since magic is innate, each person's power level is set. More than 50 percent of all people capable of using magic barely have enough power to light a candle or lift a book. Those people, once aware of the existence of magic, would thirst for more, which could send us back to archaic times, resulting in war and bloodshed."

"If we can't change our magical potential, why should that worry us, or send us into war?"

"That is a forbidden topic, Collin, one we don't speak of often. Stay back after class, and I'll explain what little I can."

I gulped but nodded. Did he really want to instruct me on this topic, or was this an excuse to get me alone?

"Second point," Helmer said. "With so much of the population practicing, it would be difficult to track down wrongdoers. Magical chaos would ensue. It would take nearly all the time and effort of our strongest practitioners to police those who are weaker. Their attention would be focused on unimportant matters instead of fulfilling their potential."

He glanced around the rows of inattentive students. "Now, let's get to today's task. I'm assigning you all books for this semester." He waved his hand; the other was in his pocket likely pinching his coin, because a stack of books along the far shelf began to float over. They settled onto the tables, one in front of each student.

"When you have your book, open to page twelve and read the introduction on magical ethics. There are practical questions at the end that I want each of you to answer. You have enough time to read and finish the assignment before the end of class."

I was the only one who did it quickly, eagerly opening the book and turning to the correct page.

By the end of class, I had completed two of the five questions. They were each hypothetical situations and asked the best course a practitioner should choose under the circumstances.

"These are hard," I murmured to Omar.

Omar shrugged and passed his sheet of paper down the row to a student who was collecting them.

"Class is dismissed," Helmer said. His gaze fell to me, and I straightened from picking up my messenger bag. Apparently, he hadn't forgotten that I'd been asked to stay after.

"See ya," Omar said, then hurried out of the room with the others.

I held up my paper. "I didn't finish this. Can I turn it in tomorrow?"

His smile was friendly but forced. "Of course, Collin. We won't rush you since you're still learning the basics. Give it to me before class starts."

"Thanks. It's a lot harder to think in terms of magic."

"Understandable. It's a lot to take in. Now, can we have a quick chat?"

"Sure. About magical potential?"

"Yes. It's a very grave topic. We teach that a person's magical potential is set, fixed, unchanging. Whether you're ten or two hundred, your magic is the same. You become faster, more experienced with age, but you always have your limits. These are innate." He paused for effect, then continued. "Except that is a lie. Potential can be changed by very dangerous, very evil methods."

"Evil?"

"I won't go into specifics, but they involve eating a practitioner's heart. There are certain rites that accompany this, of course. Naturally, we don't let anyone know them. If the power hungry were able to get their hands on the spells, magical imbalance would ensue. We have these limits set for a reason. Many believe it was God who gave us these boundaries. A way to keep us from growing too strong."

"I can see why that would make some people worry. Thank you for explaining." I bent over to grab my bag.

"Can I have another moment of your time?"

My stomach dropped, but I stilled and looked at the dean. "Of course."

"It seems you've grown close to Terrence."

I tried for nonchalance. "Yup."

Helmer's dark eyes narrowed. "It's none of my business, of course, as an academic advisor. But as Terrence's father, I do have concerns."

My throat dried and I tried to swallow, but couldn't. "About what?" *That I'm so common and unskilled?*

"I'm sure you've already figured out that Terrence was not permitted into the literature program. It's not his skills that kept him out of it. He's a very talented practitioner."

"Then why?"

"Did he tell you how he got that scar?"

The hairs on my arms stood up on end at Helmer's drastic change in subject. A sense of foreboding filled me. This was not going to lead somewhere pleasant. "A boating accident."

"A lie. What happened is this: Terrence tried to increase his magic."

My jaw dropped. "But you just said..."

The dean nodded. "Terrence, as my child, had access to much more information than the average practitioner. He grew in skill quickly and became dissatisfied with his limitations. He's strong—could be stronger than me, if allowed to train to his full potential—but it was never enough for him."

I lifted a hand to my chest, wanting to release the pain suddenly welling up inside me. *My magic. That's what he's after? Will he try to kill me? Eat my heart? That would be one hell of a betrayal.*

Helmer understood some of my sudden torment, and he reached out to grip my shoulder. "Not like that. He's not a murderer. If I thought, even for a second, he'd harm a student here, I never would have allowed him on campus. No, there are other creatures with far more magic than humans. He planned to summon a demon from an alternate dimension. If he was successful, it could have altered him beyond recognition. Humans and unearthly creatures don't merge well. But he was too determined to heed the warnings."

My voice was barely a whisper. "What happened?"

"He began the summoning before I could stop him. A fire demon called Al'venarta. I prevented him from completing the ritual, but he still paid a terrible price. As the demon was forced back through their own realm, they reached out a clawed hand and struck. Their talon sliced through Terrence's neck, nearly severing the blood vessels and killing my son. Through it all, the demon laughed. They stared at us with their evil, red eyes, then disappeared back to their realm."

I shivered, thinking of red eyes.

"Naturally, Kate—Terrence's mother—and I concluded he needed to be kept from all magic. Including myself." His head bowed in sorrow.

"Why are you telling me this?"

Helmer looked at me, his eyes wet and face suddenly tired. "I should have warned you before this. Terrence is not your friend."

"What?"

"He's determined and will try to use you for his own purposes. He'll want access to coins. Or spell books. He can't have either, Collin. You must realize he has no real interest in you. You must not trust him."

I lowered my chin unable to meet Helmer's gaze. No matter what he said, could I stop trusting Terrence? "Why is he at this school, then? Why did you let him attend here?"

"He's in the business program, Collin. And all his magical transgressions were in the past. I cannot keep him from getting a college degree when he's done no crime."

I flinched, his words too similar to my own reasons for allowing Terrence to get close to me. "Yes, that's true. He's done nothing wrong." *Yet*, I added to myself.

"Yet," Helmer said, and the word sounded through the room like a gong. "You need to watch yourself. Don't let him fool you because that's the only reason he's showing any interest in you."

My spirits sank even farther.

"Please don't misunderstand me, Collin. I'm his father, and I love him dearly. But I don't want to see you get hurt."

You can't prevent it because I'll walk into his fire on my own free will. I'll let my soul turn to ash.

"Thank you for letting me know. I'll...be careful."

His hand gave me another squeeze. "That's a good, lad. Now, off to class with you."

Chapter Seventeen

Tomes passed by in a blur. My mind couldn't shake the words Helmer told me. Terrence's heat had to come from the brief contact with that fire demon. And his plans... What did he mean to do with me?

I'm so sorry. You were right, and I'm so sorry I betrayed you.

But how?

I followed Omar, Laura, and Tabitha to the cafe for lunch, but I didn't taste anything I ate. I participated in the conversation but heard nothing.

Jenkins got on a tangent about the Heel Stone at Stonehenge, and rambled for the whole hour. Under normal circumstances, I would have listened intently—the only eager student—but not today.

Even in Methods I couldn't concentrate enough to make the book lift into the air.

"Don't let it get you down," Watanabe said sympathetically. "It'll be easier once you get coins."

I walked out, still lost in thought.

I was sure I said goodbye to the others as I headed to the dorm—they went in the other direction for some reason. Finally alone, I collapsed onto my bed and covered my eyes with my elbow.

Terrence was so skilled as a practitioner. No wonder he'd freaked when Omar and I asked about his lack of admittance to the program.

And red eyes. Terrence must meld with the demon Al'venarta. That had to be what changed his appearance.

On the slopes, Terrence had said *betrayed*, not hurt. There was a subtle difference in the meaning of his words. Betrayed meant he'd broken my confidence. He'd done something I hadn't approved of. *You were right.* Maybe what I had to do was talk him out of summoning Al'venarta. Ask him not to do it, but knowing he will anyway.

I growled loudly into the quiet room. Why did it have to be this way? I couldn't decipher any more than this.

Go to the source.

My hands dropped to my sides, and I stared up at the ceiling. Could I ask Terrence? Let him know I'd been informed of his past errors and warned against him? Confess that I loved him more than words could say, and I would do anything to help him achieve whatever he planned?

Maybe he wouldn't believe me.

Well, one thing became clear after my talk with the dean. I knew more of Terrence's motivations. And I had a name: Al'venarta.

I was on my feet and out the door before I really understood what I was doing. I went to Regalia and headed straight for the library.

The gaping room was eerily silent, more so than usual. Nothing stirred. I doubted even Professor Lorel was here.

Sammuel had shown me how to use the catalog, so I went to the top floor and stood in front of the box. I didn't have a coin or a knife. I settled for biting the skin inside my lip. At the taste of blood in my mouth, I focused and said, "Catalog, please show me books about demons."

A bright line appeared on the floor and shot down the aisle, around the opening that showed the bottom floors, and to the other side of the level. I hurried after the line, following it to a row of books, all illuminated in a glowing light. I was so awed by the sight that I failed to notice another person down the row until they gave a cry of surprise.

"Sorry," I said immediately, holding out my hands in a nonthreatening gesture. "I didn't realize you were here."

I finally got a good look at her and realized it was one of the women Terrence had introduced me to in our dorm. She was petite, with long red hair flowing to her shoulders. Fresha?

She stared at me with overly wide eyes.

"It's Fresha, right? I'm Collin. We met a few days ago." I held out my hand to her.

Instead of taking it, she moved backward. Two steps. Then three. Her startled eyes never left mine. Another step, and another. Then she turned and ran.

I was only a half beat behind. When I got to the edge of the bookshelf, she was already disappearing down the stairwell along the outside wall. At my feet was a book she'd dropped in her haste to get away from me.

It didn't seem wise to chase her. Plus, it wasn't like she was here doing something wrong.

Or was she? Were nonpractitioners allowed in the library? I doubted it. Then why was she in here, sneaking around, afraid of getting caught?

I lifted the book and held it in my hands. It glowed with the light of the other books I'd searched for. A book on demons.

Pursing my lips, I focused my concentration and used my tooth to reopen the wound in my mouth. "Catalog, please turn off the search." The light disappeared.

There was no teacher to check out books right now. I hesitated only a moment before tucking the book under my arm, then hurried the way Fresha had gone. I ran out of the library, out of the hall, and around the side of the building toward the back.

At the corner, I slowed when I heard voices. I crouched and cautiously peeked around the side of the building and was not surprised to see Terrence and Fresha.

"But it was there?" Terrence asked softly, his arm gripping Fresha's shoulder tightly.

Her eyes were still wide, and she swayed a bit on her feet. Even her voice trembled. "Yes, I found it. But I was interrupted."

"By whom? A teacher?"

She shook her head. "A student."

"Damn it. It's too risky to go back now. We'll have to wait a few days. And I'll send Ham instead." Then Terrence pulled a small, metal object from his pocket. For a heartbeat, I feared he'd use it to hurt Fresha, but instead, he sliced a small cut on his palm. The blood welled up. "Return to your dorm. Forget this happened."

Fresha nodded dreamily, then set off toward the women's dorm.

After she left, Terrence stared at the wall, lost in thought. Time stretched and my legs ached from my position, but I didn't dare move until Terrence did. Finally, with another oath, he went toward our own dorm.

With him safely out of sight, I stood and rubbed at my thighs. They burned, but I forced my thoughts onto more important matters. The book. I held it out in front of me and examined the cover. It was old, the leather at the corners frayed and crumbling. The words were done in golden gilt. *Rites of Passage*, the title read in an elegant font of swirls, almost like calligraphy. I opened the first page and skimmed the introduction.

Herein lies the sacred rites to summon our unearthly lords, the Demons. To bring a Demon Lord into our realm is what we strive for, to help the human race be free of our multitude of sins. Weep when they are called forth, for they will bring with them justice for the wicked.

I shivered and closed the book. It wasn't safe to go back to the dorm yet, not if Terrence was there. I didn't have my messenger bag to hide the book. I'd have to wait. Or find a place to stash it until later.

I decided on the first plan. If I put it somewhere, another person could find it. If this book was what I thought it was, even a normal person finding it could have terrible consequences.

An idea sparked in my head. I pulled out my cell phone and texted Terrence.

I'm going to be in the cafe for an early dinner. Want to join me?

Only a few seconds passed before his reply came through.

On my way.

I squinted at the men's dorm, visible just behind a cluster of trees. Several men came and went, but I easily picked out Terrence. His stride was purposeful and his focus directed in front of him. Once he passed the side of Regalia, I ran. I moved as if the devil himself were after me. In the dorm, I took the stairs two at a time, panting as I hurried down the hallway and into our room.

It was empty. I lifted my mattress and shoved the book beneath it. Once I set it back down, there was no indication I had something hidden there.

I sighed in relief, thinking of what to do with the book.

My phone chirped and I jumped.

Where are you?

Shit, I had to hurry.

I forgot my Ethics book in Regalia. I'm heading to the cafe now.

I pulled said book from my bag. Then with one last glance at my bed, I rushed to meet Terrence.

Chapter Eighteen

Somehow, I made it through my first week at Marke Staple. The book on demons sat under my bed, untouched. I didn't have time to investigate because Terrence was hardly ever out of my sight. Did he suspect? Or was this a different part of his plan?

Friday, after Methods—Watanabe gave me a candle to light with elemental fire—Helmer came to collect me.

Dread filled me from thinking it was going to be another lecture about Terrence. Despite all that had happened and all I suspected, I couldn't push him out of my heart. We'd kissed, slept in the same bed, and given each other blow jobs every night this week. I didn't think my virginity would stay intact much longer.

"I'm being careful," I told the dean after the others, even Professor Watanabe, left the classroom.

"I know you have, Collin. That's not why I'm here. Usually, freshmen are the last to have their coins minted, as they generally just came from a primary literature program and don't have a need. However, we've bumped you up in the schedule so you can start practicing more diligently. Professor Watanabe has told me of the progress you've made in Methods, and Professor Jenkins says you've obviously been studying your Latin."

"I enjoy learning, Dean Helmer. It's all so interesting."

"I'm glad to hear that. And coins will make it much easier."

I nodded. The dean led me out of Regalia and toward Lapris Hall. As we walked, I asked, "What exactly is this Gyranium? I've heard it talked of but never in detail."

"It's a machine, of sorts. A plant-metal hybrid. It's a living thing and grown only for this purpose."

"A living machine?"

"Yes. It was developed in Japan, at the famous Fujioka Academy. But now, every school with a literature program has one. The Gyranium takes your blood and your image and concentrates them into the metal of your coins."

My coins. I knew I'd get them, eventually, but it also felt as if it pushed me one step closer to my destiny. And Terrence's betrayal.

At the door to the building, Helmer pulled it open and held it for me. My parents had come here to sign all the paperwork, but I hadn't visited Helmer's office yet. The hall was lavish, even compared to Regalia. The floors were wall-to-wall carpet, thick and regal in shades of red and gold. The paint along the sides of the corridor was a pale cream, almost yellow. Overhead, mini chandeliers hung at intervals, instead of fluorescent lights.

"This way," Helmer said, leading me down the right walkway. The left passage looked identical, with several nondescript doors on either side. Offices, most likely, for the professors on campus and other staff. We passed several such doors the way we went. Each had a plaque and a name. I spied Professor Lorel's.

At the end of the hall, the corridor intersected with another going left. The building was rectangular, so I guessed this hall ran all along the outside edge. Instead of going left, Helmer led me to the right, to a small door hidden beside a large potted plant.

It appeared to be a broom cupboard, and when Helmer used a key to open the door, my suspicions proved accurate. A mop bucket stood to one side, and on the other were several brooms and bottles of cleaning supplies. The ground was gray concrete.

"Come inside," the dean instructed, walking inside the small space.

I followed him in, hesitantly.

Once I stood beside him, he closed the door.

"Uh—" I began, but he waved his hand at me.

Along the wall beside the door was a small keypad. He punched in a code, and then the room lurched. I braced myself against the closest wall as the floor started to descend.

A secret elevator.

"The Gyranium must be kept as secret as possible," Helmer said conversationally. "There are several safeguards installed as security measures. It's not dangerous to regular people, but a practitioner could easily hurt themselves if they tried to run it on their own. Too much blood could be drawn, or the mixtures of metals might come out unbalanced. Having the machine out of the way keeps it out of mind, as well."

I nodded. His reasoning made sense, but it didn't lessen my trepidation of entering the hidden basement of a magical school.

The cupboard shuddered again, then stilled. Helmer reached out and opened the door. It now led to a large room, like a laboratory, with sterile, white walls and floor tiles. Huge lights shone from overhead, near blinding when I raised my chin to look at them more closely.

Around the perimeter were computer stations with massive metal consoles and flashing screens.

It looked like something out of a science fiction movie.

And there in the center, completing the bizarre room, was the Gyranium. Even expecting a strange plant-machine hybrid didn't prepare me for this sight. It looked like a huge, upside-down tulip, but a dark green instead of pale pastel. It had many petals that fell from the ceiling, curving out slightly as they brushed the floor. Where the flower attached to the ceiling overhead, it appeared to be a bunch of electrical wires instead of a stem. The wires ran along the length of the room, down the far wall, and connected to one of the computer systems.

"Holy shit," I muttered.

Helmer must have heard me anyway because he snorted. "If you're all set, we can get started."

I swallowed and nodded. "Um...will it hurt when it takes my blood?"

Helmer hesitated, not a good sign. "There may be some pain. The Gyranium's needle is small, but the sensation is foreign and can be unpleasant the first few times. Eventually, you get used to it."

Sudden panic filled me. "How often will I have to do this?"

"We mint a dozen coins at a time. Typically, students use a coin a month, so this should get you through the entire school year."

I relaxed.

"However," Helmer continued, "since you are just learning, it's possible you will go through your coins quicker. We don't put a cap on a student's minting, unless it becomes apparent they are misusing their coins. I'm sure that won't be the case with you."

"Of course not, Dean Helmer."

His eyes narrowed as he studied me. Finally, he nodded. "Let's get started. This way."

He walked toward the Gyranium, and I followed.

Up close, I could see texture within the dark-green petals. They flashed with faint light, as if electrical currents circled through their leafy veins. Multiple petals overlapped, hiding the center of the device. Helmer went to a specific spot and pushed a petal to the side. It revealed a hollow space, large enough for a tall person to stand in. In the open area, however, was a plush recliner. It looked out of place among the high-tech gadgetry and weird, hanging vines.

"Go and have a seat. It's best to be comfortable."

I steeled my courage and went inside, Helmer only a step behind. Bracing my hands along the chair's arms, I slowly lowered my body into the seat. It was an old chair, worn, but somehow comforting. It reminded me of my grandpa's reading chair, set in front of the fireplace where Grandma would bring him coffee with just a splash of Bailey's Irish Cream. I relaxed into the fabric as Helmer put up the footrest.

"Once I turn it on, the Gyranium will come down and draw your blood."

I was tense again and gripped the chair with my fingers. "How? I mean, how can it tell where my veins are?"

Helmer actually grinned. "Magic, naturally."

I chuckled weakly. Magic. Of course. But it didn't make my anxiety retreat. I didn't know enough about magic to know the rules and limitations.

"Try to relax. It'll be over in a moment." He gripped my shoulder, then vanished out of the petals.

Once he left, I realized the light within this enclosed space came only from the petals surrounding me. It was bright enough to see clearly, but the Gyranium's leaves tinted it slightly. Looking down at the skin of my hand showed the color to be off, adjusted just a shade darker on the green spectrum.

"This is so weird," I mumbled to myself. Would my life ever make sense again?

Did it ever make sense before? I saw a man disappear. Nothing's been normal since that happened.

A sudden flash emitted from the Gyranium, and then all went dark. I could still make out the general shapes of things around me: my hand, the armchair, my shoes on the footrest. Then, a single vine lowered from the spot where all the petals merged into the stem. The vine came down like a snake, sinuous and circling. All along its length, light pulsed back toward the stem. The tip of the vine looked pointed but not sharp enough to puncture my skin.

"Take a deep breath," Helmer said, his voice muffled through the layers of flora between us. "It's about to start."

A little ashamed at having to do so, I shut my eyes. I'd never minded needles before, but this was something entirely different.

Think of something happy, I told myself. *Something to shift your focus.*

Unbidden, an image filled the darkness behind my eyelids: Terrence from before, when I'd thought of him as the man with scarlet eyes. The picture was so vivid, more vivid than I had ever remembered before. I could see every zig and zag of the scar along his neck, the differing hues of red within the depths of his eyes, his pupils contracting upon recognizing me, tremors in his hands as he flinched away. The slim trail of tears streaming down his cheeks. The quivering of his mouth when he apologized for his betrayal.

It felt as if he were in the room with me, close enough I could touch him. I leaned forward and felt our lips connect. Incredible heat filled my veins, pumping through my blood. Nothing existed but the heat. And in that moment, he and I were one.

I moaned in ecstasy, filling with desire so strong I could barely suppress an orgasm. My whole body felt electrically charged, making all the hairs stand up on my arms.

As suddenly as the vision and sensation came, it evaporated.

A sharp pain filled my arm, and I cried out. My eyes flew open, but whatever the Gyranium had done was finished. The vine retreated up toward the ceiling, fatter now that it was filled with my blood.

I shivered and was thankful for that bite of pain to take away any signs of my surprise erection.

"There we are," Helmer said, pushing aside a petal. "How are you doing?" He hurried to my side and handed me a small towel. "Press this against the puncture. The incision is small, so it will stop bleeding in a minute."

I accepted the towel and looked at my arm for the wound. It was noticeable, a lump like an oversized mosquito bite in the crook of my arm. A few drops of blood welled up from it. I set the towel atop it and applied pressure.

"What does it do now?" I asked.

Helmer lowered the footrest and helped me to my feet. I wavered unsteadily, thankful for his arm to steady myself.

"The Gyranium takes your blood, your innate magical imprint, and combines it with your image."

I nodded. I'd seen my own coin, after all, but I'd also been shown several of my classmates' coins. "How does it take my picture?"

Helmer smiled and led me from the enclosure. "It absorbs what it sees, like a regular plant would absorb sunlight. It takes the moments you're within its petals and it converts it to an image of you. It's truly a remarkable invention. Professor Watanabe's great-grandfather was one of the members who had a hand in inventing it."

"Really? That's amazing. Are there any other applications?"

"No, not for this model. There are researchers who continue to experiment with plants of this nature."

"Doesn't magical ethics apply to this?"

The dean raised his eyebrows. "How so?"

"It's mixing machines with a living thing. Seems like it would be seen as a bad thing to experiment on it."

He paused, then nodded. "Yes, I could see how someone who didn't grow up around magic could view it that way. But the Gyranium and other such magical items have always been with nonsentient lifeforms. There's a difference between a living plant and a living animal."

"I guess."

"That might be a good discussion for next week," Helmer said musingly. "Though you'd have to explain your reasoning on the subject. I don't think many of the students considered it before."

I squirmed, thinking of all their eyes on me, but Helmer didn't seem to notice.

"And how is Terrence?" he asked softly.

"Good."

Helmer looked at me. Maybe he wanted more details?

"Uh, we play football, American football, after dinner sometimes. Omar brought a ball, and we usually have enough players to make two teams. I think he's starting to like it."

The dean accepted my explanation with a nod. "Has he expressed an interest in your Tomes books?"

"No. None." That was a lie, and I hoped Helmer couldn't read it on my face. Terrence had flipped through my books—and there was still the hidden one on demons under my mattress. Terrence would be really intrigued by that one.

Helmer drew in a deep breath. "These coins are your coins, Collin. Even with them, Terrence could access magic easier. It can lead to serious complications if he gets his hands on one."

"I know, Dean Helmer. I won't give him my coins."

He cleared his throat. "Good."

There was a flash from one of the nearby computers, and Helmer motioned me that way. At the base of a keypad was a slot. The lights around it pulsed. Helmer pushed a button beside it, and a small tray came out of the slot.

My coins. Even knowing I'd see them, it was surreal. Not because it was my face on a coin—like a president— but because of the sudden certainty of the red-eyed man being from my near future. Things were beginning to spiral down the drain, and anything I could have done to prevent it had passed.

I reached out and picked up one of the coins. It was warm in my palm. Had the other been hot? I'd worn gloves, so I hadn't noticed. Or was it an aftereffect of being freshly minted?

"I recommend refraining from experimenting over the weekend," Helmer told me. "Wait till Professor Watanabe can show you proper activation techniques in Methods on Monday."

"Sure."

Helmer rubbed his hands together. "Then let's get going. I'd say it's nearly time for dinner."

I collected all twelve of my coins and shoved them into my pocket.

Chapter Nineteen

Over the weekend, Terrence and I lounged. There was no other word for it. We hardly left our room—except to grab dinner. The majority of our time was dedicated to schoolwork, but every second was spent next to each other. Terrence sat at my desk while I read on my bed. We propped our backs against the wall, thighs touching, as I helped Terrence with a math problem. Terrence sprawled on my bed, his hand over the edge, twining his fingers through my hair as I lay on the floor, using a small bit of my blood to light the candle Watanabe gave me.

There were also several petting sessions to help us relax between assignments.

Terrence hadn't noticed my coins yet and hadn't commented on the strange wound on my arm—despite how much time we spent without clothes on. The guilt of keeping this secret from him surprised me. They were my coins, like Helmer had said, and I wasn't supposed to share. Even so, I knew Terrence would want one. And worse, I knew I'd give him one the minute he asked.

Monday morning dawned, bringing a close to the best weekend I'd ever experienced. My alarm roused me, and I must have nudged Terrence with my elbow because as soon as the blaring noise cut off, he tackled me. After a growl and a series of nips to my neck, we fell back to the mattress in a tangle of limbs.

It was some time before we rolled out of bed and started our morning routine.

After breakfast, Terrence walked with me and Omar to the entrance of Regalia. The two didn't seem so hostile this morning, which I took for a good omen.

"See you at lunch," I said and then gave Terrence a quick kiss. He headed off to his own class.

"I didn't see you all weekend," Omar said as we entered the hall.

"We were busy."

Omar raised his eyebrow. "I bet."

I grinned, too excited to keep my good cheer suppressed. "Things are finally going well. I mean it, Omar. This is the first time in my life I've felt happy."

He matched my smile with a bigger one. "I'm glad, Collin. Though it sucks you've been so unhappy."

I shook my head, following the line of students into the Theory classroom. "It hasn't been unhappiness. More like stagnation. Dormant. My sights were always set on getting here, so I hardly let myself enjoy the things around me."

"Not a healthy way to live. Maybe Helmer was right, and you should see one of the school's therapists."

I pressed my lips together. It wasn't a bad idea. But they might ask me questions about Terrence, and I'd have to lie. A professional couldn't help if I wasn't honest with them. "Maybe. Eventually."

"Better sooner than later. You don't want Terrence's betrayal to be the thing that makes you start."

I grimaced. That was a fair point.

Class passed with little incident, besides Helmer calling on me to explain my views of magical ethics in concern to the Gyranium. He told the class my fresh perspective could aid quite a few of them who took the use of magic as a guarantee.

"Look at the world through different lenses," he said. "Not only will it make you better practitioners, but also better humans."

The groans were quiet enough that Helmer didn't hear. It was comforting to see that this group of students, most British, but some other nationalities, acted the same way as American students.

When he dismissed us, I wasn't surprised when he held me back once again. Omar lowered his brow in obvious concern, but I waved him on. I knew what Helmer wanted.

"I brought all twelve," I told him, opening my messenger bag and taking out every single one of my coins.

Helmer sighed deeply, and a look of apology filled his face. "I'm sorry, Collin. If you expected me to do this, it means I am overreacting. It's not that I don't trust you. It's that I know how dedicated Terrence can be to his task. He's a very skilled manipulator. But I see you're just as capable. Keep it up. Stay diligent."

"I will."

"Now, off you go."

I didn't let the encounter ruin my day.

In Tomes, the five of us gathered on the top floor to catch up with what happened over the weekend. Omar had been to three separate parties, all of them off campus. I thought I'd been busy, but he seemed to have hardly slept.

"Maybe I can tag along next weekend," Laura said with a grin.

Sammuel shared about his rugby match and showed off a bruise the size of a baseball on his shin. "You are all invited to the next one, of course."

Tabitha shook her head. "I don't know if I can watch such pointless violence."

"It's not pointless," Sammuel argued, but he didn't change her mind.

Tabitha went down to Brighton Pier with a couple of the business students. "Next time, they said they'd take me to the Newhaven lighthouse. It's supposed to be a big tourist attraction, just a little east of here. Maison de Verre was right alongside Étang de Vaccarès, a saltwater lagoon in Camargue. I really miss the water and the smell of salt. Being down by the channel eased a lot of my homesickness."

Their eyes turned to me.

"How are things with your roommate?" Laura asked.

"Good." My grin let on more than my words though. "I studied Latin most of the weekend. Terrence helped."

"I'm sure he did," Omar said with a tone suggesting something close to the truth.

My cheeks flushed, but I didn't let my embarrassment stop me. "And I helped him with math. His accounting class actually looks kind of fun."

There was a collective groan.

"No one thinks math is fun," Sammuel said.

Omar was right on top of him. "Accounting is the most boring math field you can possibly get into."

Laura and Tabitha nodded.

"No," Sammuel said. "It's the company that made it *seem* fun. Looks like Collin has it bad."

They all agreed solemnly.

"Maybe I do." And we dropped the subject.

I was mostly looking forward to Methods and for Watanabe to show me how to use my coins. Because of that, Latin seemed to drag by.

Jenkins began the lesson with good intentions but then remembered a random fact about vortexes he'd forgotten to tell me last week.

I rushed out of the classroom when Jenkins dismissed us. I was still the last student to leave. I fell in with Omar and the others, and we walked to our Methods class. My stomach fluttered with anticipation. I'd be able to do so much more once I grew comfortable using my coins.

And then there'll be no hiding it from Terrence. I need to tell him.

"Good afternoon," Watanabe greeted as we walked in. Usually, we arrived first, as class didn't begin for another fifteen minutes. The reason she was there became apparent when Helmer stood to his feet.

I flinched. Was he stalking me?

Helmer's smile greeted us all. "Come in, and have a seat," he said, gesturing to the front row of chairs.

The others seemed just as hesitant as me, for which I was grateful. But we did as instructed. Once we were settled, Helmer moved to a chair directly in front of Omar, who sat at the center of our group.

"Since you are first-year students, I needed to have a quick discussion with you in regard to the upcoming gala."

I relaxed; at least this wasn't about me and Terrence.

"The gala," Helmer intoned, as if he'd repeated these same words a dozen times today—and likely he had, giving this same information to the other grade levels. "It's a time for students at Marke Staple to be introduced to local society. Besides our literature students, several key members of the British government will be in attendance. Other prominent practitioners will be invited, of course. This could be a chance for you to network with young professionals.

"For this event, you are able to bring a date. We recommend you only select practitioners, but if you have a friend or significant other who is nonmagical, we can make an exception, as long as you inform me before the event. We also suggest you dress in your best."

For this, he glanced at me and Omar. "Since you two might not have brought adequate formal clothing, the school can help you to borrow a set from another student."

Omar said, "I brought my tux."

My cheeks flushed as Helmer turned to me. "I don't have anything."

Helmer nodded, as if it was what he expected. "Don't worry, Collin. We'll find something suitable. Now, do you have any questions?"

Tabitha's hand shot up. "Dean Helmer, is this gala open to other schools, or to others outside of London?"

"Not usually. Why?"

"I'm sure my mother would love to attend." Tabitha's look expressed her displeasure over the statement. "I would rather her request be denied."

Helmer's lips narrowed to a thin line. "I'm not quite sure we have the authority to keep her out, Tabitha. Can you let her know yourself that you'd prefer to attend the gala on your own?"

Tabitha sighed and shook her head. "No. I guess she'll just have to come."

Helmer nodded. "Anything else?" He glanced at me one more time, but I remained silent.

"Good. Now, I'll leave you in Professor Watanabe's care. Collin, I'll be in touch about getting you an outfit."

He left, and Watanabe took the place he had vacated. She smiled broadly. "Dean Helmer didn't mention this, but I will. The gala is also a wonderful place to meet practitioners around your own age. There will be a lot of eligible men and women."

She laughed at the looks of astonishment that shone on my classmates' faces. "This is my first time here. I'll be excited to check out the locals."

Then she sobered. Somewhat. She had a cheerful disposition, a default smile on her face, even when being serious.

"So, let's hop into today's work. Collin, you've got your coins?"

"Yeah."

My classmates leaned in close to me as I removed a coin from my bag. They each insisted on looking at it and examining the spires on the back.

"Good," Watanabe said when Omar handed it back to me. "I want to walk you through using your coin. In theory, it's easier than what you've been doing, but it can also be difficult to adjust to the boost the metals give you."

She glanced at the other students. "While I get Collin started, I want you to pair up and practice one of your weakest spells."

They stood and moved to other areas of the room, Omar with Laura and Sammuel with Tabitha.

Watanabe pulled a book from her briefcase before regarding me. "How did you do with the Gyranium? It can be scary your first time."

A hint of color touched my cheeks remembering the intense pleasure. "It was fine. A bit scary, but I managed."

"Good. I'm usually not a fan of rushing new practitioners, but Dean Helmer did make a good case for you. I think you can handle your coins."

"I'll try my best."

She nodded, as if she expected no less. "The beneficial aspect of an adult first learning is you're capable of abstract thought. Sometimes, explaining magical norms to an eight-year-old can be frustrating. They can't comprehend the depth of the information. Your mind will have no problem understanding the concepts learned in this program."

A good point, and it bolstered my already raised spirits. I would learn and swiftly. I'd prove to my classmates that Watanabe was right: an adult with knowledge could excel quickly.

"Have you tried your coins yet?"

I shook my head. "Dean Helmer advised me not to. I practiced with only my blood over the weekend."

"That may be for the best. As the dean already informed you, your magical potential must be large to get noticed by Marke Staple's radar. Easing into your powers is a smart decision."

She cleared her throat, and when she continued, she was in lecture mode. "Now, as we talked last week about ways to access magic, we established that appearing normal in public is important. At the same time, practitioners are encouraged to keep coins close for emergencies. Some fasten a loop to a coin to hang around their neck. Some keep a spare hidden in a purse or a wallet. My parents keep one in every room of the house. Mostly for convenience, if you want to turn off a light, or grab the television remote, but also to be prepared should something happen. When frightened or other emotions are highly elevated, our magical production can become reflexive. Meaning, we react with the right spell without thought. This is one way practitioners learn their special; it's a spell they do by default."

I blinked at her, trying to absorb the information. It seemed like too much to plan on—having coins stashed everywhere—and not enough. What if someone broke into your home, but all your coins were in a different room?

Watanabe seemed to anticipate where my thoughts went. "Remember, coins access the easiest branch of magic: elemental. With words, you can still use lingual magic. And in worse-case scenarios, cutting yourself will free your elemental skills. We are never helpless."

"Yes, of course," I said, my voice sounding rough. I swallowed to put moisture back in my mouth. "That makes sense, Professor, but it's a lot to take in."

"It is, which is why we *do* teach children. They are not so set in their ways to question the natural order of things. Now, are you ready?"

"Yes, Professor." My words only quivered slightly, but my cheek still heated from embarrassment. There was no reason to be afraid. I wanted to learn.

She smiled at me, letting me know she was there, and I could trust her. "Good. Now, pick up your coin. Most people tend to pinch it between thumb and pointer finger, as if you're wiping crumbs off after lunch. However, I've seen several who use their thumb and middle finger, like a snap. It's whatever is most comfortable for you."

I held the coin—it was still warm, but my classmates hadn't commented on that aspect. Was it only hot to me? My real blood reacting to my contained blood?

"When you pinch it, the sensation will be the same as when you cut yourself with the knife. You'll be able to see the elemental weaves."

I hadn't thought of the magical colors as weaves, but I still knew what she meant. To me, they looked like currents, shifts within air. Taking a deep breath, I rubbed my thumb along the top of my coin.

Immediately, my view shifted. Everything grew darker, except for the lines of colored illumination making up the world around me. Nothing differed from my previous attempts to access my magic. It looked identical.

"Can you see the weaves?" Watanabe asked.

I looked at her and was surprised again to see she shimmered with a blue haze. It meant something, though I had no idea what.

"Yeah, I can see them."

"Excellent. Now, same as before, reach out to the air."

Once Watanabe gave me the candle to work with—summoning fire instead of wind—I realized each of the currents had different colors. Air looked a soft blue, like the midmorning sky. Fire was a dark orange; an artist would call it burnt orange, or something similarly fancy. Those were the only two I could recognize.

Her blue-tinted fingers tapped at the book she'd pulled from her briefcase. "Use the air to lift the book."

It wasn't difficult to spot the air currents. They were by far the most common in the room. With my blood resonating, I poked at the sky-blue strands under the book. They tensed, turning bright red as I lashed them together. Once I had enough activated—or maybe energized was a better word—I lifted them. At the same time, I lifted my hand as if the two motions were connected, physical and metaphysical.

The book lifted, all right. It lifted so fast that it sailed up over my head. My eyes barely followed its trajectory before it hit the high arched ceiling at least seventy-five feet overhead. The book collided with a loud smack, calling the attention of my classmates.

I stared on in shock as the book plummeted back toward us. Dimly, I knew there was something I could have done, should have done, to slow it. To stop it. But my mind was horribly numb.

Luckily, Watanabe had been prepared. She pinched her coin, and the book stopped a foot above the desk. She allowed it to come to rest gently on its top.

Watanabe's eyes, and everyone else's, turned to me.

I reddened with embarrassment and terror. My connection to my blood and the ether vanished. "I-I'm sorry," I stammered.

Watanabe's face hadn't even taken on a shadow of scolding. She still smiled pleasantly. "Don't be sorry, Collin. You're learning, and you did nothing wrong."

"That was amazing!" Tabitha said. "Your spell had such power and energy."

"Another reason we teach children," the professor said. "They usually can't produce this much strength on their first try."

"I'm sorry," I repeated.

"You don't need to apologize. It's good you were able to see what your spells can do, unchecked. You must be mindful, conscious, and attentive. Let your mind drift, and you can use more intensity than you meant."

I nodded, lesson learned.

"Will you try it again?"

"Yes."

Her smile grew. "Okay, go ahead. I'm ready."

I chuckled, but it had a nervous ring to it. As I pinched my coin again, the world came into magical focus. The sky-blue lines appeared everywhere. I focused on the ones under the book and activated them. Using only the tiniest percentage of my awareness, I lifted the book. It rose at a slow pace, stopping even with my eyes.

Watanabe said, "With the connection still strong, try to pull it toward you. You need to keep the ones under it still humming, but pull the weaves at the same time."

It was like patting your head and rubbing your belly at the same time. I had a hard time focusing on the currents below while activating the currents behind. The book wobbled as one of my currents slipped, but I righted it again. The book's bottom and curved spine shimmered with a bright red light. I pulled it gently, and I glided into my outstretched hand.

"Well done!" Watanabe said excitedly.

My magical connection dropped, and the world turned back to normal. I grinned at my professor shyly, pleased but not wanting to seem overconfident.

"You did amazing, Collin. Now, I want you to try that a few more times. Then we'll get out the candle."

Chapter Twenty

By the end of class, I felt as if I'd had an awakening. My coin, my magic, my grasp of the currents. They all clicked. I'd lifted two things at once before Watanabe had dismissed us. And I was sure I could do more.

As we started to gather our things, Watanabe said, "Great work today, everyone. Laura, your skill with light is improving. Omar, I want you to focus on something besides transformation; I already know you can do that well. Tabitha, same with water. Let's try to practice skills we don't already have mastered." She smiled brightly. "And, Sammuel, you're doing incredible. I must say, I am very impressed with your array of abilities."

Sammuel's smug face brought a grin to my lips. I'd seen him working and had also been impressed by his skills. There was no doubt in my mind he would be top of our class.

We headed out in a cluster. My stomach rumbled loudly, and I craved seeing Terrence to share my success and my excitement. My fingers went into my pocket and fondled the coin residing there. There was no more putting it off. I had to show him my coins.

Between one step and the next, I collided with Laura in front of me. My shoe hit hers, and with my hand in my pocket, I didn't have any leverage to steady myself. Laura tipped sideways into Omar, who caught her, but I kept falling. My mind screamed in panic—my mouth may have too—but then, suddenly, I was back on my feet.

I glanced around, wondering which of my classmates had saved me. They stood around me in a circle, several feet back.

Had I bounced?

There was no other explanation for starting to fall and then being on my feet again.

I looked up into their faces, and each wore expressions of outright shock. Even Watanabe.

"What happened?" I asked.

Sammuel advanced toward me, and I had a half second to think he meant to console me before his hands shot up and he pushed hard against my chest.

I flew backward from the force of his attack.

Then I was standing on my feet several paces away.

"Jesus Christ," Sammuel said. He came at me again.

I hurried away from him. "Professor?" I called, my voice unusually high. "Help me?"

Sammuel chased me as I ran toward Watanabe. At her side, I finally felt safe. Except, as quick as a tsunami, her foot whipped out and kicked the back of my knee. I collapsed. But then, suddenly, I was on my feet on the other side of the room.

My eyes were wide as I looked down at my hand, still shoved into my pocket. I'd pinched my coin. I felt it that time: the release of magic. I had the first two times too, but it'd all been subconscious.

Watanabe and my classmates were still staring at me, though Watanabe was smiling as brightly as I'd ever seen.

"Collin," she said excitedly. "We just found your special."

"My what?"

She came toward me, and I retreated a few steps.

Her grin became thin, more out of humor than good cheer. She held her hands up in front of her. "I won't hurt you. I swear." When she reached my side, she pulled my hand from my pocket. My fingers still held my coin. "You pinched it without realizing it. You performed complex magic without thought. Amazing!"

"What magic? What did I do?"

"You teleported."

My mouth dropped. "Teleported? But, I didn't even realize that was possible."

She nodded. "It's difficult to do successfully, but it's possible."

"I took an intensive seminar over the summer," Omar said. "I only managed to do it once."

"I can do it," Sammuel said, but it lacked his usual boasting.

"My mom can," Tabitha added. "But my dad can't. He's been struggling with it for years."

"Can you teach me?" Laura asked. "I've never even tried."

"I don't even know what I did. How can I teach you?"

"It'll get easier," Watanabe said. "You do it instinctively, but once you puzzle out how, you should be able to explain it. Your classmates would benefit greatly from your experience."

They all rushed toward me, begging for my help. Even Sammuel. I felt like the most important person in the whole world.

"Yes, of course. Once I figure out *how* to do it, I'll help you all."

It was an excited group that made our way to the cafe for a drink. They all talked hurriedly over one another, telling me how great it had been, how surprising. How I'd gone from standing in front of them, to being thirty feet away.

Terrence wasn't in the cafe yet when we arrived, and I was disappointed. I'd hoped he'd get to see the others praising me. I wanted him to know I wasn't a complete fuckup with my magic.

We grabbed our beverages while Omar explained about the seminar he'd attended at Magica Meridiem. He was still deep in the story when we sat at a large round table.

"Teleportation was the instructor's special too," Omar said. "Only four people in the whole world have it as their special. Collin, you make five."

"This is going to be big news!" Tabitha added. "At the gala, everyone will want to meet you."

That detail flustered me. I didn't want to be the center of attention. Well, here within our small group, I was enjoying it immensely. But to have all the eyes of important practitioners and high-ranking members of the British government was something entirely different.

Terrence was suddenly by my side, as if *he* had teleported. "Hey, Collin. Hey guys. What'd I miss?"

He nudged me with his hip, and I scooted over on the chair, allowing him to squeeze in beside me. The chair was far too small for this, but I loved having him so close.

They all began to talk at once, but since Omar was closest, it was him Terrence listened to. "We just found out Collin's special."

Terrence raised his eyebrow. "Oh?" He looked to me, and in his eyes was a deep hunger. I could almost swear I saw a flicker of the red within them. "What is it? Must be something amazing to cause this much excitement."

"Apparently, it's teleporting," I answered.

For a moment, the lust in Terrence's gaze flashed a hundred times brighter, but he quickly masked it with an encouraging smile. "Teleportation? That's amazing, Collin. It's so rare. How did you find out?"

"In Methods."

That wasn't good enough for my classmates. Laura launched into the story of how I'd instinctively pinched my coin after running into her. At the mention of coins, Terrence shot me a wounded look, but again, he hid it swiftly.

"I told you it would come eventually," he told me. "And before you know it, all the other subjects will come too."

My classmates nodded, and I was happy with their encouragement.

"You guys feel like eating now?" Omar asked. "I know it's early, but I'd rather just do it now."

"I'm not hungry," Terrence said and got to his feet.

"Me neither." I stood too. "Walk with me back to our room?"

He hesitated and I could tell he was pissed. But, he finally nodded.

"See you guys later," I said, and waved.

As we walked out, Terrence didn't try to grab my hand, or playfully bump his shoulder into mine. He was silent. And it unnerved me.

Again, I feel like I'm the one betraying him. Maybe that's why he retaliates. Maybe I deserve what he does.

Once we were outside, I couldn't hold back any longer. "I can explain."

"I'm sure you can."

"Please, don't be like this. I didn't hold this back to hurt you. I did it because of your dad."

Terrence stopped walking, and he turned to me. "What's Helmer got to do with it?"

"Can we wait until we get to our room? I'm not comfortable talking about this out here."

His eyes narrowed, but he nodded. We continued on our way, and his posture relaxed slightly. At least the silence wasn't hostile now.

In our room, I sat on my bed. It wasn't a surprise when he sat on his. He was still angry, and I didn't blame him.

"Helmer told me about your scar," I said without preamble. "He told me about Al'venarta."

Terrence's face paled, then went a vivid scarlet. "So you don't think I'm trustworthy now? You think you're better than me because I've been banned from magic?"

I stood from my bed, and in one swift motion I was on my knees in front of him. "No, never. I care about you, Terrence. It took all my strength to keep this from you. I didn't want to hurt you more."

He calmed visibly. "What do you mean?"

"Helmer. He told me you'd manipulate me. That you'd use me to get access to coins and spell books."

Terrence opened his mouth again, but I didn't let him speak.

"He saw you kiss me the other day. He felt obligated to warn me of your real desire: power. But, Terrence, I don't care about any of that."

He shook his head. "You're not making sense. Why didn't Helmer's warning make you run the opposite direction from me?"

"I'm telling you his warnings didn't work. They could never change my feelings for you."

"Then why didn't you tell me about your coins? Why lie?"

"Because Helmer's been checking up on me. He made me show him all my coins this morning. I knew he'd want to see them. So I couldn't tell you about them until he relaxed. It was to protect you, Terrence, I swear."

Terrence reached out and gripped my hand. He tugged, and I got to my feet, before sitting beside him.

"So much is going on that I don't understand," I said, leaning to press my forehead against his hair. "But I know I'm fond of you. I want to be with you, grow closer to you. You can use my coins here in our room, but I can't let you take them yet. Give me another few weeks. Helmer will stop asking. Then you can have all of them if you want."

"If your special is teleporting, we can go into the Gyranium and make our own coins."

"No."

"But—"

"No. Something like that will get us both expelled. I'm allowed to go through my coins fast. I can get more minted. You can use mine."

He nodded and took my hand into his. "Okay."

I closed my eyes and breathed his scent deeply. The book. I had to tell him I had the book. I pulled back, and he turned to face me. "There's something else."

"What?"

I stood and lifted my mattress. I pulled out the book and handed it to him.

His hand shook as he accepted it. "But this... Where did you get this?"

"Fresha dropped it in the library last week. I grabbed it. I knew you'd want it."

His eyes met mine with a sharp jerk. "Then why hide it under your bed?"

I sighed. "Haven't you heard a single word I said? Helmer is spying on us! Maybe you don't have any self-preservation, but I do."

The ferocity left him, and he relaxed his body, slumping over the book in his lap. "I do too. But I've waited so long, Collin. I'm getting impatient."

I returned to his side and wrapped my arm around his back. "I know. But please wait just a bit longer. I'll help you in any way you want. But we need to hold back until Helmer's guard is dropped."

He was silent for several moments. "Collin. When did you find all this out?"

"Last Friday."

"You knew I'd tried to summon a demon, and you still want to be with me?"

"Yes."

"Why?"

It was time for some honesty. "Because, as hard as you try to manipulate me, I know you can't do it."

He met my gaze again, his eyes not angry, but questioning. "What?"

"Since we met, you've used every trick to worm your way into my good graces. You pounced on me the moment I revealed you reminded me of someone I once knew. You've schemed and lied for the past three weeks."

He made to pull back, but I cupped his face in both my hands, holding him still. "All of it was pointless, Terrence," I said softly. "I will give you anything you ask. I will do anything you command. I have had feelings for you since we met. You don't need to manipulate; I'll go anywhere you say, willingly."

A shadow of something shifted in his eyes, like a drape revealing a hidden treasure usually kept guarded. He was open, free, himself. The first time I'd seen it since that day on the slopes.

I surged forward, pressing my lips to his. It had been so long since I'd witnessed that vulnerability in him. It made me want to weep and do everything in my power to protect him.

"Nothing will change the way I feel about you." I retreated and looked into his face, willing him to understand the sincerity in my voice, in my promise. "Remember that, Terrence. Nothing will change it."

He nodded, and the hidden veil did not return to his eyes. He stayed open to me.

Oh, God, I thought. *I'm falling in love with him.*

We kissed. "Terrence," I said, my voice breathy and full of need. "Will you have sex with me?"

Chapter Twenty-One

Terrence led me to the shower. He turned on the water and waited for steam to build up before pulling me inside. The water was almost scalding, but not nearly as hot as the touch of his skin. He took his time running his fingers over me, touching my face, my arms, my stomach, my legs. He caressed me everywhere, and I sensed the devotion and care he embedded in each touch.

I'd told him of my inexperience, and I knew that was what caused his deliberate actions. He got me ready for him, not rushing to it like a finish line.

"Please," I said, my cock hard and straining. "I need…" But I had no idea what. I wanted him inside me, but I also craved a deeper emotion, a melding of our spirits as well as our bodies.

"I don't want to rush, Collin." His voice was soft, barely heard over the falling water. "I want you to enjoy this."

"I will. Just…please. I need you."

His roaming hand stilled as he kissed me. Eager and promising. Hinting at what was to come. "Turn around."

I faced the wall and pressed my arms against the slick surface.

"I'll go slow. Tell me if it's too much, and I'll stop."

I nodded impatiently, knowing I'd never stop him.

"Do you trust me to do a spell?"

"You can do whatever you want to me."

He chuckled softly as he ran his fingers up and down my back. "Didn't anyone teach you about safe sex?"

"I want you to come inside me. I want to feel you."

He trailed his lips across my shoulder. "That's why I'm going to do a spell. It protects against pregnancies, STDs, or anything else dangerous that might transmit through our fluids."

"Do it."

He muttered a string of words—presumably Latin—but nothing I'd learned from my picture book.

Then I heard the sound of what must have been a lube bottle open, before the quick *smack* of Terrence rubbing his hands together—likely to warm the liquid. Then his fingers were gently probing at my asshole. At first, they circled the sensitive skin. I tensed at each brush of a fingertip. But soon, I grew accustomed to the feel, and my body ached for more.

As if sensing I was relaxed, Terrence pressed on. His index finger slipped inside me.

I groaned as the intruding digit entered and had to force my hips to keep still. My instinct was to arch back. But I refrained. I wanted him to fuck me. We could try it another way the next time.

"How does it feel?" he asked. He moved close to me, causing his erection to rub against my hip.

"Wonderful."

"Ready for more?"

"Yes, Terrence. Please."

He slipped a second finger inside. He worked in and out of me at a measured pace.

I bit my lip to keep in a desperate whimper. Soon, I'd begin drooling, the feeling was so delicious.

"More," I begged.

A third finger and I tensed at the sudden pain. Terrence froze. "Just breathe," he said. With his other hand, he reached around and grabbed my dick. He stoked it lightly, going from base to tip and back again. "Breathe."

I sucked in air, focusing on the sensation assaulting my cock, not the stretching of my asshole. Soon, my body relaxed, and the pleasure in the front and the back escalated sharply.

"Terrence," I said, my voice rough and shaking. "Do it."

He stepped away. I looked over my shoulder as he added more lube to his hands and worked the lather onto his cock. It was a beautiful sight, and it shot more spikes of desire deep into me.

"I'll be gentle," he said again as he came close to me.

I laughed, though it was a bit high-pitched and almost hysterical. "If I wanted gentle, I would have said so. Fuck me, Terrence."

He growled, and immediately the head of his cock was at my entrance. Despite my words, he still entered me slowly. It was drawn out and the most blissful experience I'd ever encountered. His prepping had worked, because I felt no pain, only a tingling pleasure.

"Terrence," I said, leaning against the wall. "Oh God."

He grabbed my hips and pressed in as deeply as he could. "I'm going to fuck you now. Hard. Is that the way you want it?"

My whole body trembled at his words. "Yes. Please. I want..." I cut off as he began to move. A quick shift, pulling him out, then bringing him back in. This time, the whimper got out.

"Collin, you're so sexy." He moved his hips again, faster this time. One of his hands left my waist and trailed up my spine. "Everything about you is sexy. You're perfect."

I groaned as he shifted, even quicker. I had no words to beg for more, but he must have sensed my desperation. His thrusts gained a rhythm, in and out, in and out, until he was sliding so fast that my body shook from the force.

I lowered my hand from its resting place along the wall and wrapped it around my cock. It was hard and unyielding, and the feel of it added to my building ecstasy. Terrence's was just as rigid, filling up the deepest part of me, touching me where no one else had.

"Gonna come," I called. I squeezed my cock as I came, a sharp gasp escaping from my throat. Semen gushed out onto the wall, sliding down to join the falling water circling the drain. My breath sounded ragged to my own ears, and specks of light filled my vision.

I heard Terrence cry out, too, and suddenly his grip on my hips tightened. He was in so deep I could feel the base of his cock twitch as he filled his come inside me.

One more languid minute passed, each of us frozen in our roaring pleasure, and then Terrence pulled free.

There was a bit of pain as he removed himself, but it was hardly noticeable over the sweet satisfaction pulsing through my body. I turned to him, and he came to me. We met beneath the shower's spray, water soaking us as we kissed.

"Terrence." I sighed deeply. "That was amazing."

He nibbled his lip, and I was surprised to see him so uncertain. "You sure? I've never topped before, and I was afraid I'd mess it up."

I chuckled and tightened my hold around his waist. "It was perfect. Everything I wanted."

He grinned. "Next time, let's try it in bed. I think I could get a better angle."

I nodded, already eager for another round.

We rinsed off and toweled dry, then climbed into my bed. We snuggled close, Terrence's face pressed into my neck.

It wasn't even dark outside, but the comfort of Terrence's presence beside me and the release from the sex had me tired. I shut my eyes and almost drifted to sleep before Terrence's soft words roused me.

"Growing up was hard."

I made a noise of interest, asking him to continue, without words.

"My family is...complicated. They're all practitioners. Powerful ones. My dad. Uncle Francis. Aunt Gloria. My cousins: Remy, Elli, Lisbeth."

"Lisbeth? The one who goes here?"

He nodded, causing his hair to rub against my cheek. "Francis's daughter. Uncle Francis is Helmer's brother. He works for the government. A high position." He sighed. "There was so much pressure. I was the youngest, the slowest. They made fun of me. I studied harder. I pushed myself past the limit. I made myself great."

He fell silent.

"But it made them afraid?" I asked.

"I don't know. Maybe. But I will be more powerful than them. Than all of them. I promised myself I would."

"Why?"

"I don't know," he repeated.

"You're perfect the way you are."

He mumbled something and buried his face deeper against my neck.

This time, when he quieted, I did fall asleep.

Chapter Twenty-Two

Over the next two weeks leading up to the gala, Terrence helped me with my teleporting. Though I could do it instinctively, I couldn't control it completely. His encouragement forced me to try harder. Again and again.

After three days of extensive attempts, all of a sudden, my body and mind melded, and my magic was the bridge that connected them.

"It's so simple," I told my classmates during Tomes the next day. "It's about believing absolutely. I don't have to teleport across the room. I enforce the concept that I *am* over there so firmly that my magic compensates."

They nodded with varying degrees of understanding.

After that, Terrence asked me to teleport with him.

"Hold on to my hands, and take me with you. It's possible. I've seen it done in emergencies. Helmer once teleported with a student to Dr. Vivaan's office."

We tried it. The first few times, I left him behind. But after a while, I got the hang of it. It helped if he was closer to me.

With this avenue opened to us, we teleported somewhere almost every night. Sometimes we stayed close, like the pier to see the English Channel. As my confidence grew, we ventured farther, going to London and walking around for an hour or two. We went all over the country, observing the beautiful rolling hills in the north or the swelling seas off the cliffs of Dover. We found places with no one around for miles, and we lay naked beneath the dying sun.

It seemed as if my life were perfect. I had everything I wanted, everything I needed, and Terrence was beside me through it all.

Then, two days before the gala, I came back from Methods and found him reading the book on Al'venarta.

"What are you doing?" I asked, setting my bag beside my bed.

Terrence looked up. "Finishing my research. I think I'm ready for this."

I blinked in surprise. With him open and real to me, there was no need for him to summon the demon. I got him the way he was supposed to be, and he didn't have to do anything dangerous. Apparently, he didn't agree.

"I thought we weren't going to do that."

He lifted his eyebrows. "What? Why not?"

"Because we've got each other. We don't need to do that now."

He laughed, but when my expression didn't change, he stopped. He sat up and regarded me. "I've worked my whole life for this, Collin. I'm doing it."

"But it's so risky. You can hurt yourself. Hurt others."

He tilted his head to the side. "What's with you? You're the one who helped me get this book. I thought you agreed this was a good idea. If I gain Al'venarta's power as well as my own, they won't be able to keep me out of the program. I can study magic again."

No, this is all wrong. Things are perfect the way they are, and now he wants to push them off-balance again.

I walked to his bed and knelt in front of him. I took his hands in mine, entwining our fingers. "You are studying magic now. You have my coins." I'd given him one to keep yesterday. "You have the books I brought from the library."

He shook his head, and I was surprised by the sorrow in his eyes. "No, Collin. That's not enough. I want more."

"You have me," I added softly. "Why isn't that enough?"

He looked away, and it felt like a knife went through my heart.

A knock on our door pulled our attention. Terrence shoved the book on demons under his pillow. After it was hidden, I went to the door.

My mother stood there.

"Collin!"

My mouth fell open as she flung her arms around me, pulling me tight against her chest.

"Mom?"

Right behind her was a smiling Helmer. "Hello, Collin. May we come in?"

I backed away from Mom and looked over my shoulder to Terrence. His face was contorted with obvious displeasure. He got to his feet. "I'll leave you guys to catch up." He walked out of the room, brushing past Helmer without a word.

Once Terrence was gone, Helmer sighed. "I'm sorry for doing that."

I doubted it, but I gestured for them both to enter. Mom looked around the room; it was no different than at the start of the semester.

"What are you doing here?" I asked. When she looked at me sharply, I added, "Not that I'm not happy to see you. It's just so unexpected." I shot a questioning glance at Helmer.

"I was invited for the gala," Mom said excitedly. "I can't believe you didn't tell me about your studies, Collin. Magic. I can hardly get my mind around it."

My eyes flew wide. I'd told Helmer *not* to tell my parents. What the hell was he up to?

"I didn't want you to worry. Besides, I figured you'd think I was crazy if I told you."

Her lips thinned to a line. "It did take some convincing on Dean Helmer's part, I'll admit. Magic. And in our little boy." She put her arms around me again.

I relaxed into her embrace, breathing deeply the scent of her perfume. I'd missed her, missed Dad and Mindy, and Rocket. I called them at least once a week, but it wasn't the same as having her here.

"I'm glad you're here, Mom. But I can't believe you spent that much on an airplane ticket."

"It was our treat," Helmer said. "The school board thought it unfair that Mrs. Frey didn't know the truth about the program, or about your potential. We wanted to fix it."

"Dad couldn't come?"

Mom shook her head. "No vacation time left. And let me tell you, he's as jealous as a toddler. He said he didn't want me to come if he couldn't. As if I should have turned down Dean Helmer's invitation."

I nodded. That was sort of the way I looked at mine and Terrence's abilities. He wasn't in the program, but I was passing all the information onto him. I was an adequate replacement. But he didn't think so.

"I also brought your suit from home. You can wear it to the gala."

I glanced at Helmer again. Terrence had lent me one of his suits, navy-blue slacks and jacket with a purple paisley tie. It already hung in my closet.

Helmer cleared his throat. "Now that you're here, Mrs. Frey, why don't we have a seat and discuss a few items?"

Here it was, the real reason Helmer had brought my mom three thousand miles across the ocean. Mom must have got scent of my rising anger.

"Is there something wrong, Dean Helmer?" She sat down on Terrence's desk chair.

I sank onto Terrence's bed beside her—mostly so Helmer didn't have a chance to accidentally see what was under his pillow.

"He's concerned about my boyfriend," I said. At least getting it out in the open would show I held no guilt on the subject.

Mom's eyebrows rose. "Boyfriend? Collin, why didn't you tell me you had a boyfriend?"

"Because I didn't want it to get back to Dean Helmer."

Helmer snorted but said nothing.

"Why not?" Mom asked. "What the issue with him?"

"He's my son, for one," Helmer said.

My mom's face went scarlet. I knew her well enough to read the rising fury in her thinned lips and narrowed eyes. "And it bothers you he's dating my son?"

Helmer lifted his hands and quickly said, "No, that's not the issue, Diane. Terrence is bisexual and has never tried to hide it."

Mom relaxed. "Then what *is* the issue?"

"Terrence has been banned from the literature program," Helmer continued. "In his youth, he attempted something dangerous and pays the consequences of his mistake even now."

"Terrence? Your roommate?" She made a humming noise. "That does complicate things. I'm assuming you boys are being safe? Using protection?"

It was my turn to redden. I cleared my throat. "Mom, let's not have that discussion right now."

"Terrence," Helmer pressed on, "has been manipulating Collin and using Collin's access to magic to further his own ambitions."

Mom turned to Helmer, her features sharp again. "Manipulating? How? Why?"

"He has not," I cut in. "Terrence hasn't done anything like that."

Mom ignored me. "If you think Terrence is a risk, why is he even in this school?"

Helmer sighed. "He's done nothing wrong. Not yet. You know I could not judge a student on crimes they haven't committed. But, I have several students keeping tabs on him. He will be stopped before he can do anything harmful."

"Collin, are you one of the students spying on him?"

I growled low in my throat. "No. I wouldn't do that to him. I love him."

Helmer and Mom both looked startled. Well, it was true, and I wasn't going to keep it hidden any longer. Not when Helmer dragged my mom all the way here to tattle on me.

"You're being unreasonable, Collin," Helmer said. "I warned you of this danger. I told you to be careful."

"Sweetie," Mom said calmly, like she was explaining to a child why they couldn't get a new toy. "If Patrick has concerns, you need to listen. You're an adult now, and that means making responsible decisions."

"You've got it all wrong, Mom. I don't want you to take this personally, Dean Helmer, but to keep punishing Terrence like this is wrong. He made a mistake. Instead of treating him like a criminal, you should have helped him see how to use his powers for good. If he's dangerous now, it's only because he had no other option."

Helmer's face paled at my words. But at the last, he snapped angrily, "So you do know what he plans? Tell me, Collin! The lives of students are on the line."

I shook my head. "A father should see his son first, not dwell on how his mistakes reflect on your family name. There's still time. You can fix this."

"I had no say over his punishment," Helmer said. "It was out of my hands."

"Even so, you still could have been a father. He struggled, and you left him to his misery alone."

"Collin," Mom cut in. "You don't know the difficulties of parenthood. I don't think you have a say in how Patrick handled things."

"All I know is the man I love felt abandoned, so he reached out to something else."

Helmer abruptly turned to the door. "I can see I won't convince you to help. Mrs. Frey, you'll be staying in the same room you used last time. Perhaps we can talk later." Then he left.

Mom frowned after him, but quickly turned it onto me. "I can't believe you'd say such things, Collin. I raised you to be more respectful."

"You also *raised* me. Helmer stepped away from Terrence after the incident. He doesn't have a right to say such things about Terrence when he gave up his own responsibilities."

She shook her head. "You don't know all the details. And I'm sure what you heard is skewed. If Terrence feels wronged, he'd refuse to see the other side."

"Helmer had a chance to explain it, to make me see, but he didn't."

"He doesn't owe you an explanation."

"He does if he wants me to side with him over Terrence." I sighed, suddenly very tired. "Sorry he dragged you all the way over here to get in the middle of a family squabble."

Mom reached out and gripped my hand. "Sounds like more than a squabble. How are you holding up, kiddo?"

Time for some of that honesty again. "Mom, I'm the happiest I've ever been in my life. Being with Terrence is like a dream."

She smiled, but it had the indulgence of someone who didn't believe a word of what was said. "I'm sure he's great, Collin. But at your age, these things come and go."

I raised an eyebrow. "I can't believe you're trying to tell me that I'll get over him."

"Well, you've only known him a month, Collin. It seems awful quick."

My laugh was bitter, and even Mom heard it. This honesty thing was getting out of hand.

"Mom, I've known Terrence since I was twelve."

She blinked, startled by this statement. "How is that possible?"

"Remember when we went to Colorado to the ski lodge? I met him there."

Her eyes narrowed, thinking back to that trip.

"Do you remember our last night there?" I asked. "When I came back, shaken and scared."

Slowly, she nodded. "I do remember that. You'd been out in the cold too long. Your father and I were afraid you'd catch sick."

"I wasn't cold. I'd had a...paranormal encounter." I laughed again, still lacking any mirth. "I was always so afraid to tell you, afraid you'd think I was crazy. *I* thought I was crazy."

Alarm showed on her face, and her hand tightened on mine. "Collin, tell me what happened. Did he do anything to hurt you?"

"No, it wasn't like that. Before I went down the slope, I saw a coin in the snow. I picked it up and saw this." I pulled my coin from my pocket and handed it to her.

She took it and flipped it over to examine both sides.

"It's how we access our magic. The easiest way, at least. I found that coin, Mom. A coin with my face. A coin that said *Marke Staple* on the back."

Raising her eyes from the coin, she stared at me, unbelieving. As I knew she would. To give my argument more weight, I pulled out my sketch pad. I flipped to a page toward the front and handed it to her.

"I drew this two years ago."

She eyed the drawing as her jaw dropped.

Seeing I had her now, I continued with my story. "When I saw the coin, I was confused. Why would it have my face, my *adult* face, on it? Then, I heard someone approach. A voice speaking in a British accent. It was Terrence. Terrence from now, or from a few weeks or months in our future. He saw me, recognized me, and sobbed. He babbled on and on about betraying me, and how I was right, and he was sorry. Even as young as I was, I could tell the torment he was going through. My heart opened to him, and it's been open to him ever since.

"After apologizing to me and promising he'd come back to me, he took my coin and vanished. My life changed that day. I researched Marke Staple, did everything in my power to get here, and I found him again. He doesn't know we've met before, Mom. It's all in his future. But I know he regrets whatever it is he'll do, and I know he'll come back to me a changed man."

She shook her head, denying my words, or the fact Terrence was redeemable. "Why didn't you tell me sooner? You could have trusted me, Collin."

"No I couldn't. You would have signed me up for a psychiatrist, put me on meds, tried to make me believe it hadn't happened."

"That's not true!"

"Then how did Helmer convince you magic was real?" I was just guessing, based on my understanding of my parents and their views.

She flinched, so I knew I was close in my assessment. "He...he called last week and informed us you were studying magic. He apologized for not telling us sooner; he thought we knew. I, uh, called him a psychopath and told him our lawyer would be in touch in the morning and we'd be removing you from school as soon as possible."

"Exactly."

She pinched her lips. "In ten minutes, we had an FBI agent on our doorstep, escorting Minnie Randolf—the state governor—and Lyle Smith—the state *practitioner*. They proved quite efficiently that magic is real." She shivered just a bit. "Patrick called us back and invited us to the gala."

"And if I had told you at the age of twelve that I saw someone from the future?"

She lowered her head, and I was surprised to see she was crying. "I'm sorry, Collin. Like you said about Patrick, maybe your dad and I weren't there for you as much as we should have been."

I stood up and wrapped my arms around her. "You and Dad are the best parents. You did everything for me, especially supporting me when my sexuality didn't evolve the way you thought normal. It was Terrence then too. I've known about him for so long, Mom. I knew I only wanted to be with him." I squeezed her extra tight, willing her to believe my words. "You're going to have to trust me on this. Whatever happens needs to happen. I thought I could get Terrence to change without sum—" I cut off, not wanting to reveal too much. "Without doing what I think he did. But he's not the same man I saw in Colorado. Not yet."

"This doesn't make any sense, Collin. How do you know he'll change the way you think he will?"

"Don't you think kids need to make their own mistakes to learn their lessons? I know you let Mindy get dumped by that boy senior year. You knew he was cheating, but you couldn't convince her. She had to find out for herself."

"I suppose."

"The same has to happen with Terrence. And he promised he'd come back to me. He wouldn't have done that if he didn't learn something from this encounter."

She nodded against my chest. "I trust you. Let me know if there's anything I can do to help."

Chapter Twenty-Three

When Terrence came back, I was waiting for him. No doubt he thought I'd be at dinner with Mom, but I told her we'd have to eat late. She understood and insisted she needed a nap, anyway, to catch up from the jet lag.

"Are you okay?" I asked as he entered.

"Peachy."

I stood from my bed and went to him. He didn't pull away, but he didn't step closer either.

"I talked with my mom. Things are okay now."

"Sure they are, for you. What about me? Helmer never stops prying. I hardly talked to him for the past eleven years; now he's there every time I turn around."

"Will you come sit with me? There's something I need to confess." I tugged on his arm, but he didn't budge.

"Confess? That you've been one of his spies all along? That I actually trusted you when I knew I shouldn't have?"

"What? No! That's not how this is. I love you!"

He shook his head with a sneer. "I should have realized what was going on. You loved this guy from Colorado so much, but you sure forgot about him quickly. I'm such a fool." He pushed past me and went to his bed. He took the book out from under the pillow.

"Please, wait," I begged. "Let me explain."

"Why the hell should I?"

"Because you're the man I met in Colorado."

The anger in his eyes dampened but didn't vanish completely. "What?"

I went to my desk and grabbed my sketch book. I handed it out to him.

As he flipped through the pages, I said, "After that encounter in Colorado, I learned how to draw. It was the only connection I had to him. So I drew, and drew, and drew. His arched eyebrows. His small nose. His horrible, ugly scar along his neck."

Terrence glanced up at me, then back down to the sketches. When he turned from one page to the next, he froze, staring down at an exact replica of his own face.

"This man I met made a mistake. He said he did something to betray me. That's how I know doing this is wrong. It may seem like it would work, but it'll only hurt us."

"Collin, what are you saying?"

"I'm telling you the truth. I kept it inside so long, afraid to give you this last piece of the puzzle. It's like a prophecy, and I'm terrified you having this knowledge will fuck things up."

"I'm the man you met in Colorado?"

I nodded. "I've cared about you all this time, Terrence. I nearly died when I recognized you my first day here. Over the past few weeks, the feelings I had for him—for *you*—have grown stronger. I'm falling in love with you."

"But how is it possible he and I are the same?"

"I have no idea. It's in our future."

His eyes were wide and his face pale. "This isn't a trick?"

I took my drawing pad back and tossed it onto my bed. "No. It's the truth. I've known you were out there for nearly a third of my life."

"Collin." He sighed and reached out to me.

I hurried into his arms.

"I don't understand," he said.

"I don't either. But I know when I'm with you, everything is all right."

"You don't want me to summon Al'venarta?"

I hesitated. "I don't think we can avoid it. But, please wait until my mom leaves. If something were to go wrong, I don't want to worry about her getting caught in any of it."

He nodded.

"And promise me we'll do it together. I can be there to help."

"I promise."

He leaned forward and pressed his lips to mine.

I reached up and sank my fingers into his hair, holding him in place. Our kiss deepened as our passion kindled. Terrence nudged me backward, and I walked toward the bed, dragging him with me.

At the edge, we collapsed onto the blanket. We wiggled until we were all the way on, Terrence's weight pushing down on me.

"Will you fuck me?" I asked. "Just like this?"

He nodded, his eyes already glazed over with desire. "I've been wanting to try this for a while, Collin. Will you let me use more magic?"

I groaned at his suggestion. "Yes. Do anything you want. My coin is in—"

"I don't want your coin. I'm going to use your blood."

A piteous whimper escaped my throat. "Please," I begged.

After he muttered the same Latin spell, he quickly peeled off his clothing. I tore mine off just as fast. With him naked above me, my whole body trembled with anticipation.

"Please," I said again. "I need you."

He lay atop me, aligning our bodies perfectly. His lips found mine, and the kiss turned rough, animalistic. My mind went wild with longing as instinct took over our actions.

Then, Terrence took my bottom lip between his teeth and bit down—hard.

I gasped in pain and pleasure. Blood trickled from a small gash.

Terrence's tongue licked at my blood, and his eyes flashed with lust. I felt an invading force push at my asshole. It wasn't physically Terrence, but it was the manifestation of his magic. The currents slipped inside me. A few at first, working to get me stretched. Then he increased them. They pulsed as they worked in and out, loosening me without any hint of pain.

I thought back to my encounter with the Gyranium, how its magic had caused my body to burn with desire. Terrence's magic on me had the same effect. My skin felt on fire, my muscles scorched, and my voice cried out my building pleasure.

"God, Collin," Terrence muttered. "You're incredibly sexy."

"Fuck me, Terrence. Fuck me, now!"

He growled and nodded. He lifted my legs to get a better angle. With the currents of magic still inside me, he shoved his cock into my asshole.

I nearly screamed from the impact of it. My blood still dripped from my lip, and suddenly, my vision shifted. I saw the ether, the currents, the bright colors of the magical world. Above me, Terrence shone like the sun. He was a bright red, and it radiated out of him like a halo.

He thrust his hips forward with a grunt.

I wanted more. So much more. With my magic, I activated the air currents behind his back. I pulled him toward me, forcing his chest to mine. I held him there, as close to me as he could get without causing us harm.

The angle shifted, but he still kept up his movements. His hips bucked and his connection to magic still pulsed inside me.

He kissed me, the blood from my lips mingling between us. The sharp taste of metal filled my mouth as Terrence filled my body.

It was too much. I cried out as I came, but Terrence swallowed the noise with his lips. He was a half heartbeat behind, his thrusts becoming erratic in the glow of orgasm.

I released my hold on him, but he still stayed perched atop me, slowly kissing me. The bottom lip was sore from his bite, and his soft touch along the wound made my softening cock twitch.

"You're not satisfied?" he asked, noticing my reaction.

"I am. More than satisfied. But I think I enjoyed it rough."

He chuckled and gently pulled his body free. "I liked it too. I'm glad you let me try."

"You should have asked sooner."

He laughed again and nuzzled close to me. "I was afraid you'd say no."

I shook my head and kissed the bridge of his nose. "Terrence, when are you going to see that I will never tell you no?"

A smile bloomed on his lips. Sweet and charming. My heart ached at how pure it was. And I knew he loved me as well.

"Are you ready for dinner?" I asked after he pulled away.

"Yeah."

"Mind if Mom joins us?"

His lips curved. "Of course not. Though we'll have to shower first."

Chapter Twenty-Four

"Now remember," Helmer said as we all stood to leave. "The gala is tomorrow night, and I expect all of you to be on your best behavior."

There were mutters of acknowledgment, but mostly the students talked excitedly about the upcoming event.

"I can't wait," Tabitha said as we followed the crowd out of the classroom. "I bought my dress at the Lanes last weekend. One good thing about my mother being here is she can buy me some new outfits."

Laura nodded. "I love the market. I got my dress at Snooper's Attic, and it's amazing!"

Sammuel said, "Personally, I'm partial to the She Said Boutique."

Omar's snort let me know there was some joke in what Sammuel said, though I didn't get it.

"My mom brought my suit, but I think I'd rather wear Terrence's." I'd already informed my classmates of my mom's surprise visit—though not Helmer's real reasons for summoning her. Omar suspected, I was sure, but I hadn't gotten him alone to share what had happened.

Tabitha smiled warmly, but Sammuel laughed. "It's like the boyfriend shirt, right? Does he think you look sexy in it?"

"He thinks I look sexy out of it," I retorted with a smug grin.

Sammuel's eyes flew wide for half a second before he exploded with laughter. He threw his arm over my shoulder. "That's why we love you, Collin. You seem so vanilla on the surface, but underneath we know you're rainbow sherbet."

"I always thought he was cookie dough," Omar said.

Laura shook her head. "Mint chip."

I looked at Tabitha. Surely, she had a guess too.

She grinned sweetly. "You can be any ice cream you want, Collin."

I chuckled and put *my* arm around her. We surely looked weird, me and Tabitha and Sammuel walking down the hallway with our limbs all tangled.

When we got to Tomes, we broke apart. I was already digging in my messenger bag for my research paper. I'd finished it late last night and was ready to turn it in a full week early. My classmates wandered around in separate directions while I headed to the second floor to find Professor Lorel. She sat at her usual seat with a book on the table in front of her.

"May I turn this in, Professor?"

She glanced up from her book and then held out her hand. I gave her my paper, printed out at the school's computer lab first thing this morning.

"Your topic was dragons?" she asked as she glanced at my title page.

"Yeah. It was a lot more interesting that I initially thought. Most people think dragons are myths, so it was nice to see historical records and facts."

She smiled. "Most primary school students turn in papers on dragons. Can we try for something a bit more advanced for your next one?"

I grimaced. "Yes, Professor."

"Why not look more into your special? There are several books on teleporting. Try the top floor."

"Sure, Professor." It actually was a good idea, but I didn't appreciate that she nearly called me juvenile. Anyone, on learning dragons really existed, would want to study them.

I left her and went to the fourth floor. At the catalog, I asked it to find me books on teleporting. When the line zoomed down the aisle to the left, I followed.

There were a handful of books in the middle of one shelf all lit up by the catalog. However, the line still continued down and around the corner. Curious as to why the books wouldn't be together, I went in that direction. The line illuminated a path straight down the side of the library to the far back corner. There, on the top shelf, one book flashed with light.

When I pinched my coin to turn off the catalog, the line vanished. I stood on tiptoes to reach the large book. I pulled it off the shelf and hefted it in my hands. I needed both to support its weight. I flipped to its cover and read, *Curiosities and Wonders.*

I didn't know if it was possible, but I pinched my coin again. "Catalog, please show me the passage about teleportation."

Nothing happened that I could see, but I began to flip through pages. Eventually, I found a page with a glowing title.

"Teleportation and Time Travel," I read aloud. I nearly dropped the book. Time travel? I knew Terrence went back in time, but I never considered it would be my special that sent him there.

I hurried to the closest table and started reading. After the first few paragraphs, I flipped back to the beginning and read the introduction. Apparently, this book was a collection of essays on conspiracy theories, most not even believed by practitioners who were used to ideas being odd and far-fetched.

Conspiracy theories? Looks like I had a question for Professor Jenkins in Latin.

I checked out the book from Professor Lorel who eyed it with barely veiled disgust. I remembered her earlier warning about a more advanced topic. Well, this was about my special. She shouldn't complain when I took her advice.

I shoved the book into my bag, then went with the others to the cafe.

Of course, my mom was there and wanted to meet all my friends. I struggled to keep my cheeks from heating.

"My mom should arrive tonight," Tabitha said, and I eased a bit. At least I wouldn't be the only student with a parent tagging along.

"I look forward to meeting her," Mom said, smiling. She seemed to vibrate with energy. She was in a really good mood, probably buoyed by the fact that my dad couldn't be here too. It made her feel special.

Terrence joined us, and I stayed silent as the others entertained my mom. Terrence laid on the charm extra thick. He needn't have bothered. Mom said she trusted me, and that extended to Terrence too. She had to see the depths of my feelings for him. I knew she'd be supportive.

"Maybe I'll run out to this Snooper's Attic after lunch," Mom said. "There's got to be something there I can get for the gala."

I wrinkled my brow. "I thought you said you brought a dress from home."

A touch of pink colored her cheeks. "This is my one chance to go shopping in a foreign country."

I laughed and held up my hands. "You don't need to justify your actions to me. My suit is blue, and my tie is purple if you want to match."

Her face lit up even more.

We said bye to Mom, then headed to Regalia. Terrence held my hand snuggly within his own. At the door, he kissed me, then hurried to his own class. I watched him go until Omar pulled on my sleeve.

He grinned at me. "You can ogle him later. We're going to be late if we don't go now."

"Not like Jenkins would even notice." But then I remembered I had questions for him.

We sat in class, students already pulling out phones to occupy themselves during Jenkin's lecture. The professor, as usual, sat at his table with his eyes downcast until the exact minute class began.

He stood and addressed the class. "Good afternoon. Today we're going to take a look at the root word—" He cut his words off as he noticed my raised hand. "Yes, Collin?"

"Professor, I checked out a book that has an article about time travel. It was a little vague though. With your expertise, I was hoping you could elaborate."

"Time travel? Well, that was an area I studied when I was completing my degree. I'm no expert, but I do know about most of the leading theories."

He glanced around the classroom before returning his gaze in my general direction. "There's a lot of debate on this topic. We aren't even sure which branch of magic it would fall under. Lingual? Could we find words powerful enough to send a person to the past or the future? Elemental? Could a person teleport not to a different location, but a different time as well? Maybe a branch we haven't discovered yet?

"There's also the possibility of syphoning off another's power. For instance, if we could tap into a vortex, like the one in Egypt, there would surely be enough power to bend space and time. However, researchers haven't been able to draw even a gram of power out of an established vortex. Which leads practitioners to think they have been established for a specific purpose, possibly—"

Not wanting another tangent about vortexes, I cut in. "So teleportation can do it?"

He blinked several times, but then nodded. "In theory, yes. Now a person with a teleportation special..." he trailed off, his eyes widening. He almost met my glance but quickly returned his eyes to the floor.

So that's it. My teleportation special has to be the key.

I switched my line of questioning. "How would someone attribute a spell onto someone else?"

He tilted his head. "I'm not quite sure what you mean?"

"Like if I wanted to heal someone. Omar told me it's possible with magic, and Dr. Vivaan did it to me at the start of term. How do I get my magic inside someone else?"

He made a noise of understanding. "I see. Healing is a very tricky area of study, and magical healing even more so. It also has many limitations; we are unable to fix something inherently wrong within the body. We cannot cure cancer. We cannot keep an appendix from rupturing. We cannot grow back a severed limb. What we can do is give power to the chi within a person's body and guide it to healing itself. What Dr. Vivaan did with you was to get your swelling down from the knock to your head and give a little jolt to your electrolytes—making you feel more energized. Simple, really."

I nodded. Putting my powers into Terrence. It made sense.

Professor Jenkins was still talking though. "And of course with semen or other bodily fluids—"

I yelped and he stopped midsentence. "I'm sorry, Professor, but what are you talking about?"

The rest of the class perked up at the mention of that word, same as I had. Jenkins seemed a bit flustered when he realized all his students' eyes were on him.

"I, uh, I said that we attribute our magic to our blood, but all of our bodily fluids contain trace amounts. Blood does have the highest concentration of magic, and it is easier to harvest a practitioner's blood to meld with coins than...other fluids."

"I bet some would enjoy the other more," Sammuel whispered to me, with a nudge of his elbow on my arm. "The Gyranium could be altered to suck instead of poke."

Omar groaned softly. "I can't believe you're making jokes about having sex with a plant."

Sammuel shrugged and his grin stretched wider.

Jenkins cleared his throat. "I seem to have gotten off subject."

Mallory, a junior, who had long, blonde hair pulled over her shoulder in a braid, raised her hand. "Why don't we have a magical health course? I think the guys would benefit from hearing about how a woman's period affects her magical abilities during menstruation."

Jenkins's face went scarlet, and he wobbled on his feet.

"Go on and tell us about it," Kiaan said. He was a sophomore, with dark hair that reached his shoulders.

"Class," Jenkins said but softly. And his voice trembled. "Let's get back to Latin."

"Think about it," Mallory said. "If blood is the main activation ingredient in magic, what do you think happens?"

Tabitha leaned forward interestedly. "What about losing your virginity? Does that impact anything?"

"Yes it does," Mallory answered. "Which you would know if we had a magical health course."

"Class," Jenkins called again, but there was no way he'd get them to stop now.

Mallory stood and moved to the front of the whiteboard. All questions about time travel were pushed from my mind as Mallory detailed how puberty affected men and women's abilities to interact with magic.

Lark, a senior with short-cut brown hair, raised his hand. "What about magic during sex?"

I nibbled on my lip, still tender from Terrence's attention yesterday. Magic and sex mixed well.

"Collin knows the answer to that one," Sammuel said.

I flinched as all eyes turned to me. "What? No I don't!"

Sammuel grinned. "Then why'd your face go red? Does magic work in place of lubricant?"

There was a collective noise of interest from nearly every throat.

"Class is dismissed," Jenkins nearly wailed. He fled from the class faster than anyone else.

The students filed out slowly. Omar came up to my side as I put my bag over my shoulder. "Have you done it with magic?"

I glanced around. The only ones still paying any attention to me were from my same year. No harm in admitting it, then.

"Yeah."

Tabitha came closer. "What happened?"

I bit my lip again and willed my face to stop growing hot. "It *does* aid with lubrication."

Sammuel hooted. "I knew it! If we get a health course, we should get a sex course too! You'll have to teach it."

"I don't think that's something the administration would approve."

"Why? We're all adults."

I laughed. "But is Jenkins? Maybe we shouldn't have talked about it in front of him."

"Don't worry about him. I'm sure he has to sign all sorts of waivers to work here. Never know what can happen when you work around magic."

Chapter Twenty-Five

In Methods, I graduated to earth. Or ground. Watanabe gave me a jar of dirt to play with. During class, I dumped it out onto a desk and attempted to move it. The dirt's currents were a light pink like earthworms. Odd, since I figured they'd be brown.

With only a little effort, I could shape the dirt into spheres or squares. By the end of class, I'd formed it into a rectangular prism.

"Good work, Collin," Professor Watanabe said. "You seem to have an affinity for ground. You worked it much quicker than the other two."

"I like the ground currents...or, ah, weaves, I guess. When they wiggle, they do look like worms."

She smiled. "See if you can get all of it back into the jar. If not, I can help."

"Sure, Professor. Can I take the jar with me?"

"Yes, I want you to practice over the weekend. Even though the gala is tomorrow, we still have our studies."

We walked out of class and to the cafe as was our custom now. Mom was already there with Terrence seated beside her. When we joined them, Mom greeted us cheerfully.

"Omar," Mom said. "Thank you for giving me your mom's contact information! I think she'll be a great help once I get back home. She's a lovely woman and so proud of you!"

I would have squirmed if Omar's mom had said something like that to me, but Omar only smiled and nodded. "I wanted to give it to Collin our first week here, but he didn't want to bother you with all the magic stuff right away."

Mom frowned at me. "Yes, well, it'll be helpful going forward." Then her smile was back. "Patrick let me borrow one of the cars and chauffeurs to drive me down to the pier. It was beautiful to see, and I found a perfect dress for the party tomorrow."

It was funny to see my mom so excited. I'd been so afraid of her negative reaction to magic that I never wondered how she'd feel when proof was offered. She saw it as something wonderful and new. I saw it that way, too, but her ideas on it were purer. Mine was to a particular end goal. Even now, most of my desire to learn stemmed from wanting to help Terrence.

Do I have an interest in this for myself? Yes, there is desire, a wanting to learn something so unbelievable. But I am so far behind. I'll never catch up to my classmates.

At first, I'd been optimistic, driven. Now, a month into my studies that optimism faded. A more realistic look replaced it.

I like it, but there's no way I can make a career out of it. A position in the government? Not for me. What other options did I have?

"You okay, kiddo?" Mom asked, gripping my hand.

I forced a smile. "Yeah. Just tired. It's awfully draining working with magic."

Her grin became mischievous, an expression I'd never seen on her face before. "Terrence let slip that it's possible I have magical potential too. When you come visit us next, I want to try."

"I can't come home till summer. You want to wait that long?"

She gave me an odd look, like I was being stupid on purpose. "Can't you teleport? You can come home tomorrow."

"How do you know that?"

"Terrence told me."

I shot Terrence a scowl, but it bounced off his cheerful smile. "Well, even if that is true, I've only teleported a couple hundred miles. Going across the ocean is a different matter."

She patted my hand. "I'm sure you'll figure it out. We expect you both home for Thanksgiving."

"We won't miss it," Terrence said.

"Are we invited too?" Sammuel asked. "I'd fancy trying an American cooked turkey. And maybe one of those apple pies."

"Apple pies aren't for Thanksgiving," Laura said. "You eat pumpkin pies."

Sammuel shrugged. "Any kind of pie will do."

Mom laughed. "Of course you're all invited! Then maybe we can pop over and meet Omar's mother in person."

I growled. "Hey, I'm not a taxi. I don't even know if I'll be able to get that far." But as I said it, I knew I would. My powers would send Terrence to Colorado. That was nearly five thousand miles. Florida was closer than that.

Still, the sentiment stayed. I wasn't going to bus people all over the place just because I could.

Mom dropped the subject, but I saw that she wouldn't forget this. Likely it would be the topic of every one of our conversations from now till then. She understood how to weaken my resolve.

We ate an early dinner; then Terrence and I accompanied Mom to her guest room. Though small, it was still bigger than our dorm. Plus, it had a couch and a television. The three of us sat and watched cooking shows. Having Dad there too would have been icing on the cake. My mind dwelled on how he'd react to seeing Terrence's hand in mine or his head resting lightly on my shoulder.

Mom and Dad came to terms with my identity as a demisexual in my late teens. They wanted to understand, and more, they wanted me to understand myself. I saw a therapist for a year and a half, and afterward my life made much more sense. I couldn't experiment sexually with any of my friends or acquaintances, and I came to terms with it. I could, however, experiment with myself to thoughts of the red-eyed man's gaze.

And here I was, with Terrence on my left, Mom on my right, and a silly television show droning on about the proper ratio of coarse sugar to brown sugar to make the best cookies. If every day were like this, I'd be the luckiest man in the world.

Around ten o'clock, Terrence began yawning.

"You boys better head off to bed," Mom said, rising from the couch. "I'll have to fly home on Sunday, but this has still been the best vacation I've ever had. I'll miss having you kiddos around. The house has been too quiet since you left, Collin."

"We'll come visit," Terrence said. He went to her and pecked her cheek. "I'll convince Collin to give it a try. We'll come home every weekend."

Mom's eyes sparkled. "Thank you, Terrence. Have a good rest of the night, boys."

Chapter Twenty-Six

The campus was abuzz the day of the gala. Terrence and I met my mom for breakfast, but the lines were long. Everyone was up early, even the business students. They were excited about the high-profile people we'd have visiting. No one I knew, but apparently many were local celebrities.

Tabitha's mom trailed after Tabitha as she walked toward our table. In her wake, several people gasped or muttered softly to their companions behind their hands.

When Tabitha had mentioned her mother wanting to come, Helmer had implied he didn't have the authority to tell her no. I wondered who she was; obviously someone important. Terrence must have known because he gave a start when he saw her and quickly got to his feet when they joined our table.

"Mrs. Fabron," Terrence said, rushing forward to take her hand. "It's an honor to meet you. I'm Terrence Smith, Dean Helmer's son."

Tabitha's mom, tall and lithe, but with Tabitha's same delicate features and blonde hair, nodded as she shook Terrence's hand. "Lovely to meet you, Terrence." Her voice had a soft, drawn-out accent: thick but still clearly understood.

Terrence gestured to me. "And this is my boyfriend, Collin Frey. He's Tabitha's classmate."

Mrs. Fabron's gaze turned to me. She smiled, but it didn't seem to reach her eyes. "Yes, Collin. Tabitha has told me so much about you."

"And this is my mom, Diane," I said, waving my hand for my mom to come over.

Mom, unable to read the vibes in the room, rushed toward Mrs. Fabron and hugged her.

Tabitha and I both squeaked.

"It's a pleasure to meet you," my mom gushed. "I'm so excited to get in contact with other parents. We didn't realize Collin had magic until just a few days ago. It's been such a whirlwind." She stepped back and smiled up at Mrs. Fabron, who stood half a head taller.

Mrs. Fabron blinked rapidly, but then smiled sweetly—very reminiscent of her daughter. Her eyes brightened, and she reached out to take my mom's hands in her own. "Diane. Lovely to meet you too. If this is all new to you, it must be very overwhelming. Maybe we can have coffee together this afternoon? I'd be happy to explain anything you don't understand."

My mom's face lit up. "That would be wonderful, Mrs. Fabron."

"Please, call me Pierrette. We have no need for formalities."

Tabitha made another noise, like a cat being stepped on.

"Will you join us?" Mom asked.

Mrs. Fabron nodded.

Mom hurried to grab another chair from a nearby table and set it down next to hers. Mrs. Fabron sat.

When she did, I saw two men in dark suits on the periphery of the room walk closer and take up positions at opposite ends of the cafe. They were far enough away to not intrude, but close enough to intervene if needed. Security guards. And powerful ones, by the way their shirts stretched over broad shoulders and taut torsos.

Mom and Mrs. Fabron fell into a quick conversation about the gala and what to expect. At one point, Mrs. Fabron waved her hand, and one of her guards went to fetch her a coffee. When he presented it to her at the table, my mom finally noticed the security detail. She reappraised Mrs. Fabron, but it didn't slow their discussion.

Tabitha sat next to me, her eyes wide on her mother. "She's acting so friendly," she whispered, loud enough for me to hear. "I don't think I've ever seen her treat another person like this."

"She doesn't have any friends?" I asked.

Tabitha shook her head. "Ever since I was little, Mother's been in a position of power. She always told me to be wary of who wanted to get close to you. I think she feels your mom—with no magical background—can't be a threat."

"My mom isn't a threat," I agreed. "Though I'm still shocked she hugged your mom without asking."

Tabitha shivered. "The last person who did that was my aunt. She flew ten meters backward. I'm really, really glad she didn't do that to your mother."

I was glad, too, but my mom might have deserved it. Still, I was happy we'd averted the crisis, and everything was fine for now.

"Tabitha, do you mind if I ask who your mother is?"

She sighed. "She's a minister in the French government. The Minister of the Armed Forces. She's in charge of our military."

My jaw dropped.

Tabitha nodded. "She's very high in the chain of command. We have the Prime Minister over regularly. It's actually quite exhausting. Going to school here has given me a respite from all that."

I grinned. "You miss it a bit, huh? The pomp?"

Pink touched her cheeks. "A little. Let's say I'm excited for the gala. And that will be enough to satisfy me for the rest of the school year."

Eventually, we grabbed some breakfast and ate. Terrence appeared to want to hover near Mrs. Fabron, but my mom had a monopoly on the discussion. So he settled next to me while shooting covert glances at the pair.

"You want to talk to her?" I asked after swallowing a bite of pancake. "I'll call my mom over here if you need an in."

Terrence hesitated but shook his head. "No. There'll be time at the gala. Your mom looks happy; it would be rude to interrupt."

We finished eating, but Mom and Mrs. Fabron still had their heads close together.

"We better leave them to it," I told Tabitha.

She nodded gratefully.

"See you later, Mom," I said.

Tabitha muttered a similar farewell.

Our mothers barely looked over and gave us brisk waves.

Once outside, Tabitha sighed again. "She can be so overbearing."

"You'll have to talk with Omar about that. His mom's the same way, he said."

Tabitha lifted her shoulders. "Maybe it's something to do with being an only child."

Terrence barked a laugh. "Not really. I'm an only child, and Helmer hardly acknowledges my existence."

I flinched at the hurt in his tone—though he tried to say it nonchalantly. Maybe Mom had been right yesterday, saying I couldn't judge because I wasn't a parent. But, looking at so many miserable people, seeing how their relationships with their parents affected so much of their lives, really made me appreciate my own. They were far from perfect, but they tried so hard to give me balance.

Tabitha shook her head. "I'm used to it. She's been like this all my life."

I saw a flash in Terrence's eyes. His father, at least, hadn't always treated him as a criminal. At one point they'd been happy.

"Well," Tabitha said, as we reached the fork in the sidewalk, "I'm going to start getting ready."

I pulled my phone from my pocket and glanced at its screen. It was only ten in the morning.

She seemed to understand my shock. "Mother hired someone to come over and do my hair for me. It'll take a few hours to wash, dry, and curl." Her smile was forced.

"Hey," I said, suddenly reaching out and grabbing her hand. "If your mom is busy with my mom, maybe she won't notice if you go missing for a few hours. You can come hang with us. We'll go to the Swift Unicorn."

She blinked a few times before her lips began to curl up. "You mean it?"

"Yeah! Right, Terrence?"

He nodded. "I know the owner. He'll let us hide there, if need be."

Her smile grew. "Let's do it."

"You'll love it there," I said. "It's real cozy."

"Thank you, Collin, Terrence. I appreciate this."

Chapter Twenty-Seven

It was early to be drinking, but we couldn't turn down mimosas. Terrence wrinkled his nose at the mixture—he liked harder stuff—but nodded once he got a taste.

"So, the gala's tonight, huh?" Alfie, the bartender, said after dropping off our drinks. The place was busy, and the scents of breakfast filled the room. I wished I hadn't filled up on school-made pancakes. One of the servers kept bringing out plates of steaks and eggs, and they looked delicious.

"Yes," Tabitha said enthusiastically. "It'll be exciting to see some of the locals. Richard Hyde. Malcolm Williams. Charles Evans."

Alfie chuckled. "All the eligible bachelors, I see."

Tabitha didn't even try to hide her intentions. "I'd be much happier marrying outside my country. Mother has a line of suitors ready for when I graduate—she *did* want schooling to come first. But I'd rather beat her to it."

"Good for you, Tabitha," Alfie said. "Don't forget, no matter who your mum is, you've got to live your own life. Now, this round's on me, friends. Need something to eat?"

I shook my head, as did Terrence, but Tabitha eyed one of the servers. "Maybe something sweet? A scone?"

"Coming up." Alfie set off to the kitchen himself.

"I think he likes you, Tabitha," Terrence said under his breath.

"What?"

"I've been in here with many, many people, and I've never seen him so attentive."

A pretty pink glow touched her cheeks. "Really? He is rather good-looking. I like his arms."

My mind had a picture of who Mrs. Fabron had picked as a possible match for Tabitha. The barkeep, with his shirtsleeves rolled up to show off his tattoos, was not what I envisioned. I was all for helping Tabitha find a few hours of independence, but I didn't want to be on the receiving end of Mrs. Fabron's fury if Tabitha showed up at the gala with this man on her arm. I didn't want to make a habit of telling off my friends' parents.

"This place is nice," Tabitha said, glancing around. We sat in armchairs in front of the empty fireplace. "We drink a lot of wine at home, but not too much beer. We'll have to come back sometimes to sample what they have."

Terrence smiled. "Collin and I come here at least once a week. You can join us."

"I'd like that." Her eyes fell on Alfie as he approached, and the pink on her face turned darker.

Alfie set down a pumpkin scone on the table. "There you are, Tabitha. Compliments of the chef."

Tabitha let out a delighted giggle.

Terrence got to his feet. "Alfie, we hate to trouble you, but Collin and I have to get back to campus. Tabitha needed a break, but I just remembered I have a study group, and Collin promised to help me with my algebra. We don't want to leave Tabitha by herself…"

Alfie didn't even hesitate. "Why don't you come and sit up at the bar, love. I'll keep your plate filled, and you can tell me all your troubles."

"You sure I won't be in the way?" she asked, standing as well.

"Of course not. I'd appreciate the company." He picked her plate back up and led her toward the other end of the room.

"I am good," Terrence said. He reached out his hand toward mine and pulled me to my feet. Once standing, he didn't let go. "Come on. I've got plans with you, and it doesn't include any math."

I laughed and hurried to his side. I leaned into him, loving the closeness of his body. "Oh yeah? Like what?"

We exited the Unicorn. The chill of the morning hit me hard. I'd be doomed once winter actually arrived.

"Get us there fast, and I'll tell you?" He showed me a toothy grin.

I pulled him in close, and with my right hand, slipped my fingers into my pocket. I pinched my coin, envisioning us in our dorm. And within a heartbeat, we were there.

Terrence didn't waste any time. He pressed his lips to mine roughly.

"Uh-uh," I said, leaning away. "Use your words. Tell me what you're thinking of doing to me."

He chuckled and nuzzled into my neck. "It's what I want you to do to me. Collin, I love you." He lifted his head and met my eyes. "I really do. So much."

My throat tightened and moisture filled my eyes. "I love you too. I always have. I always will."

His smile was bright and beautiful.

I lifted my hand and sank my fingers into his hair. The strands were soft, and the motion caused him to moan.

"Collin." He moved in close, our lips a breadth away from touching. "I want you to fuck me."

My whole body tingled from his words and his nearness.

"Would you be willing to do it?" he asked.

I nodded, brushing my lips against his. "Yes." I nudged him backward, toward my bed, but he didn't move.

"When we first did this," he said hesitantly, "you didn't want slow."

I remembered. He'd been considerate, wanting to ease me into it. I'd needed it quicker. "But you do?" I asked, reading his body language.

"With you, I want to feel everything."

My grip tightened at those words. *With you.* It brought to mind all the past lovers he'd had. I had no right to be jealous. He had no idea I was out there waiting for him. I had the advantage of foresight—or maybe prophecy.

"Every inch of you," he said. "Every piece of you you're willing to give."

I kissed him. "You already have all of me. I don't have anything else to give."

His smile was so sincere it hurt my chest.

I nudged again, and this time he went. We fell onto my bed, me on top. Terrence felt delicious below me, needy and already starting to moan as I rubbed against him. Remembering his request for slow, I shimmied down his body and began to lift his shirt. I laboriously pulled it up, paying attention to each inch of flesh as it was revealed. He squirmed but didn't insist I speed up.

Once his shirt was off, I made similar work with his pants and briefs. I ran my fingers over his skin, traced delicate circles on sensitive areas, kissed and nipped and sucked at anything within range.

"Collin," he said breathlessly. "I'm gonna do the spell."

I nodded, determined to learn it sometime soon. Once he'd finished the Latin words, I said, "Roll over."

He complied, then sank down onto his elbows.

Slow, I reminded myself. *Slow.*

The allure of him threatened to overwhelm me. Seeing him in this position, ass in the air, vulnerable and wanting, made my mind so fuzzy I could barely keep my thoughts focused.

I squeezed his cheeks, and he groaned his encouragement.

Slow.

Bending over, I licked up his crease.

He gasped, a piteous sound, and my cock twitched in longing.

I repeated the motion, easing my tongue along his skin, dipping as low as his balls and running up past his hole.

Another groan from Terrence, and I had to close my eyes to keep my mind on my task. Doing this slow was hard, but I wanted to give Terrence everything he desired.

Up and down I licked, stopping now and then to prod gently at his asshole. When he began to move his hips backward against my tongue, I knew he was ready for more.

I straightened and slipped my finger into my mouth, coating it with saliva. He was plenty wet from my attention, but I wanted to ease this as much as possible. Sure enough, my finger pressed into him without resistance.

"Collin," Terrence called with a sharp intake of breath. "God, yes!"

Terrence's inner heat blazed. He ran hot anyway, but this was like a bonfire, enticing and drawing me like a moth to a flame. As I worked my finger in and out, I wrapped my other hand around my own cock. It ached with need and felt harder than ever before.

I slipped a second finger inside him, and a low, contented moan came from his lips. My cock spasmed in my hand. He was alluring without even trying.

"More?" I asked.

He made a noise of assent.

My third finger joined the others. Terrence's cry was rapturous. His hips rocked back against me, bringing my digits in farther. I'd been on the receiving end enough to realize the thickness of three fingers applied pressure against his prostate.

"Collin," he purred.

"Are you ready?"

He nodded.

I pulled my fingers free, and he whimpered.

"Let me lie on my back," I said, shifting beside him. "I wanna see your face."

I got into position and Terrence went to my cock. He licked it a few times, then took me fully into his mouth. We worked up and down, coating me with his wetness. Satisfied, he straddled me.

He gripped my cock with both hands as he settled atop me. Guiding me gently, he situated my throbbing tip at his entrance. The heat against my sensitive skin was a million times better than feeling it with my fingers. If I wasn't careful, I'd come the minute he sank down. I bit the tip of my tongue to keep the building bliss at bay.

Terrence sat there for a few minutes, rubbing my cock along his asshole. His eyes closed, and his features turned angelic as he gently rubbed back and forth.

I bit my tongue harder.

He opened his eyes and must have seen the desperation on my face. He grinned. "Too slow?"

"No," I answered. "I want to give you what you want."

"What if we compromise with medium?"

I laughed, but the vibration of my body made Terrence bounce against me. I turned it into a groan.

In answer, Terrence shifted his hips backward and impaled himself on my cock. It was deliciously, sweetly hot, and oh so slow. I squeezed my eyes shut tight, wanting to embrace this sensation, to saturate my whole being with it. I needed this memory to be firmly etched in my consciousness.

"Terrence," I gasped as he sank lower. "It feels so good."

"You too," he said, and his voice had a sharp edge to it.

I glanced up at him and saw something close to pain on his face. "Terrence?"

"Shh. I like it, Collin. Let me do it this way."

I nodded and tried to relax my tight muscles. Maybe I hadn't prepped him well enough. Maybe we needed something better to act as lube. Maybe...

He finally got all of me in. He perched atop me, staying perfectly still. Red blotches colored his cheeks and a slight sheen of sweat covered his skin.

I worried that it was too much for him, that it was hurting, but he seemed to read my sudden fears.

"You feel so fucking good, Collin," he said. He gazed down at me, and his eyes were bright and sparkling. "I want to feel you inside me for as long as possible. I know this is torture for you, but...God! It's so good!"

"I want to please you, Terrence. Use me however you want."

The shimmer in his gaze darkened. "Use you?" His lips curled up slightly. "Maybe I will another time. For now, I better get to it before you have a breakdown."

I chuckled, but again, the movement made me super aware of my position inside Terrence's body.

He began to move. With his knees positioned to either side of my waist, he rocked his hips in a graceful arch. The compression on my cock shifted and increased with his movement. I moaned to let him know I liked it. He understood because he repeated it, arching his hips forward and to the left. Then forward and to the right. Then he dipped backward, and the new angle made my breath catch.

This time, when I bit my tongue, I broke the skin. I reached out to my magic, and my vision shifted. I grabbed air currents and used them to grip onto Terrence's erection. His eyes widened momentarily; then the pleasure within them spiked.

"You like it?" I asked, my voice breathless. "Can I keep going?"

He dipped his head, and I used the currents to stroke him. Touching him with magic was an entirely different feeling than using my hand, but not unpleasant. I liked the feel of his skin, but with the currents, I could make the touch featherlight. It was a mere brush of magic to flesh. Terrence gasped, but he didn't pick up his pace.

He continued his slow ride, up and down along my cock. The precision he used pushed me up to the edge of orgasm.

"Terrence," I said in warning.

His smile was sly, as if he liked seeing me in agony. But he sped up his bouncing, and I sped up my strokes along his cock.

"Please," I said, nearly a whine.

He laughed, full throated and delighted. Then he came, his dick spasming in my magical hold. I nearly cried as I let myself cross the boundary. I'd held myself balanced at the tipping point for so long, once I let go, I felt like I was falling. Plummeting through time and space. The air swirled around me.

Terrence surged forward, bringing his lips to mine. The physical sensation grounded me, bringing me back to my own body. For half a second, I'd been afraid I might teleport somewhere accidentally.

"Jesus," I said under his assaulting kisses. "Goddamn."

He chuckled again. "That good, huh?"

"Hell yes. That was beyond amazing, Terrence."

He shifted his hips and climbed off me. "I wasn't too mean?"

I shook my head. "We can play around with that some more. The buildup made the payoff vibrant. It was...extreme."

He nuzzled into me, but I knew there was a coy grin on his face. For taking a bottom position in this, he'd still been more of a top. I nearly laughed. One day, I'd be able to do the same to him.

We fell into peaceful silence.

"Don't fall asleep," he said, his voice reverberating against my neck. "We need to get ready for the gala."

"Just a half hour. We can do a power nap."

He moved in closer and, surprisingly, didn't argue.

Chapter Twenty-Eight

At quarter till five, Terrence and I met Mom outside the dorms. Her dress was chic, short, and frilly. A lot different from any other outfit I'd seen her wear. The pale-lilac color did match my tie.

"Look at you," she said, pulling on the bottom hem of my jacket. "So handsome."

"You look amazing, Mom. I bet Dad will be even more upset he can't see you in that dress."

She preened. "I'll take it home with me. Dad can still enjoy it."

I laughed, then offered my arm to her. On the other side, Terrence did the same. She linked her elbows with both of ours, and we started down the sidewalk.

"How was your time with Mrs. Fabron?" Terrence asked as we sauntered toward Regalia Hall.

"Wonderful! She is such a sweet woman. Did you know she serves in the French government? She's pretty important."

"I knew," Terrence said with a chuckle. "But Collin didn't."

Mom shrugged. "We're both new to this, so don't sweat it, hon."

"I'm not sweating it."

"Well, I don't want you to be nervous. Pierrette told me how anxious everyone is to talk to you. Your teleportation abilities have them all agog."

I looked over at my mom and raised my eyebrow. "Agog?"

She blushed, but didn't retract her statement. This place was having a weird effect on her. I guess I'd acted out of the ordinary since coming here, too, so I couldn't blame her.

At the entrance to the hall, a large crowd of people lined both sides of the sidewalk. Some I recognized as business students, who were not invited to this event. They held cameras and talked excitedly to each other. Standing closer to the door was a journalist and cameraman. They filmed the guests as they entered, even stopped one or two as they walked by.

"This wouldn't be covered on regular news, would it?" I asked as we approached the line of people waiting to get inside.

"Nah, but there are channels that cater to practitioners. And special networks unavailable to regular people."

Mom gasped softly. "That's so cool! I'll have to make sure your dad and I get it at home."

I laughed. Had I really been worried she'd pull me from the program? She was ready to join the community faster than I was.

At the door, two people stood as guards—their sharp, dark suits looking very much like Mrs. Fabron's security detail. I gave my name and Terrence's, as my plus one. Mom said hers and added that she was invited by Helmer himself. The woman who stood on the right waved us through almost immediately. As we passed the threshold, a tingle went down my spine.

Terrence caught my shiver and said, "Wards. There'll be a million in place tonight. Helmer couldn't live with a scandal happening on his watch."

I took his hand in mine and gave a squeeze. "Let's enjoy ourselves tonight, okay?"

He grinned. "I know I will. You might not."

"Why?"

"When people find out who you are—" He cut off as a large man approached us.

"Collin Frey?" He stuck out his hand to me. His accent had a soft Southern drawl. "A pleasure. I'm Marcus O'Roark."

He looked like he wanted me to recognize his name, so I said, "Oh, yes, of course. Nice to meet you."

He smiled easily.

Terrence put a hand to my shoulder. "I'll go get us some drinks."

I nodded, but O'Roark was already starting up the conversation.

"When Patrick informed us of your special, we were all pleasantly surprised. Naturally, though, you understand that such a talent could make people nervous."

"Nervous? How?"

He laughed as if I said a joke. "You've got the full backing of the British government already, but we'll make sure things are dealt with when you get home. We're not suggesting you wear a tracker—"

"A tracker?" I broke in. "Like a GPS ankle monitor?"

He laughed again and even slapped my back. "Oh, nothing like that. Unless you make some poor choices. But we're not anticipating that."

I straightened my jacket to cover up my shiver. Was he threatening me? Warning me, at the least?

"I don't have plans to do anything illegal, Mr. O'Roark."

"Collin's a good boy," Mom added, to my horror. "But is it really possible to track someone with magic?"

"Yes, Mrs. Frey. But as I said, we aren't considering that avenue." An unspoken *yet* hung to the end of his sentence.

"Omar told me that four other people have a teleport special. Do you keep tabs on them?"

"Only one is an American," O'Roark said. "And that's between him and the government."

I grimaced. Of course this obviously government official wouldn't give me any information.

O'Roark noticed my displeased face and patted my back again. "You see the potential threat with such a unique and rare special? Certain precautions need to be taken to ensure magical powers are not misused."

"I understand that, Mr. O'Roark. If someone could teleport easily, they could go into banks, or even into the White House." He started to nod, but I pressed on. "However, Omar said he's taken courses on teleporting. That means it's possible for others to do it as well. Why do I need to be singled out if many others can duplicate what I do?"

He blinked at me a few times, and I realized I was showing my ignorance again.

"Collin, specials are something entirely different from normal magic. Yes, Lilly James, the instructor you're thinking of, can assist others in teleportation. However, with specials, the magic goes down deep." He chuckled softly. "This is something you learn in Theory class, but I know your circumstances are a bit unorthodox. The difference between magic and a special is complex. Even if someone learns to teleport, they will never have your precision, or your stamina, or your ability to go long distances."

He paused there, tilting his head slightly. "How far have you managed to go so far?"

I thought of lying but knew it would not aid me in anyway. "A couple hundred miles."

He shook his head. "The most skilled teleporter couldn't do that, even if they practiced every day. You see?"

"But what about a normal special? I mean, Omar's is transformation. Does it also lack the same kind of limitations?"

"Yes, a special is something so powerful that the results of your magic are astronomical in scale."

"The vortexes?" I guessed. "Is that a theory that it came from someone's special?"

He laughed. "You have Elai Jenkins this year? He's a big supporter of that belief, though we have no proof. But the reasoning behind it is sound. A special is beyond powerful."

I nodded slowly. "Yes, I can see your concern."

"Thank you for your understanding. Well, I've taken up enough of your evening. We'll be in touch soon."

Then, he walked off into the crowd.

"Who was that?" Mom asked.

I glanced around the room, looking for Terrence. He'd know for sure. But I didn't see him. Maybe the line for drinks was long, considering everyone who was here. I spotted Omar with Laura, and I waved to them.

"I'm not sure, Mom, but I bet Omar can tell us."

The two joined us. Omar was dressed in a sleek and shiny gray tuxedo. Laura wore a dress in a complementing shade of blue. Her hair was done up in an elaborate braid, leaving her face completely open. I wasn't shocked to see a long scar along the outside of her left eye, but I was surprised.

"Hello," my mom greeted them happily. She threw her arms around both of them. "Are you enjoying yourselves?"

"Yes, Mrs. Frey," Laura answered. "It's so exciting. Special events like this in Canada are always well attended, of course. But being so close to so many countries really opens the playing field. I mean, I saw Kurt Schmidt, the *Vizekanzler* of Germany." At our confused looks, she added, "He's a sort of vice chancellor. And there's Edvige Romano; she's the Italian Minister of Justice."

"Do you know who that guy is?" I pointed to O'Roark standing next to an older American student. "Marcus O'Roark?"

Omar nodded. "He's the Secretary of Homeland Security. I'm surprised you didn't recognize him."

I shrugged, kind of embarrassed at my lack of knowledge. "I never really paid attention to politics. But him being in charge of homeland security makes sense. He just gave me a warning about my special."

"That's weird," Laura said. "How do they even know you'll decide to go back home?"

My mom gaped at her. "Of course he will."

Laura smiled. "But what if he likes it here and wants to stay? Or if he wants to teach at a foreign academy? There are so many other avenues available. Seems odd that they'd warn you off before you've even made any decisions."

"That's the American way," Omar said. "Assess things before they turn into threats."

I never considered not going home, but it was an option. Not an appealing one, at the moment, but it was there.

"Even if I would choose that, Laura, I'd still go home to visit. They know my family lives there, so I'd have to show up sooner or later."

"Good point," she said. "Best to deal with you now, get the official warnings in place."

I glanced around the room again, looking for Terrence. Maybe he'd found a celebrity and had to introduce himself. I grinned. He'd enjoy this just as much as my mom.

I was about to excuse myself from Mom and my friends, but then a young woman approached. Omar and Laura offered quick bows of their heads, so I did too. She introduced herself as Leslie Fairchild, a local practitioner, but I could tell there was more from Omar's and Laura's reactions. She chatted with me, inquiring about my special and dropped hints about meeting up for dinner. I answered that dinner would be lovely, if I could bring my boyfriend along. She agreed without hesitation, but a lot of the sparkle left her eyes after that.

She eventually left, but another replaced her. Then another, and another, and another. I lost track of Mom, Omar, and Laura. I was constantly surrounded by strangers, all of them asking after my special, wanting to know what I planned after graduation and asking if I'd be interested in meeting them again.

I worked Terrence into every conversation, but that didn't deter some of them.

I was polite and courteous, but I wanted to get away from them. To find Terrence and my friends. But every time I turned around, another person was waiting to speak to me.

A sudden tug on my sleeve made me glance to my left. I'd expected Terrence, smiling and happy to be in the spotlight with me. But it was Omar.

"I need to speak to you," he said urgently.

My stomach dropped, and my heartbeat doubled in pace. "Excuse us," I said to the people around us, and then I allowed him to pull me into a secluded corner. "What's wrong?"

"I just found out right now. Terrence was kicked out of the party."

"What!" He hushed me, and I lowered my voice. "What happened?"

"Apparently, he ran into his uncle, who was surprised to see him. They got into an argument, and Terrence tried to perform magic. But his uncle beat him to it. Flung him across the room. Then Terrence was escorted out."

"Shit! When did this happen?"

"Almost as soon as you got here."

"That was nearly an hour ago! Fuck! I need to go."

"Are you sure?"

"Yes! He'll be pissed and hurt and..." Desperate? Desperate enough to complete the summoning spell? If he still thought himself weak compared to his family, then yes. "But he promised me we'd do it together," I muttered.

"Do what?" Omar asked.

I shook my head. No time to explain, so I used our secret code. "Red lightning. I need to go to our dorm."

"I'll go with you."

I looked at Omar, and my heart ached with affection. He was an amazing friend. "You sure?"

"Yes."

We ran toward the door. Luckily, Mom didn't see us. I spied her talking with Mrs. Fabron by the buffet table. She'd have wanted to come too, and I wouldn't allow that. I knew that Terrence was summoning a demon, and I couldn't put her in danger.

Outside, the sun was dipping low on the horizon. Many of the gathered people looked our way as we hurried by. But we didn't hold their interest for long. None yelled at us or followed after.

We made it to the dorm in record time. I bounded up the stairs, Omar's long legs easily keeping up with my panic-fueled haste. I threw open the door to our room, my coin held tightly in my fingers, ready to send out currents or something. But it was empty.

Just to be safe, I inspected the bathroom. He wasn't in there.

"Collin, there's a note on your bed."

I left the bathroom and went to Omar. He had a sealed envelope in his hands. I took it, swallowing past a lump in my throat. I ripped off the top and pulled out a handwritten letter. I read quickly, then went back to the top and read it again.

> *Collin,*
>
> *Sorry to lie to you, but this is something I need to do for me. I can't stand being like this any longer. I won't let them treat me this way. I remember my promise about your mom, so this is the only way I can do it. I'm going down by the water in Newhaven. I'll be far enough away that no one there will be hurt if it doesn't go well.*
>
> *I love you.*
>
> *Terrence*

"Newhaven. Where's Newhaven?" I knew I'd heard it before, but my mind couldn't function. Fear and betrayal and hurt and anger all piled atop one another. Fear for him attempting this alone. Betrayal because I knew he needed me there, and he knew it too. Hurt that his pride suffered so much, and anger at his family for making him feel this way.

"It's a city to the east."

I remembered now. "A lighthouse, right? Didn't Tabitha go there?"

Omar nodded. "What are you going to do?"

"I need to be there. This is it. The moment I have to send him back. I need to get to him!"

"Can you wait for us? I'll call the others. We're all willing to help."

"No, I don't want you guys to get hurt."

Omar gripped my shoulder. "You feel betrayed because he left without you. We'll feel the same if you go without us."

I met his gaze and saw the sincerity in his words. I nodded. "Okay, but we need to go fast."

"I'll call Laura, and she'll get the others. I'll have them meet us outside."

Chapter Twenty-Nine

"All right, so spill," Sammuel said as he and Laura and Tabitha joined us. "What's the urgency? I'll have you know, I had Leslie Fairchild hanging on my every word."

"Terrence is in trouble," I answered. "He's summoning a demon, but it's not going to go well."

Tabitha tilted her head. "How do you know?"

"I... I met him six years ago. He came from my future to his past and told me."

Sammuel laughed. "Time travel isn't possible, Collin."

"I don't have time to convince you," I snapped. "If you're here to help, then help. If not, go back to the party."

Slowly, Sammuel nodded. "I'll help."

I turned to Tabitha. "I need to get to that lighthouse in Newhaven. You have pictures or something I can see?"

"Yes, I've got some on my phone." She pushed a quick series of buttons and then turned the phone to me.

I accepted it and swiped through the few she had. Nodding, I handed it back. "We're going to have to teleport. Do you trust me?"

"I do," Omar said immediately.

"Me too," Tabitha said.

Laura nibbled her lip, and Sammuel couldn't quite meet my eyes.

"Take one of the cars," I told them. "Meet us there."

Laura shook her head. "No, we need to go with you now. Come on, Sammuel. This has to be done."

A surge of gratitude filled me, and I reached out to take Omar's hand. We formed a line but stood close to one another.

Suddenly, a voice called out, "What are you doing?"

I jumped and dropped Omar's hand and my coin. The metal fell to the cement with a *clink*, and rolled a few feet away. Professor Jenkins was walking up to us, out of the staff dorm, in normal jeans and a shirt.

"Why aren't you at the gala, professor?" Tabitha asked.

He shrugged. "I don't like crowds. Why aren't you five there?"

"Just taking a breather," Omar said.

"We don't have time for this," I hissed. I glared at our professor. "Terrence is attempting harmful magic, and we need to go help him. Now, run along and tattle to his father."

Jenkins glanced at my chin. "Tattle? I won't tattle. Is this the time-travel thing you've been worried about?" At my perplexed look, he chuckled. "You think we teachers don't converse with one another? Mirah told me about the book you checked out. And combined with your questions in class, it's obvious it's on your mind for a reason."

With no reason to keep it secret, I dropped all pretenses. "Yes, Professor. I'm going to send Terrence back in time. But we need to go now!"

"If you have no objections, I'll join you. I'm curious to see if it's even possible. You seem so sure, which suggests something from your past convinced you it is."

"You can come, just hurry."

I picked up my coin; then we joined hands again, Jenkins grasping onto Sammuel's. I held the coin in my fingers, worry and fear fueling my magic. *Terrence. Please let us not be too late.*

I pinched the coin.

The smell of salt and water hit me, as did a strong gale of sea wind. I glanced around in the dying sunlight. We were on a large, but narrow, concrete pier that extended several hundred feet into the English Channel. Out toward the water, a lighthouse stood at the center of a rounded area. I couldn't see Terrence, but I knew he was that direction.

I let go of Omar's hand, and I darted down the pier. It didn't occur to me that my classmates were unused to the effects of teleporting. I'd practiced almost every day, and my mind and body accepted the fact I was in a new location easily. But before I'd gone a few feet, I heard their footsteps behind me. Or maybe it was only Jenkins.

"Terrence," I called as I rounded the lighthouse. "Terrence!"

I skidded to a halt. He was there, in the jeans and gray shirt I remembered. He stood on the edge of the low wall, his focus out on the water. At my desperate cry, he turned to me.

"Collin?" He jumped down off the ledge and came to me. "What are you doing here?"

"You promised you wouldn't do this without me. I need to be here!"

"This has nothing to do with you. I need to prove that I can do it."

"Your worth doesn't come from your magical abilities."

His eyes narrowed. "It does in my family. You've seen them. I want to belong. I want to be my father's son again."

I wrapped my arms around him. "This won't do it. Nothing will convince him."

"I have to try. I won't give up."

The others came around the lighthouse and stopped. Terrence glared at them.

"What are they doing here?"

"I brought them to help."

"I don't need help," he spat. "All this time, I thought you understood. I was willing to let you stand by my side when I came into my power. But you doubt just as much as my family." He pulled away from me.

I grasped for him, catching his shirt in my fist. "I don't doubt. I know you can do this. I believe in you, now more than ever. I want to stand at your side, to be with you always. Please, Terrence. Please."

He only hesitated a second before taking my hand in his. "Let's do this."

I joined him up on the ledge. Below us, the water churned a frothy white along the jagged rocks that lined the pier's base. Bits of spray caught the wind and dampened my face and hands. My fingers tightened on Terrence's, and he squeezed back.

"Al'venarta," Terrence intoned. "*Ostende tuam veritatem reducunt...*"

Out in the water a swirl of gray vapors began to spin. Small at first, but as Terrence continued his words, it grew larger. Soon, long tendrils shot out of it like fingers, swirling around its center faster and faster.

"*Et vocavi te in hoc mundo!*" Terrence shouted.

A shockwave of energy flew from him. My grip on his hand kept me from flying back from the force, but my classmates weren't so lucky. They all fell to the ground. Only Jenkins stayed on his feet, his coin pinched in his fingers. He'd created a force field around himself, but it dissipated when the magical flare passed.

Jenkins helped Omar and the others to stand; then they approached me and Terrence at the ledge.

The swirling vortex was even larger now. Terrence turned toward me, and I met his gaze. His blue eyes glowed with an unearthly lust. He wanted this power more than anything.

"It's finally happening," he said, his voice trembling with desire. "We're so close."

"How do you mean to bind them?" Jenkins asked.

Terrence shot Jenkins a glower. "I've studied this since I was seven. I know what to do."

"But this is Al'venarta. You've encountered them before."

Terrence's angry features softened. "Yeah? So?"

"And, if I'm not mistaken, this creature gave you that scar."

Slowly, Terrence nodded.

Jenkins continued as if he were lecturing in class. "That means Al'venarta has access to your blood."

Terrence paled. "But that shouldn't affect anything now. It was ages ago."

"You may be more correct than you think. We've no idea how their dimension is, compared to ours. Ages, you say. And ages it may be. For Al'venarta it could have happened a century ago. A millennia."

"And it could have happened ten days ago. Your speculations are pointless."

Jenkins shrugged, then glanced out at the water. Among the swirling wisps of the vortex, a shape was beginning to form. "We'll need a plan if it doesn't go as you wish."

"I'll handle it, Jenkins."

A sense of foreboding filled me. I knew this didn't go well or else Terrence wouldn't have been so broken when we met before. I hoped Jenkins was dwelling on what to do, but I'd be damned before I mentioned it. I didn't want Terrence to think my faith in him wavered.

The demon's outline became more substantial. And larger.

Terrence cleared his throat. "They look a bit bigger than I remembered."

When the demon was clear enough to make out their features, I made a noise of disgust. Their skin was a bright red and gleaming like wet blood. All along their body were random patches of black scales that resembled armor. Their arms—there were four of them—sprouted from their side and were tipped in single, sharp claws. Their legs ended in cleft hooves. And their head...

I shivered and swallowed to keep bile from rising up my throat.

The demon's head was a mass of horns, covering every inch of their skin above their eyes. Some curled, some extended straight out, and others looked to be broken, ending in jagged edges. Their mouth was more of a beak with black lips that came to points. And their eyes—the deep red I remembered seeing only once before—glared with an uncontainable rage.

The creature opened their beak and shrieked, the sound cutting across the water like something physical. All around us, the world seemed to still at their cry. Then, they solidified completely and plummeted into the water of the channel.

A desperate mewl came from their mouth—obviously pain induced.

"The water will hold them," Terrence said. "It'll weaken Al'venarta's innate fire magic."

"Do it now," I said, wanting to cover my ears to keep their horrifying sounds out. The sight would haunt my dreams; I didn't need audible triggers to go with it. "Use my coin. Quickly!"

Terrence dropped my hand but didn't pull my coin from his pocket. Instead, he made a sign over his chest, his pointer fingers steepled and thumbs tucked inside. "I don't need your coin yet," he said. Then he began to chant words in Latin. His fingers kept shifting, interlocking and then releasing, quicker than my eyes could follow.

Al'venarta's howls of misery gained intensity, and then a beam of white-hot light shot out from Terrence's body and zoomed toward the demon. Even from this distance, I could see the beam connected them heart to heart.

For half a second, I breathed in relief, seeing Terrence had it all under control. Then the demon's noises turned into a deep rumble. Laughter. A shiver ran over my whole body from the sound.

"Terrence—" I began, but then, the light connecting him to Al'venarta shifted to a dark red.

Terrence flew backward. His body hit the side of the lighthouse, then crumpled to the ground.

I jumped off the ledge and raced to him.

"Stop!" Jenkins yelled, and my steps froze. Not on my own account; my professor blocked me with a wall of solid air. "Don't touch him, Collin."

"Why not?" I demanded. "I need to save him!"

The wall disappeared, and Jenkins stood beside me, gazing down at Terrence's form. He was unconscious, eyes closed, chest rising and falling at an alarming rate.

"It's the blood. Can't you see? Al'venarta's had all this time to prepare. Their magic is far superior to Terrence's."

"I know."

He glanced at me, almost surprised enough to meet my gaze. "You know?"

"Yes, I knew this wouldn't work. I knew he'd fail."

Jenkins's scoff had the hint of disbelief. "And you let him try it anyway?"

"He wouldn't have listened no matter what I said. He had to do this. I knew it had to happen."

"Time travel?"

"I'll explain later. For now, we need to send him away before Al'venarta comes any closer."

Jenkins glanced over his shoulder. "You better hurry. They're on their way."

I looked, too, and was shocked to see the large creature—and getting larger as they approached—moving with a speed unfathomable to my mind. Something that big couldn't go that fast. It broke the laws of physics!

Idiot. And I teleport my entire body from one location to another.

"Any tips, Professor?"

"The magic you're about to attempt is very powerful. Summon an equally powerful memory, something to help you focus."

I nodded.

"And," he added hesitantly, "remember what I said about fluids. If you two have...uh...been intimate, use that to your advantage."

I pinched my coin and my eyes adjusted to the ether. Terrence's body still glowed red, but it was pale now and growing fainter. Al'venarta's aura was dark as midnight and pulled in any light from around them.

Focus, I scolded myself. *You can do this.*

With my blood's magic singing in my veins, I could pinpoint all of my essences inside Terrence. Saliva from our kisses. Skin cells from holding hands. Even my semen from earlier today. All of these held traces of my magic. Of me. To add a bit more, I bit my lip and dipped my finger into the blood that welled. I coated it along Terrence's lips and it glistened in the fading light.

"I love you," I told him softly. "I remember your promise, and you'd better too."

I cemented the image of Terrence in the snow, made my mind accept it as fact, because I knew it was.

Another pinch of my coin, and he vanished.

The light connecting him to Al'venarta evaporated on the spot. The demon let out a horrible scream of fury.

"What do we do now, Professor?"

Jenkins grinned. "I thought you'd never ask."

Chapter Thirty

"Omar," Jenkins said, "I need you to transform into an imitation of Terrence. The demon will realize eventually, since the heartbeam won't connect you, but they should be disoriented enough to be tricked momentarily."

"Sure, Professor," Omar agreed immediately. He pinched his coin, and suddenly a life-size copy of Terrence was standing beside me—where Omar had just been. I looked into the Omar's eyes and was surprised to see a shimmer of Terrence's soul lurking deep within. If I didn't know better, I would have accepted Omar as my boyfriend.

"Laura," Jenkins said. "Music, please."

I blinked in surprise, wondering how that would help anything.

Laura didn't hesitate. She pinched her coin, and suddenly a flute was in her hands. She placed it up to her lips and blew a single note. It resounded through the air, piercing the night with its pure, clear sound.

Al'venarta stilled.

"Tabitha, Sammuel, we need help on the water. Tabitha, can you get Sammuel close to the demon? The two of you should be able to wrap them in water and freeze them in place."

"Yes, Professor," Tabitha said. Then the two of them jumped off the edge of the pier.

"Collin."

I turned to face him. Jesus, the man *did* have a plan. I felt worthless; I'd been willing to let Al'venarta wreak havoc on the world, only concerned about mine and Terrence's future. People could have gotten hurt, or killed, without Jenkins here to help us.

"Yes, Professor?"

"I need you to teleport me to Al'venarta's shoulder. We can take some of their blood and send them back to their own realm."

I nodded, not trusting my words. I was as culpable as Terrence. Letting him make this mistake put guilt on my head as well.

We watched as Tabitha and Sammuel zoomed toward the towering demon on a circle of frozen water. Laura's musical note still held Al'venarta transfixed, but their eyes were starting to refocus.

"Wait till they have Al'venarta trapped," Jenkins said, but he grabbed my hand in preparation.

Just as the demon began to wake, Tabitha and Sammuel were in position. Tabitha motioned threads of water to wind their way along the demon's arms, legs, and chest. Once they held the creature, Sammuel froze them, turning them into a solid binding.

"Now!" Jenkins said.

I pinched my coin, and we were suddenly atop the demon's shoulder. Al'venarta roared their displeasure at being held, but for the moment, Tabitha and Sammuel had it caught.

Jenkins dropped to his knees and pulled a small switchblade from his pocket. He plunged the knife into the demon's skin, and droplets of green blood trickled out. After scooping some into a glass vial, also retrieved from his pocket, Jenkins stood and grabbed my hand again.

"Time for us to go," he said.

With a pinch of my coin, we were back on the pier.

"Back away!" Jenkins called to Tabitha and Sammuel. He didn't wait to see if they obeyed his order. He poured the green blood on the cement ground. Poking his finger into the blood, he smeared it across his other hand. Then, with his blade, he sliced his palm so his blood and the demon's blood mingled. A sizzling sound emitted from the connection, and the scent of burning rubber assaulted my nose.

"Al'venarta," Jenkins intoned. "*Ad a quo factum est. Iam vos mundi sunt, hoc interdictum.*"

The creature shrieked again, and another swirling vortex opened above their head. The chains of ice shattered as Al'venarta was pulled upward and into the abyss. As they disappeared, they lashed out with arms and legs, but nothing was close enough for them to reach. They were swallowed by the tendrils and were gone.

I sagged against the side of the lighthouse, finally allowing my limbs to give up. My whole body shook with adrenaline now that it was over. Omar and Laura were by my side, and Tabitha and Sammuel appeared a moment later.

"Everyone okay?" Jenkins asked. "No injuries?"

We all shook our heads.

"Now, where is Terrence?" he asked, meeting my eyes. I was startled to see that they were a deep brown, almost black. "I want answers."

I launched into the story, leaving nothing out. Omar had heard it before, but the others gasped as I detailed my coin, Terrence's red eyes, his ominous words, and how he had vanished right in front of me.

"I knew he had to do it," I tried to explain. "The way he was wounded and so broken; I knew I wanted to help him, Professor. I love him, and I only wanted him to come back to me."

I realized I was sobbing, and I hid my face in my hands.

"I don't know if he ever comes back."

Someone pulled at me, and I went willingly. Omar held me tight, but then Laura put her arm over my shoulder. Tabitha slipped her hand around my waist. Sammuel patted my hair. Under their support, I broke down further. I wept uncontrollably, holding nothing back. I'd been so stupid, but I knew, given the chance, I'd do it all over again.

"We need to get you back to school," Jenkins said. "All of you. We dealt with Al'venarta quickly enough, but traces of their magic will linger. We can't hide what happened."

"My fault," I said with a sniffle. "I'm sorry I got all of you involved. I'll let Helmer and all the others know it was my fault. He told me not to let Terrence access my magical items, and I did. It's only right that I be expelled."

Jenkins nodded, but Omar said, "We'll have to see. Don't worry about it until you know that's what's going to happen."

"Are you strong enough to get us back?" Jenkins asked. "Or should I call for a car?"

I got to my feet, wobbling only slightly. "I can do it."

We took ahold of each other's hands, and just as I was about to pinch my coin, a grunt sounded from the other side of the lighthouse. My heart leapt into my throat. I loosened my grip on Omar and ran around the lighthouse.

Terrence lay on the ground, his gray shirt soaked with sweat. He raised his head and locked scarlet eyes with mine. The shame and self-loathing there nearly broke my heart. He lowered his head, tears already dripping down his cheeks.

"It was me," he whispered. "I didn't really believe you. But it was true."

I dropped to my knees beside him and embraced him. He tried to pull away, but I held tight.

"I love you," I said immediately. "I've loved you all this time."

"How can you?" he wailed softly. "After all I've done? After everything that's happened? I don't deserve your love. You should have let Al'venarta kill me."

"Hush," I said, running my fingers through his damp hair. "Don't say anything else. We'll get it sorted out, okay? No one was hurt. There's no damage done. It's not as bad as you fear."

He raised his eyes to me, and my heart skipped a beat. This was the Terrence I'd fallen in love with. Except it was more now. I'd seen him evolve, let down his walls slowly. Overcome some of his inner struggles. And now, the feelings inside me were so large they hurt. I didn't think it was possible for me to love him so much. And in ten years, twenty, thirty, I knew my love would continue to grow.

I helped him get to his feet.

"The stress of time travel must be taking their toll," Jenkins said. He placed a hand to Terrence's forehead. "He's burning up."

"No," I said. "That's from his connection to the demon. I don't think we can fix it." I looked at Terrence. "We need to get you to Dr. Vivaan. Can you handle teleporting once more?"

He nodded. "That was the easiest part, you know. I've never been good at it, even with your help the past few weeks. But knowing I promised you, I was able to do it so easily. I did little jumps at first. A few days. A few weeks. I worked up to a few months, then a few years. In all, I passed through seven years, nine months, and twenty-two days. That's two thousand eight hundred and fifty-three days, Collin. Almost seventy thousand hours. Over four million minutes. And I teleported through them all because I knew you waited here for me."

I kissed him there in front of everyone. We both had tears on our faces, adding a saltiness to the heat and spice of his mouth. It was comfort and stability and so nice after a hard trial.

"We'll make it through," I said. "You and me, together."

"Yes," he whispered against my lips. "Together."

I took his hand, and he took Jenkins's, who took Omar's. We made a link and then pressed our bodies close. I pinched my coin, and we vanished.

Chapter Thirty-One

We landed outside the dorms, almost at the exact location we'd left from. A few people walked around, but there was no cry of panic or hysteria. The people here didn't know yet that a demon had been summoned thirty miles away. There was no doubt in my mind they'd know eventually.

I dropped my shoulder and put it under Terrence, helping him to stay upright.

"I'll go get Dr. Vivaan," Sammuel said and took off at a run.

"Let's get him to his bed," Jenkins suggested.

Omar got on Terrence's other side and supported his weight.

Laura ran ahead and opened the door to the dorm. It was slow going, getting up the stairs, but I didn't want to do any more teleporting. At our room, Tabitha held the door as Omar and I dragged Terrence in. I started for his bed, but he stopped us.

"That one." He pointed to my bed.

Omar and I got Terrence lying down, and his eyes fluttered shut.

"He'll be all right," Jenkins said, as if reading my thoughts. He went to sit on the opposite bed, and Tabitha and Laura joined him. "He's just exhausted. Remember, teleportation isn't his special, but he went through seven years in less than a day. Probably fifteen hours, if I had to make an estimate. His body and mind need to catch up."

I nodded and sat next to Terrence on my bed. I picked up his hand and held it in my own.

"What will they do to us?"

"I don't know."

Omar was standing in the doorway, his phone in his hands. "Don't worry about it now," he repeated. He looked up at me and winked.

It was only a few moments before Dr. Vivaan was rushing into the room, followed by Sammuel, my mom, and Dean Helmer. Helmer's face was pale, and he looked to have aged ten years. When his gaze fell on Terrence, his hands covered his mouth.

"Is he...?"

Vivaan's fingers were already on Terrence's head, with her coin held in her other hand. "He's alive," she said, eyes shut. "Let me concentrate."

The room fell into silence. Mom walked to me and hugged me tightly. Helmer seemed paralyzed and stayed in the doorway.

Suddenly, Terrence's eyes fluttered open, and he groaned softly.

I smiled down at him, willing myself not to cry. "Terrence? How are you feeling?"

"Like shit," he answered, his voice rough and still weak. He glanced around the room, and when his gaze met everyone's, most unconsciously flinched from the blood-red hue. But not Helmer. It was Terrence who twitched and dropped his eyes when they looked at each other from across the room.

"Terrence," Helmer said, sounding strangled.

"Maybe we should give them some privacy," I suggested and started to get to my feet.

Terence pulled on my hand. "No. I'm tired of running from this. Even with everything that happened tonight, that's still the same. Dad, I really fucking hate you."

"I know," Helmer said, and tears began to leak from his eyes. "It was my aim, dear boy. I wanted you to hate me, to stay away from this school. To stay away from magic. I didn't want to be a constant reminder to what you did, so I stayed away."

Terrence blinked rapidly, and his grip on my hand increased. "What are you saying? That you pushed me away? On purpose?"

"Your mother and I decided it was the best course of action. Obviously we didn't think it through well enough. Instead of forgetting about me and magic, you fixated on it. The wound inside you grew and festered. All of it my fault for not being a better father."

"I thought you didn't care... I thought you hated me for bringing shame on the family."

"Of course I care. And you've never once shamed me. I'm proud to be your father, Terrence, even if I'm an old fool who's made more mistakes than I can count."

Terrence was crying again. I stood from the bed and motioned Helmer forward. He came, but slowly, as if a sudden move would make Terrence bolt.

"There's still time," I said. "We can fix things."

Helmer nodded and looked at me gratefully. Then he got to his knees beside Terrence and took his son into his arms.

My mom draped a hand over my shoulder. "You did good, kiddo," she whispered.

I shook my head. She had no idea what I'd done tonight. How careless I'd been. How reckless and self-centered. I didn't deserve praise.

We gave Terrence and Helmer a few minutes alone—or as alone as they could be with eight other people in the room. The rest of us gathered at the foot of Terrence's bed, and we kept our voices low.

"There's no lasting damage," Dr. Vivaan said. "A few days of rest and he'll be all better." She eyed the rest of us. "You better let me check all of you, as well."

I waved away her seeking hands. "I'm fine." The others repeated similar statements.

"Are you going to tell me what happened?"

"I'm curious about that myself," Helmer said, drawing our attention. He sat next to Terrence, and they both seemed calmer.

"I summoned Al'venarta," Terrence said. "And luckily, my boyfriend had enough sense to bring reinforcements to send them back. I owe you my life, Collin. And so do the people of Newhaven. It could have been catastrophic if Al'venarta made it ashore."

"No," I began, but Omar nudged me in the ribs.

"We all hand a hand in it, sir," Omar told Helmer. "We all knew bits and pieces of what Terrence planned, but we never tried to stop him. If he's guilty, we all are."

Surprisingly, my classmates all nodded.

I gasped. Had they been the spies Helmer sent to gather information on me and Terrence? Had Omar? If so, he'd been a lousy agent. I nearly laughed at the thought. It didn't matter. I knew I'd be expelled, and it was the best outcome. I wasn't to be trusted with magic.

Suddenly, Lisbeth was standing at our door. Behind her, a dozen other faces peered in. "We're guilty too," she said. "We all had chances to corner Collin and beat the truth out of him, but we didn't. If you expel him, you'll have to kick us all out."

There was a loud chorus of agreement outside the room. Just how many of the students had assembled?

"I don't want to stay in the program," I said. Everyone's eyes whipped to me, even Terrence's. I met his gaze. "I was a temptation to you. If you can't use magic, I won't use it either. If I had to choose between the two, you're the one I want. Now and always."

He smiled, and it softened the harsh edges in his eyes. At least the two of us would be okay, whatever happened. Then he said, "I don't want you to give it up for me, Collin. You have real skill, and you can go far once you're trained. And you won't be a temptation. I don't want to use magic anymore. When Al'venarta took hold of me..." he trailed off, and a tremor shook through his body. "It's like getting better from an illness. You don't want to be near what made you sick in the first place."

"But—" I began, but Terrence cut me off.

"If the school doesn't expel me, I'd like to finish my business degree."

Tabitha spoke again. "If Terrence is expelled, we're all leaving too."

He shot her a surprised look, and she smiled softly.

Helmer got to his feet, shaking his head. "It's not that simple."

"Why not?" Jenkins asked. "I feel everyone involved learned a valuable life lesson. No harm was done, aside from a few of us suffering from nightmares from here on out. The consequences we paid already more than make up for any wrongdoings we've committed."

Helmer hesitated, then nodded. "Perhaps you're right. This could have been worse, but it wasn't. We'll have to explain to Francis what happened, but there's no reason for it to become public knowledge. There's a spin that can work for us." He patted Terrence's shoulder. "I suggest we let everyone have some rest. We'll discuss this more tomorrow. Yes," he said, holding up his hands to forestall the sudden voices of the gathered students. "I'm well aware of your demands. We won't do anything drastic. I promise."

Everyone began to file out of the room, but I stopped my classmates and Jenkins. "Thank you," I said. "If it hadn't been for you, this could have had a very different outcome."

"That's what friends are for," Omar said. "You two get some sleep. We'll see you tomorrow."

Sammuel threw an arm over Jenkins's shoulder. "Who knew you were so cool, Professor? How old are you again?"

"E-eighteen," Jenkins answered.

"We might just have to induct you into the group." He shot me a grin. "No need to worry, Collin. Jenkins *is* old enough." Then he laughed and pulled the professor out of the room.

Tabitha and Laura gave me quick hugs, and Terrence, too, before they left.

Omar was last, and I nearly started crying again as he wrapped his arms around me.

"Thank you," I repeated. "Through all of this, you've been my rock."

"Don't worry," he said with a chuckle. "Next year, I get to be the one who comes up with the crazy scheme."

"Deal."

When he left, it was only my mom staring at me like I was some strange creature.

"You've grown so much, kiddo," she said. "Even in the past few hours. I wish your dad was here to see this. He'd be as proud of you as I am."

"You shouldn't be," I insisted. "I fucked up big-time."

"That doesn't change how a parent feels love, or pride, for their children. You made a mistake, but you faced the consequences." She gave me a quick peck on my cheek. "You too, Terrence. I'm proud of you."

His eyes welled up with tears. "Thank you, Diane."

She smiled and kissed his forehead. "Now, you two do need some rest. I'll see you in the morning."

She left and when the door shut behind her, I hurried to the bed. I didn't bother taking off my clothes, just climbed under the covers and snuggled in close to Terrence's warmth.

"I'm sorry," Terrence said.

"I'm sorry too. I think I manipulated you just as much, if not more, than you did to me. But, can we promise not to do it again?"

He chuckled softly, causing his body to vibrate against mine. "Promise."

We fell asleep, and though I knew there would be nightmares about this night, in that moment all was at peace for the two of us.

About the Author

Foster Bridget Cassidy is a rare, native Phoenician who enjoys hot desert air and likes to wear jackets in summer. She has wanted to be a fiction writer since becoming addicted to epic fantasy during high school. Since then, she's studied the craft academically—at Arizona State University—and as a hobby—attending conventions and workshops around the country. A million ideas float in her head, but it seems like there's never enough time to get them all down on paper.

For fun, Foster likes to take pictures of her dachshunds, sew costumes for her dachshunds, snuggle her dachshunds, and bake treats for her dachshunds. In exchange for so much love and devotion, they pee vast amounts on the floor, click their nails loudly on the tile, and bark wildly at anything that moves outside. Somehow, this relationship works for all involved.

While not writing, Foster can usually be found playing a video game or watching a movie with her husband. While not doing any of those things, Foster can usually be found in bed, asleep.

Email: FosterBridgetCassidy@gmail.com

Facebook: www.facebook.com/FosterBCassidy

Twitter: @FosterBCassidy

Website: www.fosterbridgetcassidy.com

Other NineStar books by this author

Breaking His Spell

Also Available from NineStar Press

Connect with NineStar Press

www.ninestarpress.com

www.facebook.com/ninestarpress

www.facebook.com/groups/NineStarNiche

www.twitter.com/ninestarpress

www.tumblr.com/blog/ninestarpress